–Book One–

MIKEY BROOKS

Published by:
Lost Treasure Publishing & Illustrating, an independent studio.

Summary: When a nightmare named Fyren takes over the gateway to Dreams it falls on Parker, Kaelyn, and Gladamyr – the Dream Keeper – to stop him.

ISBN -10: 1-939993-03-2
ISBN-13: 978-1-939993-03-8

DEDICATION

For Brooklyn, my constant star.

CONTENTS

ACKNOWLEDGMENTS

This book started out as a dream and flourished into reality.
There are so many people who have helped this come to pass.
My wife, Brooklyn, she is my best friend and first editor and
without her no one would be able to make sense of what I wrote.
My children, who regularly sacrifice daddy time so that I may
continue to live in a dream world. My sister, Stephanie, who has
remained my truest confidant and never lets me forget my dreams.
My editor, Cas Peace, who dedicated herself to making my book
shine with radiant glory and loved it so much she wrote me a song.
My wonderful angels in the Authors' Think Tank who continually
support me and make me feel like I am worth something.
My teachers, who taught me lessons not only in the classroom but
in life. And last but certainly not least, my family and friends,
for whom without a dreamer cannot dream.

THE LULLABY

By: Cas Peace

Come hear the lullaby, softly it's calling you,
close your eyes and hear what it means.
Let go of your waking, your slumbers are taking you
into the Crossing, to cross into Dreams.

Come hear the lullaby, softly it speaks to you,
now is the time all your dreams to forsake.
Come hear the lullaby, gently it carries you
over the threshold, and back to Awake.

CHAPTER ONE
THE CROSSING

Parker was about to assassinate the general of the goblin army. It wasn't murder, it was an assignment. He tried to justify what he was about to do as he jumped from the rooftop and landed just above the battlement wall. It was the perfect spot to scout the camp.

The goblins filling the keep were everywhere, sharpening blades and axes or gathering weapons for the impending battle. A large troll in the right hand corner of the space below, hammering solidly on a sword large enough to split three men into six. He spotted his target.

The general of the goblin army, a large brute with gold braids that hung down his chest. Not only had he ordered the burning of Parker's home village, he had ordered the death of Parker's family and friends. This monster, this villain, was the reason Parker had set out on his journey to seek vengeance upon the unjust. This was the creature responsible for Parker swearing allegiance to the Mightercore army, who quickly gave him the role of assassin-scout.

Parker maneuvered his way down the wall, careful

not to move too fast or his invisibility cloak would lose its power. He placed his foot in one crevice, then his hand in another. After a few moments of skilled climbing, Parker found himself precariously positioned just behind the golden-haired brute, leaving only a small distance between him and his foe. In quick session, Parker could ignite his blade with the magic of the Mightercore and his target would be no more. He positioned himself to strike, raising his sword and whispered the incantation that would release the blade's power—

"Parker."

He ignored whoever was calling his name; they did not matter. All he saw was the villain before him. The completed spell ignited Parker's sword with a blazing haze of blue fire, and he had to act fast.

"Parker!"

He swung too late.

The goblin general had already turned. He struck, forcing Parker back against the rocky battlements. Parker parried the attack and thrust forward with a low slash. The general sidestepped and lunged forward again. Parker parried and rolled away from the wall. A lightning spell was the only magic he had left. If he could find enough time to call out the incantation, he could have the general radiating electrons from every appendage.

He rolled until he was a good ten feet from his opponent, then quickly stood. Thrusting his hand into the air, he called down the lightning. The sky filled with a brilliant white light. The crack of thunder reverberated off the walls. Parker briefly closed his eyes then opened them, praying he had hit his target. As the white dust began to clear, he made out an image before him. He peered at it, his heart thumping.

The screen went black.

"Parker, I've called you three times. Now get off that machine and go do your homework."

Sitting on the floor staring fixedly at the television screen, Parker ground his teeth. It had taken him three days to get that far in the game, and now it was lost. His mom had insisted he plug the game station into a socket that had a switch so she had ultimate control, but only one other time had she actually turned the whole system off before he was able to save his game.

"Mom, you don't have any idea what you've—"

"Parker, I have every idea what I just did. I have a law degree—I know everything. Now get going on your homework so you can be on your way to getting your own doctorate."

"Mom, you don't understand. I was almost—"

"Parker, I'm not going to tell you again. If you get your grades back up then you can have more game time."

"But—"

"I'm not arguing." She stood there, hands on hips. Parker imagined she stood that way in the courtroom, whenever someone tried to defy her. It was a hopeless cause. Arguing with his mom would only get him grounded. Parker growled and tossed his controller on the couch. "Look, honey, if you get an A in your Math and English classes and at least a B in Spanish then you can have more game time. Grades are important, Parker."

Oh great, here it comes, another speech on how good grades merit rewards. Bla, bla, bla. As if on cue, she launched into it. Parker half listened. He kept thinking about the game and when he had saved last. It must have been before he made it across the battlefield. *Man, that had taken forever to cross.* Maybe if he could just turn the TV back on and check his status he could—

"Are you even listening to me?" His mom was tapping her middle finger on her hip. Parker tried to remember what she had been saying. Something about grandpa wanting a phone call in Spanish, or something.

"Sure Mom, I'll call him later." He smiled, acting the attentive son.

She wasn't buying it. "Sometimes I wonder why I even try."

"Mom, I'm sorry. I just kind of tuned out."

"You're just like your father. Maybe it's hereditary or something. All the men in the Bennett line ignore me when I speak, is that it?"

"I wasn't ignoring you, I was just thinking about—"

"Your game—I know! I've had enough of your games for a while. I think maybe you shouldn't play them for the rest of the night. Now please go to your room and start your homework. If you need me I'll be in my office."

Could it get any worse? Parker watched his mom, as if in slow motion, pick up his controller and take it with her down the hall. Now what was he going to do? He needed to finish that game.

Parker stomped down the hallway and made a point of closing his bedroom door harder than normal. He kicked over a pile of clothes on the floor, and then threw himself down on his bed. He was screwed! Why had he bragged about beating Medieval Assassin today? That was just stupid. He thought back to the conversation he'd had just after school let out. Connor had been bragging about playing the game and how far he had gotten.

"Yeah, I made it all the way to the training grounds

in like, an hour."

Parker grimaced. It had taken him twice as long and he'd had to start over when he got killed by a hobgoblin hiding in the trenches. Jason, Parker's best friend, came quickly to his defense.

"Yeah well, Parker's a lot further than that. Tell him."

Everyone turned to Parker. What should he say? He had barely finished his last few assignments without getting killed. If he admitted to that, Connor would make him look like a loser.

Before he could change his mind, he blurted, "I beat the game last night."

The conversation that followed was a blur. Everyone had shouted, cheered, and slapped Parker on the back. He felt great and sick at the same time. Jason called Connor a loser and his beaming face fell.

Loser—the one word no one ever wanted to be called in junior high. The word scared Parker more than anything. He imagined what his friends would say if he told them he actually never beat it. They would call him a loser for sure. Rule number one in the teenage world: never get called a loser.

"She is such a loser!"

"No, she's a *fat* loser."

Kaelyn tried to ignore the laughter and hurtful comments from the group of girls. She had promised herself she wouldn't cry today, or give them the satisfaction of knowing they had affected her. Today would be different. She walked up to the girls and smiled at each one.

They sneered back.

"How's it going?" she said.

"What's it to you, Freak Show?" Tiffany, the glorified leader of the group, asked.

Kaelyn didn't know what to say. She tried to be polite—wanting desperately to make a friend. She had been at this new school for almost a month and the other girls still treated her like she was ... a freak.

"What are you staring at? OMG, can someone puh-leeze tell her to go away."

"Freak Show, the losers hang out in D hall. You know, Resource," Taylor, the short redhead offered.

"But . . ." Kaelyn stammered.

"But what, loser?"

"OMG! She wants to be our friend." The group of girls started to laugh and tears itched behind Kaelyn's eyes. She couldn't cry, and give Tiffany's mob yet another thing to tease her about. She took a deep breath and let it out.

"Look, I'm just trying to get to my locker. I need my binder for class."

The girls' smiles immediately fell. They all turned to look at the lockers behind them, counting out each other's until they pegged the one that had to be Kaelyn's.

"How did you get a locker next to us?" Brianna, the tall brunette of the group asked.

"I—"

"I bet it was her Freak Show aunt," said Tiffany. "She voodooed her way into making it happen."

There it was again, another remark about her Aunt Zelda. *So what? Zelda chose to be a psychic, what was so bad about that?* Kaelyn could think of a million different professions that sounded worse, like a lunch lady or even a person who cleaned up road kill. She wanted to say something, to tell them her aunt was actually really cool, but every time she opened her mouth nothing came out.

"OMG, people are starting to look," Brianna said, trying to hide Kaelyn behind her tall form.

"This is not happening . . . just not happening," Madison whined, tossing her blonde locks from side to side.

Brianna looked up and down the hall. "They're going to think she's one of us!" she whispered. "Everyone will think she is—"

"You cannot have your locker next to us. You'll have to go." Tiffany glared at Kaelyn.

Kaelyn glared back. Who were they to tell her where she could or could not have her locker? It wasn't like she asked to be given a locker next to Tiffany and her band of Plastics. They had nice clothes and hair out of a teen magazine, but so what? That didn't give them the right to push everyone around. Kaelyn felt a surge of energy rise inside her. She wanted to fight, to stand up to the bullying, but her shyness wouldn't allow her. The energy vanished and her glare turned to a glazed stare. She was a lone gazelle and the Plastics a pride of vicious lions.

"Now," Tiffany began, still glaring at her, "we're going to go to the bathroom and when we come back, we expect you to have your things cleared out. Got it, loser?"

"Sure." Kaelyn looked at the floor. Tiffany's Plastics marched in unison down the hall and Kaelyn kept her eyes down, the tears now leaking. *Why'd you give in?* She felt the urge to rip off Tiffany's head and yet she agreed to do what Tiffany said. *What's wrong with me?* She wiped the tears from her cheeks and began pulling her things out of her locker.

They had won. Again. Kaelyn could kick herself. Instead she kicked her locker door. It slammed shut and a few kids gave her the 'weird eye' as they passed. She wished they would just ignore her, but how could anyone ignore a cry baby?

Her dad had always told her that no one was big enough to make you feel small. But what did he know? He never had a hard time making friends. Her dad had been a social butterfly. Kaelyn had turned out to be his complete opposite. She preferred books and drawing pads to shopping and socializing. At least, she thought she did. A part of her wanted to be like Tiffany, so confident with so many friends. But she wasn't Tiffany.

Kaelyn had to accept that she was now living a nightmare. She was a loser.

A smile crept across the Dream Keeper's immortal face as the purple glow illuminated the dark space in front of him. Any moment a figure would emerge from the light. He waited patiently, calculating the time in which the event would happen. In the distance, a soft lullaby could be heard, calling forth the spells and opening the passages to the mortal world. Within the light, a shape formed. Little by little, the shape expanded and stretched and soon a child stood before him. She was dark skinned, with wide brown eyes that glimmered at the Dream Keeper. Her light pink nightgown, which ended just above her bare feet, rippled in the breeze blowing in from the mortal world.

Capturing the child's trust with his gentle smile, the Dream Keeper reached out his hand. She took it and he led her from the light, following the path that would lead them to the border wall. They walked in rhythm with the far off lullaby, and the purple glow behind them dimmed to blackness.

At the end of their walk, the Dream Keeper and the girl stood on a great wall. It had no visible beginning or end, stretching far into the black spaces of Dreams. The Dream Keeper looked to his left and examined the land on that side of the wall. It was dark and misshapen. No recognizable color could be seen, they seemed to change with every shift of wind blowing across the carved surface. Far beyond the wall, and deep into the land, an eerie fog drifted ghostlike across a realm plagued by madness. It was a dark world but even so, the nightmares that called it home were darker still.

The Dream Keeper knew the Mares fed off the fear of mortals, hiding themselves in shadows waiting for innocent prey to come. He felt evil watching, and a cold chill ran down his back. A strange, inner tugging pulled on him, bidding him entry into that dark land. With conscious effort, he turned away, and looked toward his right.

Sunshine radiated the sky with perfect clarity. The land to the right of the wall was covered in luscious green grass, dappled with wind tossed sprouts of heather. Trees with gold and green leaves winked and twirled in the warmth that blew across the field. The Dream Keeper smiled and knew that the child, whose hand he still held, smiled too. She lifted a finger and pointed to a cloud of butterflies that flew across the open grass.

The Dream Keeper wished more than anything that he could leave her here in this world of bliss. He wished she could cross over the border wall and enter that land of enchantment. Yet, he could not let her. The Dream

Keeper's smile faded as he turned to look again at the dark land behind them. With a heavy heart, he stepped from the wall, leading the young child into the darkness.

"This is where I must leave you for a time," he said, his voice soft.

"But I don't want to stay here alone."

"It won't be long, little Lydie. I will be back. But this is where you are meant to be tonight. I wish it could be different."

The Dream Keeper paused. Lydi's brown eyes filled with tears. Her hands shook. He could tell she was afraid of being left alone. But the Crossing called. The lullaby hadn't ended and he knew the light would return, bringing another mortal to the world of Dreams. The Dream Keeper cleared his throat and knelt down, facing Lydie.

"Little Lydie, don't you know how brave you are?"

The little girl shook her head.

"Well, I do. I know you are one of the bravest little girls I have ever met. You must continue to be brave for just a bit longer."

"But I'm scared. Won't you stay with me?"

The Dream Keeper gazed into the brown of the girl's eyes and saw his reflection there. His own eyes betrayed what he must do. In the distance, he heard the lullaby beckoning him back to his post, back to the Crossing. He wiped a tear from Lydie's cheek and tried desperately to hold back his own. She was just too young to leave alone.

He pulled the child in close and whispered in her ear so as not to let any of the shadows hear. "If you get too scared, Lydie, say my name and I'll come find you. Just say it once and I'll be there."

"What's your name?" she asked.

The Dream Keeper hesitated only a moment before whispering, "Gladamyr."

Lydie started to repeat the name, but the Dream Keeper put a finger to her lips.

"Only use it when you have dire need, for you can only use it once."

She nodded and the Dream Keeper stood.

"Sweet dreams, little Lydie." With that, Gladamyr pulled a golden key from his pocket, slid it into a hole that hovered in the air before him, turned it, and left the girl alone in the dark land of Mares.

"You've done it again, Gladamyr, and this time I am going to have to report you."

Gladamyr stared fixedly at the piece of pink ribbon in his hand. A piece of ribbon the little girl had given him in return for rescuing her from the nightmare she had fallen into. A smile crept across his face at the memory of placing Lydie back into the glow of the purple light. The thought of her waking and re-entering Dreams was a hopeful thought. Perhaps this time she would be allowed to cross over into Favor and far away from Mares.

"You aren't even listening to me, are you?" His boss's shrill voice interrupted Gladamyr's thoughts. The Dream Keeper looked up from his ribbon and into the face of a dreamling. Her cheeks turned a shade of red that clashed with her skin's normal light blue. Her once sapphire eyes were now a raging scarlet. She was about to lose her temper.

"No, I was lost in thought," he replied. "I'm sorry, Cerulean, really I . . ."

"You are going to lose more than a thought if you

don't get yourself together. This is the fourth time you have been caught violating the return code. I do not want to have to tell you this again, but it seems I must." She cleared her throat and then shuffled through a stack of files on her black shiny desk.

"Dream Keeper's Nocturnal Code, page forty-six, paragraph two, reads as follows: 'Under no circumstances is a dream keeper to divulge his or her name to any being from the mortal land. Such divulging of said name will grant instant return of the mortal being to the world of Awake, leading to unbalance in the realms of Dreams. Furthermore, the usage of a dream keeper's name, if used in Awake, will grant unknown re-entries to the mortal. In consequence, the mortal will then have power to call on that dream keeper at any time while in Dreams. Such divulging of a dream keeper's name must be reprimanded harshly and adequate penalties must be enforced.' I can continue on to the list of suggested reprimands unless you can give me sufficient reason to not punish you."

"I know I violated the return code, and I am aware of the power that divulging my name gives to the mortals, but I had to——"

"How so, Gladamyr? Did this mortal child threaten you in some way? Did she——"

"It just wasn't right leaving her there, is all. She was scared, she didn't want to be in Mares. She wanted to——"

"What she wanted was not her choice, Gladamyr. There is a necessary balance to be kept. It is not the responsibility of the mortals to choose what land they visit while in Dreams. It is not a dream keeper's responsibility either——"

"Yes, I know this——"

"Do not interrupt! It is the responsibility of the

keeper's council to determine where each mortal will be sent. It is up to them to check the balance of the realms and then instruct you on who goes where. You do not hold the authority to out-maneuver the council. Any variation in the orders given and you will be deemed insubordinate. And that, I am afraid, is not a trait we look for in a dream keeper."

A heavy silence fell on the small room. Gladamyr fixed his eyes on the pink ribbon in his hand. He thought once again of the girl from the mortal world; her dark skin that matched her eyes, the many braids in her hair and the pink nightgown. Pink. Little girls always seemed to wear pink when they slept. Was there something about that specific color that helped them to sleep? Or was it, perhaps, natural for little girls to wear that color? Gladamyr had seen many girls wearing other colors, but the ones in pink stood out the most for him.

"Gladamyr?" The dreamling's voice was calmer.

He looked up to see that the red had faded from her face, it was now a normal shade of blue. Her eyebrows lifted and pulled together, almost a look of concern. For a moment Gladamyr thought she actually might be pretty if not for the fact she was always mad at someone.

"I'm sorry, Cerulean. I really am," he said softly.

"Are you feeling well, Gladamyr? You seem very . . . I don't know . . . out of sorts perhaps? Or is this just a trick you are trying to play so that I don't go ahead with filing that report on you?"

"No."

"No, you're fine, or no you are not playing a trick?"

"I'm doing just fine and no, I am not playing a trick. I may have been a Mare once upon a time, Cerulean, but I'm no trickster. I know what I did was wrong, and if you want to file a report, then do it. I don't want you getting in trouble either."

"You know, Gladamyr, I would let it slide, but this is the fourth violation and the third time this year that you have broken the return code and it's only February. I am going to put in the report that you have been harshly verbally reprimanded and will be put on suspension for a week."

"For a week? Oh, come on, Cerulean, I need to work. I can't just sit around and—"

"Rest! Rest is what you need, Gladamyr. I think you should take a break from the Crossing and relax. Better yet, leave Teorainn all together. Why not visit Mares for a little while? Don't you have some friends to visit there? Or perhaps one of the cities in Favor? I heard that Éadrom is wonderful this time of year. The point is, Gladamyr, I am giving you this time to reflect on what you need to do to better yourself—so that in a week, when you return, you can be top notch. The council is getting very strict recently, and it won't just be your job on the line the next time you mess up. I am telling you this last part not as your supervisor but as your friend."

Gladamyr left Cerulean's office confused. He didn't know whether to be upset or elated. He liked to work—no, he loved to work. If he didn't have his work, he would do nothing but sit for eternity in his apartment sulking about his early life mess-ups. But then again, he hadn't been outside Teorainn, the border city, since starting his job at the Crossing nearly a decade ago. Perhaps Cerulean was right. Maybe he did need a break from the mortals and their trips to Dreams.

"So how did it go? Were you totally stoked when

you beat the game? You know Connor has been trying to beat it for like a week now and can't get past the training stage. He's such a loser."

Parker felt the bottom of his stomach twist into a tight knot. That word, 'loser', scared him more than anything else in the world. He dreaded ever being called it. He knew that it would just take a few times for someone to overhear his name and that word together for his life in junior high to end.

Forget about being anything ever again—except a loser. Parker cleared his throat and looked at his best friend. Jason seemed eager for him to supply the details.

"Okay, so I got past the battlement's wall and into the goblin keep by using the invisibility cloak I got from the old hag in the southern Mightercore city. It worked great—except you have to move really slow. Seriously, it took forever. Then I found the general. At first I tried to use the fire magic on my sword but it didn't work out, so I used the lightning spell on him and—"

"Wow, you totally beat the game then, didn't you? You are totally awesome, dude—we have to tell Nick and Tyler. They won't believe this. And just wait till we tell Connor, he's going to look like such a loser. You know that Austin stayed at Zach's house this weekend? Yeah, they said they were going to beat it too, but I bet they didn't even get as far as you did last week."

The bell rang and students in the hall started running for their classrooms. Parker followed Jason as they dashed for 'B' hall and made it to their seats before the tardy bell rang. He glanced up at the large clock above the door, and for the first time in his life begged that math class would never end. Time, however, was not on Parker's side and the three periods flew by without pause. He wondered why every other day dragged on forever, but today seemed to be racing. He got to his next class just as the bell rang and kids jumped to their seats. Mr. Martinez, despite the fact that no one was listening, continued going over the homework assignment they'd been given.

"Make sure you all proofread your papers before you turn them in. Just because this is Spanish doesn't mean you can use bad English."

Parker walked as slowly as he could toward the door. Jason stood in the Hall with Nick, Tyler, and Austin. They signaled with their hands and notebooks, calling out for him to hurry. He didn't see Connor with them, but knew he would be in the cafeteria. Connor liked food. Parker was just stepping through the doorway when—save!

"Mr. Bennett, can I get you to help me carry these boxes to the library?" Mr. Martinez asked. A smile stole across Parker's face. He nodded. At that moment Parker promised himself to proofread his Spanish paper three times before handing it in. When he turned toward the Hall, he saw his friends' sulky faces. He shrugged and whispered that he would catch up with them later. Obviously bummed, they headed off in the opposite direction.

"Thanks for giving me a hand with these. My wife donated some of her collection to the book drive."

"No hay problema," Parker said in perfect Spanish.

"Good, ¡bien hecho! Your Spanish is improving. I'm looking forward to reading your paper."

"Your wife collects a lot of fantasy novels," Parker remarked, looking at the box's contents.

"That's my wife . . . le encanta de los libros . . . she's loved fantasy since she was your age. Her favorite book was *The Hobbit.*"

"Great movie!"

"Yeah, but back then it was only a book. You had to use your imagination to really see it. It's not the same anymore. Once a book gets more than a few thousand copies sold it's turned into a movie, then why read it, no?"

"I guess."

The library was one of the few places Parker hadn't been to yet. He rarely read books, let alone checked them out. And why even do that when everything you ever wanted was found on the internet?

Bottom line, he preferred games to books. The room was completely empty except for a few tables and chairs and a mass amount of large imposing shelves that filled more than half the space. It was so quiet that Parker could hear the air escape from his sneakers every time he stepped. Mr. Martinez set his box down on a half-moon desk in the middle of the room. Behind it sat one of the oldest women Parker had ever seen. Her stark-white hair matched her wrinkly, crushed, newspaper skin. He could almost see words in the lines and folds of her skin.

"Thank you, Javier. I take it these are for the book drive?" she asked.

"Si, my wife decided to part with a lot of her collection; she's into spooky romances now. You know the ones with vampires, ghosts, and things?"

"Like the rest of the teenage girls I get in here. Don't bother introducing me, Javier. I know this boy."

Parker hurriedly searched his memory for any recollection of the old woman. She didn't look at all familiar. He blurred his vision to see if that would make some of the wrinkles disappear so her face would become recognizable, but nothing.

"You've got to be Little Lizzy González's boy . . . or is it still Bennett? These new age women . . . I don't know whether they keep their married names or not anymore. Back in my day you married a man and were stuck with his name until the day you ate dirt."

"No, she still goes by Bennett. How do you know my mom? Did she help handle a case for you?"

"Heavens, no. I said 'I do' and I meant every word, even if he drove me mad with his snoring and stinky feet. No, your mother was my best customer when I worked at the public library. She'd come in every day and read all sorts of books. She started like most kids your age with the fun magic stories, then she went to the lovey-dovey books and it wasn't long before her favorites were the boring law books. She changed once she went to college; she used to be a dreamer."

Parker didn't believe it, *my mom a dreamer?*

Kaelyn found that the best place to eat her lunch was in the girls' bathroom outside the library. She had grown tired of trying to sit at table after table only to be told that the seat she was about to sit in was already taken. Then, one day, she made the mistake of trying to sit at Tiffany's table of Plastics.

Half the girls stared in shock and the other half mumbled incoherent acronyms. "OMG! AYSOS? MKAY . . . n00b." Tiffany, on the other hand, looked her up and down, smiling viciously the whole time. Finally, after what seemed like forever and next Tuesday, Tiffany asked Kaelyn to sit down. Stunned, plastic faces dropped.

"You're new here, aren't you?" she said with a

perfect smile. Kaelyn couldn't help but look at her teeth. They were bright white and every one an orthodontic heaven. Her lips glimmered glossy pink and her eyes a royal blue. Even her hair shone a silky yellow, reminding Kaelyn of a Barbie doll. "So where did you move from?"

"Glasgow. It's in Scotland."

"You don't sound Scottish."

"Well, I only lived there for a little while." Tiffany sneered at Kaelyn like she was lying. "My dad liked to explore new places. I was actually born in the U.S."

"Oh . . . so what brought you back? Did your dad get bored with all the European traveling?"

"No . . . he . . . died."

"Oh, that's just terrible." Tiffany's perfect wax smile gave Kaelyn the creeps. It made her feel she was being led into a trap. "So you moved back here with your mom?"

Kaelyn was quiet for a moment then shook her head. "No, she died when I was a little girl."

"So you're an orphan . . . how terrible! Did they find you a good foster family in town?"

"No, I live with my Aunt Zelda."

"Zelda? That's a funny name." The Plastics laughed along with Tiffany. The uneasy feeling increased and Kaelyn began to get up from the table. "Oh wait, I know your aunt! Isn't she the crazy lady who claims she is a psychic?"

"I know her too!" Brianna giggled. "What a freak!"

"That's right," Tiffany agreed. "A freak . . . freak . . . freak . . . freak . . ."

The Plastics chanted the word over and over. All the kids in the cafeteria turned to see their latest victim. Some joined the mocking chant and soon, every eye was on her. Kaelyn hurriedly pulled her legs out from under the table but her right ankle twisted. She fell to the floor, landing in her salad. The unbearable chanting and laughter increased. Kaelyn hobbled from the cafeteria trailing a line of lettuce. The next day, Kaelyn found her sanctuary in the bathroom.

It really wasn't all that bad. No one seemed to use it, so it was always clean and never smelled. Plus it gave her time to work on her homework, or draw. Kaelyn finished off her tuna fish sandwich and eyed her backpack. Because of Tiffany and her eviction notice, Kaelyn's backpack was ready to bust at the seams. She had to find a way to get rid of half the stuff before her back became permanently damaged. With effort, Kaelyn lifted her bag and headed out the bathroom door— CRASH!

The contents of her backpack flew in a million different directions. Books flopped to the ground and paper swooshed in the air. Kaelyn's leg buckled. She dropped to the floor.

A boy fell on top her.

"I am s-o-o sorry!" the boy said, red faced.

"No, it's my fault I should have looked before . . . ouch!"

"Sorry."

"No, not you, something is digging in my back."

The boy stood up. Kaelyn recognized him at once, Parker Bennett. Kaelyn was not the type of girl to have a crush on a boy but if she was, Parker would be that guy. Taller than most of the guys in ninth grade, his dark brown hair and chocolate brown eyes made her breath stop for a moment. He had freckles, but they only made him look cuter.

Kaelyn noticed him her first day of school. He was in three of her classes and she sat next to him in one of them. Although he had never taken any notice of her, she secretly hoped he knew her name.

Parker reached down his hand and Kaelyn took it.

"I'm really sorry."

"It's okay, Parker. I'm not hurt."

Parker looked at her and she could tell he was trying to figure out where they met before. "I'm really bad with names," he tried.

"It's okay. I'm Kaelyn. I just moved here."

"Oh yeah, I think you're in one of my classes. Geez! Girls sure do carry a lot of stuff in their backpacks."

Kaelyn scanned the mess. The Hall mimicked a tornado strike. Books, paper, tissues, pencils, pens, and candy wrappers were everywhere. She quickly bent down, picked out some of the more personal items and buried them in her bag.

"You never know what you're going to need," she said with a smile. Parker shook his head and helped gather items. Kaelyn did her best to shove papers, binders and books, but no way was everything going to fit. After a desperate push, the bag's zipper split, so she left most of the books out. Parker picked up a paper with a drawing of a pegasus she'd doodled during first period.

"This is pretty good. Did you draw it?"

"Dude, where have you been?"

Kaelyn and Parker both swiveled toward the boy coming up the Hall. It was one of Parker's friends, Kaelyn knew, but she couldn't remember his name. She could have sworn Parker cringed when he saw his friend. Maybe he didn't want to been seen with her. After all, half the kids in the cafeteria had called her a freak the week before.

"Hey, man," Parker said, handing Kaelyn her

drawing. "I had to help Mr. Martinez in the library."

"Well come on, Zach and Austin beat the game and want to see what you did to get past the general."

"Sure, um, see ya 'round, Kaelyn."

Kaelyn watched as the two boys walked down the hall.

"Dude, why are you hanging out with that girl? She's such a loser."

Kaelyn didn't hear Parker's response, but she could have guessed. She had been branded the moment she arrived at this school. It didn't help that her aunt was an infamous, self-proclaimed psychic. No wonder she was a loser.

CHAPTER TWO
THE KEYS

The seven moons of Éadrom glowed brightly, casting hues of pale blue upon the beach. Gladamyr glanced toward the vast ocean before him and breathed in deeply. It had been decades since he took a moment for himself, and he loved it. True, he only just arrived in Éadrom minutes before, but that was all it took for the grandeur of the ocean city to hypnotize him with its magic. The wind whispered that he could live there forever, and he almost agreed with it. He leaned back in his hammock and swung his body into the wind.

Looking over his shoulder, he saw a man and two little children running down the beach. The man laughed and kicked the waves as they hit his legs. The water splashed up into the air and the two children danced in the reflected moonbeams.

Gladamyr wondered which one of the three figures was the mortal visiting Dreams. Whomever it was, he thought they were pretty lucky to be brought to such a wonderful place for the night. The man reached down and picked up one of the children, and the boy laughed with glee. The other child suddenly melted into the surf, and Gladamyr knew at once the boy in the man's arms was the dreamer.

He had seen it before. People come and go in a mortal's imagination. The boy must have just wanted a moment alone with the gentle man. The scene wasn't anything extraordinary to Gladamyr. He had seen a thousands of mortals call up such moments from the past, or bends in time. Anything to spend just one more minute with the person they loved. He had seen husbands conjure up their deceased wives, and mothers their lost children. Gladamyr smiled as the boy chased the man round the beach, calling out over and over 'Daddy, Daddy.'

Another figure appeared on the beach and Gladamyr knew that the boy's wonderful moment with his father had come to an end. It was Felix, a dream keeper, come to take the boy back to the crossing—to return to Awake. Perhaps, Gladamyr thought, the child would return tomorrow and be able to see his father once again. It was wishful thinking, for only on the rarest of occasions did a mortal come to Éadrom. Gladamyr watched as the boy saw Felix standing on the sand. He heard Felix call out the boy's name and beckon him closer, but the boy hesitated. He didn't want to leave, not yet. He rushed to his father and wrapped his arms around the man's neck.

"Don't let him take me, Daddy! Please," he cried.

The father—who had been dressed in shorts and an open shirt—transformed into a solider bedecked in a tan and brown camouflage. The boy cried out and held onto his father just a little longer, until the solider dissolved into the water. Slowly, the boy turned to the dream keeper, and Gladamyr watched as they walked away from the beach. Felix pulled a golden key from his pocket and inserted it into the air. With a quick turn of his hand, Felix and the boy vanished into a purple mist. Gladamyr heard the faint sound of a lullaby calling the boy back to Awake.

He got up from the hammock and walked over to where the father had been standing only moments before, catching a glimpse of a silvery chain and identification tag as it washed away with the surf. He had to wipe away the single tear that had forced its way down his cheek. Even in the beautiful ocean city, Gladamyr, the Dream Keeper, could not escape the sadness of his job.

"You are becoming too emotionally attached to the mortals."

Gladamyr turned to be confronted by two different faces, one the scowling face of a man with green skin, and the other the smiling face of a beautiful woman. Both faces belonged to the same dreamling. Jaynus, whom some called Two-face. She-he-them, had worked for a short time at the Crossing but had been let go due to the lack of cooperation from the always grumpy Mare side. At times, it seemed to Gladamyr, that Jaynus was constantly fighting a battle with two individuals trapped within the same body.

"Did you hear me?" the female side of Jaynus asked in a gentle voice.

"Of course he heard you. He turned around, didn't he?" answered the gruff male side. "Why are we over here in the first place? I told you I was hungry and wanted to find a concession stand."

"We will find a concession stand in a moment. Remember, it's my day to be in charge, not yours."

"But I'm hungry."

The dreamling started to walk away, then turned

around, and then turned around again, then completely lost all balance, crumpling to the sand. The female side started to sing softly and the dreamling's body rocked back and forth. Within a minute the gruff face slumped and his eyes closed. Jaynus stopped singing, stood up, and shook the sand from her legs and arms.

"I'm sorry you had to see that, Gladamyr, but my brother gets a little cranky when he's tired and hungry. It was best to put him to sleep for a while. Sometimes I have to do that so I can get a break from him."

"I understand," Gladamyr said, although he really didn't. He had no idea what it was like to be permanently stuck to another dreamling. It wouldn't be so bad if that other dreamling was sweet and kind, like the woman side of Jaynus, but the grumpy man side would be intolerable. Gladamyr remembered when Jaynus had worked at the Crossing with the male side in charge; he had done nothing but complain and scold the mortals for dreaming in the first place.

"We were watching you just now with the mortal child. You really are too attached to them, you know."

"I'm not. I just feel they should have more of a choice, is all."

"You think I'm wrong? When was the last time you looked in a mirror, Gladamyr? You don't resemble a dreamling at all. You make yourself look more mortal every day with that shifting trick."

"I'd rather look this way than . . ."

"What? Like me? Looking like a dreamling isn't a bad thing for a dreamling. Of course, there isn't another dreamling with two faces strapped to one neck, but that is what happens when you are born too close to the border wall. I'm just saying what I feel, Gladamyr. We're not part of their world."

"But we could be, Jaynus. Why does everything have to be black or white, dark or light? Why does an innocent child have to be put in Mares while some criminal is allowed to go to Favor?"

"That little boy got to come to Éadrom—"

"But for how long? And how often do you see that happen? Did he have a choice when he got to leave? The moment his visit to Dreams actually became about him, Felix came and took him back to Awake. They should have more of a choice, is all."

"I get what you're saying, Gladmyr." Jaynus dropped her gaze to the sand. "I know what it's like sometimes not having a choice. I'm stuck to a brother who is fully of Mares in his mind, and it contradicts the things I feel being fully of Favor. But still I accept who I am."

Gladamyr looked at Jaynus, then down at the sand. Acceptance was a word he had a hard time with. He couldn't accept the fact that mortals had no control when they visited Dreams, and he couldn't accept the fact that he was a Mare when he didn't feel like one inside. He changed his appearance to resemble mortals because that's what he felt he was. Mortals could express traits from both Mares and Favor at the same time in one body. They were a lot like Jaynus, with one less face.

"Look, Gladamyr, a sand dollar."

Jaynus reached down and picked up the shell. A pattern in the shape of a star was etched into the shell's surface.

"I've heard these have special powers," Jaynus said, turning the shell over in her hand. "They're supposed to bring good fortune to the person they belong to. I want to give it to you, Gladamyr—"

"You don't have to—"

"No, I want you to have it." Jaynus held out the sand dollar.

Gladamyr took it. It was weightless in his hand.

"Thank you, Jaynus."

"You're welcome. I better go before my brother wakes up. He'll wonder why we're still here and not getting food."

Jaynus walked down the beach. Gladamyr turned his attention to the shell he held. With a finger, he traced the star shape over and over. He almost wished what Jaynus said about it having special powers was true, but he knew it was just a shell.

Smiling, Gladamyr put the shell in his pocket. He felt something hard and cold and pulled out two iridescent keys. Each was uniquely different, much like the mortals they belonged to. One key had swirling, crisscrossing patterns that formed its head, while the other was all sharp angles.

Gladamyr sucked in a deep breath, it was against the rules to take a key from the Crossing. He had intended to take back the keys at the end of his shift, but had been called away when Lydie said his name. He didn't think about them again after he got suspended. He had to get the keys back to the Crossing before they got warm; before the mortals they belonged to tried to enter Dreams.

Parker had done it! He made it the whole day without having to talk to his friends about Medieval Assassin. It took as much skill avoiding his friends as it did to get to the final level of the game. *Skill?* Okay, it was luck. *Let's face it man*, Parker told himself, *your butt*

survived out of pure luck.

It wasn't skill that Mr. Martinez asked him to help in the library, or that he ran into the new girl who happened to make him miss lunch period. Luck had triggered a fire drill and fate got him asked to be a student monitor. It was luck that Mrs. Cunningham said she had a headache and that talking in the classroom was forbidden. And it was luck that Parker had to go to his therapist after school and wasn't able to go to Jason's house. *Luck, yep, it was all dumb luck.*

"Sounds like it's a good day for you to buy a lottery ticket," Dr. Gates, his therapist, agreed.

Parker's parents had been divorced for well over a year, but his mom still insisted on him going to counseling sessions. *Counseling sessions*—Parker preferred to call them therapy sessions. It sounded cool to be so messed up in the head that you had a therapist at the age of fourteen.

Plus, Dr. Gates was cool. He wasn't a hundred years old, and he never asked stupid questions like, "Parker, how does that make you feel?" or "what does this random blob of paint on this canvas remind you of?" Parker just kicked back on the couch and talked about normal stuff, like gaming. Dr. Gates played a lot of Xbox and was really into this game about World War II.

"So what's the new girl's name?" Dr. Gates asked as he passed over a bag of Doritos.

"Kaelyn, or something like that. I don't really remember. I heard she is totally bogus though. Jason heard from Tiffany that she tells everyone she's lived all over the world when she hasn't . . . oh, and that her aunt, she lives with, is Madam Zelda."

"The one with the TV commercials?"

"That's the one. 'Come to Madam Zelda's and your

future can be seen through your wallet.' Totally lame."

Dr. Gates laughed. "Yeah, she could have invested a little more into her advertising. How do you know she didn't travel all over the world though?"

"I don't know. That's just what all the guys say. I really don't care though."

"So is she cute?"

"What? Please don't tell me we have reached the point in our sessions for me to start talking about girls." Parker grabbed a pillow and threw it at Dr. Gates.

"Hey . . . hey . . . I was just asking. What's wrong with asking whether you thought she was cute or not? You told me you thought Tiffany was cute—"

"I never said that! Tiffany's a dog. Have you seen how much makeup she wears? I've seen clowns with less makeup. Plus Kaelyn's totally not my type—"

"Oh, so that is her name . . . ."

"Whatever . . . Anyway she's been tagged a loser so life is hopeless for her."

"Life is what you make of it, Parker. If you let others dictate your life to you, then that's what makes you a loser."

"Thanks for the therapy session, Dr. Know-it-all."

"Well, that is what your mother pays me for. Speaking of which, I think she should be here any minute. We on for another round tomorrow?"

"Would my mother have it any other way?"

When the courts had suggested that Parker go to counseling, it was for one or two sessions a week, but since Parker's dad was footing more than half the bill, Liz Bennett had insisted on at least two to three visits a week.

"Probably not. But hey, I'm not too bad a guy to hang around with. Tomorrow I'm going to bring candy bars. You dig Snickers?"

"You know it."

Kaelyn finished her math homework and closed her book. She liked the satisfaction of knowing her homework was done well. There were few things that Kaelyn felt she did well. She wasn't good at picking out clothes, talking to people, or making friends. Apparently she looked like a loser. But Kaelyn was amazing with school work. Maybe they tagged her wrong at school; nerd would be more fitting than loser.

Kaelyn got up from the kitchen table and went into the living room, or what Aunt Zelda referred to as 'the parlor.' Across from the fireplace was a large ornate mirror that stretched from ceiling to floor. Kaelyn's reflection confirmed her less than tidy appearance.

Her dirty-blonde hair had grown so long that it looked stringy in places, compared to Tiffany's glossy, gold tresses. Kaelyn's eyes puffed and dark half circles shaded the bottom lids. She knew she hadn't been sleeping well, but she never thought it would make her look like an old woman. She dreamed of the same thing over and over . . . the car accident. The scar at the base of her neck where the doctors had repaired her collar bone glared at her. That didn't help her appearance, and neither did the scar across her wrist; she'd heard the girls talking about it. And just look at that waistline, no wonder Tiffany's Plastics called her fat.

She *was* a loser.

"You look so pretty, just like your mama." When Aunt Zelda wasn't playing the role of eccentric psychic she actually had a nice voice. It was calm and loving. A lot like Kaelyn's dad's voice. Kaelyn looked at her reflection and then thought of her mother. She looked nothing like her. Kaelyn remembered her mom as something special; golden hair down to her waist, perfect blue, crystal eyes, and flawless cream colored skin. Her mother had been beautiful, and Kaelyn was nothing but a sad copy that had lost all the good qualities. Suddenly her throat was tense, her eyes prickled and the tears came.

"Oh, baby, I'm sorry. I didn't mean to bring your mama up. You would think I'd be a little more—"

"It's not that, Zelly . . . it's . . . that . . . they call me fat . . . and tell me I'm a loser and a freak . . . and a . . . ."

"Who? Those no good kids at school? Oh, let me guess, it's that Tiffany Martin girl and her Barbie wannabes, isn't it? You'd think after all the good advice I give her mother she'd be a little nicer to my kin. That's it! The next time she comes for a session I'm telling her that the future shows her married to a fat, lazy plumber—cracks and all."

Kaelyn laughed and wiped an unwelcomed tear.

"Oh, Kae baby. You're only fourteen years old. Honey, what those girls are calling fat now is what they are going to be wanting come a year or two. You're built the way your mama was, you just give it time and those girls are going to be wishing they were you. Believe me when I tell you, 'cause I've seen it. Madam Zelda knows her stuff."

"I miss Mom and Dad."

"I know Kae . . . I miss them too."

"It was easier being in other countries 'cause all the kids wanted to know what it was like to be an American. Here, they act like I'm lying when I say something. They're so mean and I don't know why."

"It's 'cause you're special, baby. They see something in you that they don't have, and they are jealous that you got it. You're smart and beautiful . . . ."

"Whatever! I look nothing like Mom. She didn't have stringy hair like mine and baggy eyes and zits."

"You don't have any zits!"

"Oh, what is this right here? Better get your eyes checked, Zelly, 'cause it's the size of Texas."

"Kae, my darling Kae, you are too much like your mama. I remember when she was your age she ran all over the house complaining about the craters on her face. The very next summer her face was as spotless as could be. Don't worry, that will clear up by tomorrow. We'll just go buy you some face wash. And if you wanted your hair done, all you had to do was tell me. I do readings for a beautician down the street and she owes me a favor. As for the kids at school, just give it time. I'm sure there's someone who is just dying to be your friend."

Eerie silence filled the air as Gladamyr approached the border wall that led to the Crossing. Something felt wrong. The border wall was barren of light, and the soft humming lullaby that accompanied the mortals' passage to Dreams had stopped. Gladamyr shifted instinctively, his skin darkening from lavender to deep purple. He climbed the winding stairs that led to a platform outside the Crossing's gate. Each step echoed in the darkness behind him and his stomach churned with anticipation. As he reached the platform, a blue glow caught his attention. In less than a second the Dream Keeper shifted once more, his body shrinking and molding itself to the stair's railing.

"Is someone there?" Recognizing the timid whisper, Gladamyr slowly shifted back to his normal form.

"Cerulean, it's me."

"Oh, Gladamyr, you've got to get out of here! It isn't safe."

"What's going on? Why is the Crossing so dark and the lullaby—"

"Fyren has ordered all the keepers arrested and all activity at the Crossing to stop."

"Fyren? Fyren has no authority to—"

"He took over the council this morning."

"But how? Allyon wouldn't allow—"

"They say Allyon is dead."

Gladamyr's heart sank. Allyon had been his mentor, the one Favor he most wanted to be like. He couldn't accept the fact that Allyon was dead. It was impossible! There wasn't a way to kill a dreamling. They were immortal.

"I know what you're thinking, Gladamyr, but how else could Fyren take control of the council?"

"But Allyon was the strongest Favor in Dreams! He couldn't have—"

Cerulean put a finger to Gladamyr's lips, and they listened to the sound of approaching footsteps. She looked into Gladamyr's eyes and he could see that all her strength had been replaced by fear. He pulled her close to him as his color shifted again, blending in with the dark stone platform. Cerulean's natural blue glow faded but she was unable to put out her light. She reached up, cupping his neck and pulling him closer.

"I can't hide from them as you can," she whispered. Gladamyr could feel her lips on his neck and for a moment wished this could have happened at another time. "If Allyon is alive you must find him and if not, find a way to take back the council from Fyren."

"But Cerulean, I can't—"

"You've got to try, Gladamyr. You're our only hope."

"You weren't thinking of leaving, my little pixie, were you?"

Gladamyr didn't need to see the dreamling to know that evil voice. It was Minyon, a wicked nightmare who was attached to Fyren like a Mare to shadow. Cerulean looked at Gladamyr, but he knew she could no longer see him. His powers as a shifter allowed him to blend into darkness almost as if he were invisible. He wanted to reach out to her and protect her from the monster behind her, but he had seen the look on her face too often and knew she wanted him to stay completely still.

Cerulean turned around, her blue glow illuminating Minyon's form. The dreamling was made completely out of spiders, millions of them intertwined, making one massive whole being, tall and thin. Minyon smiled at the blue dreamling, and his teeth were large pincers. His smile, however, was not his most disturbing feature, and Gladamyr could see the two, large black widows nesting in the hollow cavities of his eyes. Their red hourglasses gleamed viciously.

Minyon cocked his head to one side. "Didn't Fyren instruct you to have all your keepers brought to the council chambers for questioning?"

"I have followed through with all of Fyren's orders."

"Oh, but our records show that not all the keepers have reported to Fyren. You seem to have missed the most important one."

"All keepers on active duty have been sent."

"The council was unaware that you have inactive keepers in your department, Cerulean. Did you forget to file a leave of absence with the council?"

Cerulean stood taller, and Gladamyr recognized some of the strength he had seen in her before. One thing he knew for sure about Cerulean; she knew her job. "Perhaps the council overlooked the report as they were being infested by a scheming Mare and his pack of dogs."

Minyon bared his pincers and the mass of spiders making up the skin of his face began to roll. A large grey spider detached itself from his cheek and crouched menacingly on the crook of his nose. Cerulean did not back down, but Gladamyr could see her fingers shake. Minyon had a reputation for being one of the cruelest monsters to ever come out of a mortal's nightmare.

"Careful now, Cerulean, I might not be able to kill you, but I can make you wish I could."

"You don't scare me, Minyon. You . . . or your master."

"Perhaps that's because you have never seen Fyren's true form."

Gladamyr felt burning at his right thigh and his muscles tightened. He knew the keys in his pocket would soon start to glow gold, and they would get hotter and hotter until he let the mortals they belonged to into Dreams. He looked from Minyon to Cerulean, and then to his pocket. Was it just him or could the others see a tiny hint of gold light glowing?

"Where's Gladamyr?" Minyon asked coldly.

"He was given a week's suspension and told to go on vacation."

"This I am aware of, Cerulean. I asked where he is."

"You think I know? He could be anywhere. Check somewhere in Mares, maybe he is visiting someone."

Minyon laughed. It was an odd sensation to hear a

mixture of barks and a clicking of pincers. Sensing the Mare relax, the grey spider hissed and returned to its nest in Minyon's left cheek. "You know as well as any other dreamling that Gladamyr would never vacation in Mares. He may be one of us in form, but not in spirit. I have to say he's Fyren's greatest failure. Now tell me where I can find him. Fyren wants all the keepers, even the disappointing ones."

"I told you, I don't know where he is. He could be anywhere in Dreams."

Minyon stared at Cerulean, his spider eyes blinking red. "Fyren will want you to repeat this to him."

Without another word, Minyon turned around and walked toward the gate. Gladamyr was just about to release his form from the platform when he saw a large spider in the glow of Cerulean's light. It stood on its back four legs, hissing up at the blue fairy. She shimmered for a second before emitting a blast of blue, blinding light.

The spider fell onto its back and Gladamyr was left blinded. For a moment his form shifted, and he felt Cerulean push something into his hand. When his vision cleared she was gone, and all that was left on the platform was a withered spider. He opened his hand and looked curiously at a small, round stone. It was a dreamstone; a stone that allowed the mortals to see Dreams as it really was. *How had Cerulean gotten a dreamstone? They were forbidden.*

Gladamyr slid his hand into his pocket and felt the two keys. They were hot and he knew he couldn't wait much longer, but he had to get somewhere safe. Fyren's cronies would be looking for him. *Where to hide?* Then he knew. Gladamyr raced down the winding stair onto the border wall, and leaped far off into the land of Mares.

CHAPTER THREE
DREAMS

P arker wore the cloak of an assassin-scout, the mottle-green color blending in nicely with the lush vegetation around him. Under the cloak was the armor of the Mightercore army. But where was he? This scene didn't look familiar; he was in a jungle of sorts. Parker didn't remember a jungle in Medieval Assassin. He looked around, trying to find something familiar, but there was nothing. Just the trunks of large trees, leaves, and vines everywhere. Wait, was that a stone wall?

Parker moved slowly through the vegetation. The armor was heavy and it weighed him down to the point of exhaustion. Finally, after great effort, he reached the stone wall. It stretched high into the air, so high that Parker couldn't see the top of it. He looked to his left, and then to his right, and couldn't see where the wall ended. It just went on forever. He turned his back and was shocked to find himself still looking at the stone wall. Panic took hold and he spun in circles, finding himself in a stone prison that reached up into the sky and disappeared.

"What a loser!" The voice echoed off the rocky walls, amplifying into a million taunting voices. "Loser, loser, Parker Bennett is a loser, loser—"

"Stop it! Stop!" Parker crumpled dizzy to the ground, the Mightercore armor clanking as it struck the stone floor. He put his hands to his ears, trying to stop the continuous chanting. *Please make it stop, make it stop,* he pleaded, over and over in his head. The voices only grew louder. This had to be a dream. He was stuck in a nightmare and couldn't make it stop. He scrabbled at the ground, trying to claw his way to freedom. He needed to escape. The fear of being enclosed was overpowering. The voices kept changing pitch and he hard Jason, Tyler, Zach, and Nick, shouting that hateful word over. Then came Connor's voice—louder and the most obnoxious. "Parker Bennett, you're such a loser . . . loser . . . loser —"

"Parker . . . Parker . . . Parker . . . ."

The chanting disappeared, but he still heard his name being called. The voice was different, soft and high pitched—a girl's voice. Parker slowly opened his eyes. He was no longer in the stone prison, instead he was in a strange land. The ground was black and cracked, with large misshaped rocks jutting out from all angles. A suffocating grey mist circled here and there like ghosts riding on the wind. The most peculiar things, however, were the trees overhead. Suspended high in the air, their roots dangled down like twisting snakes. He turned and saw the girl who had called his name. Kaelyn . . . *Kaelyn Clark, the new girl—whoa! Why am I dreaming about Kaelyn Clark?*

"Parker . . . Parker . . . where did you go?" Kaelyn was looking around as if she didn't see him.

"Kaelyn, I'm right here." No response. She turned

and turned. A look of panic came over her face.

"Daddy, watch out," she screamed. "Daddy . . . Daddy!"

"Kaelyn?"

Parker watched as a car materialized around Kaelyn. A man sat in the seat beside her. Suddenly, the car crumpled, and Kaelyn lurched from side to side. The car turned upside down and her body collapsed to the roof. The man beside her hung motionless from his seatbelt. Parker ran to help, but then he noticed another man standing next to the car. A tall, broad shouldered man with purple skin. The strange man nodded to Parker as if saying hello. Parker gave a nod back, and then turned back to Kaelyn.

"What's going on?" he asked.

"She's dreaming," the purple man said. "Don't worry, she's not hurt."

"Of course she's hurt! We need to help her."

"It was her choice to give you the dreamstone," the man said, pointing at Parker's hand. Parker looked in his hand and saw an opaque round rock the size of a silver dollar. "She insisted you take it so you could escape."

"What? I don't understand."

"That stone makes it possible for you to see Dreams as it really is. Kaelyn entered Dreams first, so I gave the stone to her. Then you came in and you started having a nightmare; common when you're in Mares. I'm sorry I had to bring you here, but it's the only place I thought would be safe. They won't look for me in Mares."

"Daddy! Daddy, wake up!" Kaelyn pulled at the broken man in the car. Her left arm hung awkwardly at her side, and she was trying desperately to unfasten the safety belt.

"Stop this!" Parker shouted. "Can't you stop it?

Look at her . . . stop this!"

"I can't. There is only one dreamstone, and I can't take you anywhere else. They'll find me."

"This is crap! Total crap!" Parker ran over to Kaelyn and tried to pull her off the man, but she kept pushing him away.

"He'll make it, just help me get him out," she cried. "Please, I can't lose him too."

Parker crouched next to the window. He called out her name, but she looked past him. Tears flowed freely from her blue eyes. He just couldn't take it anymore. He had to help. Parker pulled open the man's door and reached for the buckle. It took only a moment and then the strap released. Magically, the man's body lifted from the chair and hovered in the air. Parker reached to take Kaelyn's hand. The man and the chair disappeared.

"Parker?"

He glanced at Kaelyn and saw her staring back at him, studying him.

"What's going on?" she asked, glancing at the car that was fading away to nothing.

Parker and Kaelyn both turned to the man behind them, the man with purple skin. He seemed surprised for a moment, before giving a slight shrug. "That was unexpected. I had no idea the dreamstone was powerful enough to give sight to two mortals. I'm sorry, had I known I would have helped you sooner. I'm not one hundred percent sure how the dreamstone works."

"Who are you?" Parker asked.

"I'm a dream keeper, and you are in Dreams."

"In Dreams? Not having a dream?" Parker was getting turned around again. "Can you please explain what the heck is going on?"

The purple man, or dream keeper, or whatever he

was called, motioned for Parker and Kaelyn to follow him until he found some large stones they could sit on. Then, after checking the hovering trees as if there might be others watching, he motioned them in close to whisper.

"You need to listen carefully because what I am about to tell you I can never repeat again. It's forbidden for a dreamling to divulge the true nature of our world, but right now both of our worlds are in danger."

"In danger? What do you mean?" Kaelyn asked.

"There is a world inside your own, but you can't see it when you are awake. This world can only be seen when you're asleep; it's called Dreams. When you sleep your mind comes here."

"So we're dreaming then—this isn't real," Parker said louder than he thought. The Dream Keeper put his finger to his lips and shook his head.

"You don't understand—the dream world is very real." The Dream Keeper paused for a moment and let out a deep breath. "My world is divided into two realms: one called Favor and the other Mares. When your mind visits Dreams, you must be taken to one of these realms during your stay. You see, the people of your world keep our world in balance and as long as there is a balance, both of our worlds are safe."

Kaelyn frowned. "What happens when it becomes unbalanced?"

"Our worlds merge. Then bad things happen."

"What do you mean, bad things?"

"Our historians tell us that there have been several times when the balance in the realms has tipped too far. When the balance tipped toward Favor, a large group of dreamlings escaped into your world and decided they were gods. They took over a mountain named Olympus and it took centuries for their powers to wear down. Another time, some dreamlings from Faerie Realm—that's in somewhere in Favor—made it to Awake and did all sorts of things to mortals, some good and others bad. Dragons and other beasts have also escaped."

Parker laughed. "This is great! This is the best dream I have ever had. I hope I remember all this when I wake up. Are you going to tell me now that witches and wizards and fairytales and all that stuff I learned about when I was a kid are real? Come on!"

"Parker—" Kaelyn began.

"What? This is totally bogus! Greek gods weren't dreams brought to life. And fairies and dragons—come on."

"Then how do you explain both of us being in the same dream?" she said. "How do you explain what happened just minutes ago with that stone? How do you explain this world? Or him?"

Parker turned and looked at the Dream Keeper. She did have that right. Besides the floating trees and the Doctor Seuss landscape, he was pretty weird looking. He was completely purple from his hair to his eyes. And although his face looked normal enough, there was something different about it; as though he'd lived a thousand years but not aged a day. But then Parker's practical side won out. It just wasn't real.

"Look, Kaelyn, I totally dig this dream, but come on. I've had dreams like this before. You'll see. Tomorrow we'll wake up and we won't remember any of this. You'll carry on being a loser at school, and I'll try not to become one."

The moment Parker said it he wished he hadn't. The look on Kaelyn's face was enough to break his heart. Why had he said it? Why couldn't he just play along with the dream? Why did he have to be such a jerk? Parker looked down at his hand and the stone in it. He handed it to Kaelyn and shook his head.

"Kaelyn, I'm sorry—"

"It's okay, Parker . . . really. I may seem like a loser to you and your friends, but at least I know who I am. You—you, Parker, you can't even be yourself."

Parker had no comeback. What she'd said was the truth. Hadn't he just spent all that day trying to avoid his friends, since he wanted them to believe he was something he wasn't? Parker looked at Kaelyn, then the strange, purple man. Was this guy for real? The idea of going to sleep and your mind entering a different world was ridiculous, something only a little kid could believe. Parker secretly wanted to just go with the flow, to play around with the idea of it being real, but the practical side, the adult side, that his mother had pushed him into, could not accept it. No, he was dreaming and soon he'd wake up and it would all be over. He looked at Kaelyn once more and gave an apologetic grin. Then he let go of her hand.

Kaelyn watched as Parker moved away from her, staggering and shouting for help. Part of her wanted to run after him, take his hand and force him to believe that what was happening was real. The other part wanted him to just go away. She brushed the tears from her cheeks, trying not to let what he had said hurt her anymore. She liked Parker a lot, and tried to convince herself that one day he would see past the labels the other kids had given her and see for himself.

"I know it's a lot to take in, but I'm telling you the

truth," the Dream Keeper said.

"I know you are." Kaelyn was still watching Parker. He was further away now, but she could still hear him crying out for help.

"He'll be okay. This isn't the worst part of Mares."

"I know. I just hoped he—"

"Why do you believe me?"

Kaelyn turned from Parker and looked into the kind eyes of the Dream Keeper. The purple man reminded her of her dad; he had the same soft voice and sad look. She knew her dad's sad look came from the loss of her mother to breast cancer, and she wondered what the Dream Keeper had loved so much and lost.

"I've been stuck in a nightmare ever since my dad died in a car accident. Every night I close my eyes and I'm back in the same car, on the same highway, and the same horrible things happen. But tonight you pulled me from it. You gave me this stone and I suddenly knew this was real. I guess it took me months of living in a nightmare to know when I was saved from one."

"Then you believe me when I tell you our worlds are in danger?"

"I believe you— I just hope you're wrong."

"I'm not wrong, Kaelyn. I'm not wrong at all. I just came from the Crossing where we normally bring mortals into Dreams. I found out that the council has been taken over by a Mare."

"What's a Mare—like a horse?"

"No." The Dream Keeper laughed. "A Mare is a dreamling that was created in Mares. In other words, you could call him a nightmare or a monster. Technically, Fyren's a shifter; a Mare that has the ability to change his shape at will. Dreamlings have special powers. Some have magic from Favor, others from Mares. There are only two shifters in all of Dreams, but Fyren is definitely the most powerful. Not only can he change his shape, he also can read the thoughts of mortals. He does it to become the thing they fear most."

"And now he is in control of this world?"

"Yes and no. It is the council that determines how many mortals visit each realm; they are in charge of keeping the balance. Allyon, who is the head of the keeper's council, is missing or dead—I don't know which. Fyren has taken over the council, arrested all the dream keepers and stopped all mortals from visiting Dreams. This means that when you wake up tomorrow you're going to have a lot of really grumpy mortals to deal with."

"Grumpy? Why?"

"Imagine how you'd feel if your mind didn't rest at all. With the Crossing closed, no mortal can sleep. Their minds cannot rest."

Kaelyn thought about the way she felt after the accident. The days of no sleep and the headaches that followed. Those days were wakeful nightmares. "So if the Crossing is closed, how did Parker and I get here?"

"I accidentally stole your keys last night."

"Our keys?"

The Dream Keeper pulled two old-fashioned gold keys. They reminded Kaelyn of something she might find at an antique shop or in her aunt's attic. She put out her hand to touch them, but the Dream Keeper pulled them back.

"I can't let you touch them or you would go back to Awake. Last night, when you went to sleep I took you to Mares, and I took Parker to Favor. Not nice, I know, but those were my orders from the council. I also took another young girl to Mares and that is when I got into trouble."

"She wasn't supposed to go to Mares?"

"No, she was—that was me following orders. However, she was very young and was ordered to a harsh part of Mares. I felt bad for leaving her there so I broke one of the biggest rules in the book. I gave her my name."

"How is that breaking a rule? People share names all the time." Then Kaelyn realized that the Dream Keeper had never given her or Parker his name.

"When a dreamling tells a mortal his name, it creates a magical bond between them. The bond allows the dreamling to gain power from the mortal, but it also allows the mortal to get power from the dreamling. It's hard to explain properly. But if I were to tell you my name, then you would be able to enter or leave Dreams whenever you wished."

"So she said your name to leave and you got caught?"

"I broke what is called the return code, and for it I got a week's suspension as punishment. It was pure luck that I forgot to return your keys to the Crossing before I left, otherwise I would still be on the beach in Éadrom and I wouldn't know anything about Fyren."

"Didn't you just break the name rule by telling me Fyren's name?" Kaelyn smiled. "Now that I know his name, I can just drain all his powers or something, right?"

"Afraid it doesn't work that way. The magical bond only happens when you're told the name by the one it belongs to. I don't think you can just drain a dreamling's power either, but then again I have no idea how it all works. I don't even know how that dreamstone works. I just know they are forbidden."

"You seem to be the rebel in this outfit."

"Well, I am a Mare." The dreamling smiled.

Kaelyn looked at him in surprise. He didn't look at all like something that would come out of a nightmare. True, he was tall and had an odd skin color, but otherwise he didn't look anything like a monster.

"You may think you are a nightmare, but you don't look like one to me." Kaelyn smiled and the Dream Keeper smiled back. "So, how are we supposed to stop the shifter?"

The Dream Keeper cringed. "I have no idea. I just know that we have to do something and do it quick. Imagine what your world is going to be like if no one is sleeping. I don't know if it's true, but our historians tell us that visiting Dreams is what keeps mortals alive. You have to dream or you go crazy, or something. It has to do with the creation of Dreams, but I don't know very much about it."

"It's true. My dad told me that once—that we have to sleep. It's called reaching REM, the point at which our mind is fully asleep and we dream. If no one can reach REM, then everyone will go crazy. My dad said that a person can only last so long without sleep before they start doing things they can't control—bad things, I guess."

"And if no mortals are visiting Dreams, then our world will start to disappear."

"What do you mean?"

"Without mortals to dream all this up, my world will just vanish. Every dreamling was created by a mortal. I was, Fyren was, Allyon was. If mortals stop coming to Dreams, then we stop existing. It is the conscience of mortals that keeps our world intact. I don't understand why Fyren would risk the destruction of our world."

"We need Parker to help us," Kaelyn said abruptly.

"He doesn't want to help. You heard him, he doesn't believe this is happening."

"He doesn't believe this is happening because he thinks he is still dreaming. Look, I would love to say 'fine let's forget him,' but I'm not strong like he is. I don't know much about him, but I do know Parker is a gamer, and if I know anything about gamers, they know how to get rid of a bad guy."

"How are you going to convince him to help us?" the Dream Keeper asked.

"I am going to have to confront him when we are awake. If I start talking about a dream that only he is supposed to have had, he will have to believe it was true."

"If you have to return to Awake, we won't have a lot of time to do anything. We need to stop Fyren now."

"I don't know how to stop him, but I am sure Parker will." Kaelyn paused, not sure what to say next. She knew she wasn't up for saving two worlds without some help. She had overheard Parker and his friends talk about the games they played and how they had to fight monsters and such to win. Parker had to know what to do. Plus, Kaelyn needed someone else to do this with her. She knew what she was capable of and saving the world was one thing she couldn't do alone.

She came to a decision. "I need you to give me your name and send us back to Awake."

"But with my name—"

"I can return to Dreams without having to wait until I am tired and it's all dark outside. If you tell me your name, then I can talk to Parker in the morning, convince him he is an idiot and then find a quiet place to take a nap." Somehow, she would have to get Parker to fall asleep too or she'd have to wait till nighttime for it to work. Cross that bridge when you come to it, she told herself.

The Dream Keeper glanced around, eyeing the spooky scene. Then he stepped in close to Kaelyn. "My name is Gladamyr."

"Well, Gladamyr, it's nice to meet you."

Gladamyr turned the key and the purple glow vanished. He stood for a moment watching the place where Kaelyn crossed over to Awake. A feeling of despair took form in the pit of his stomach. Could Kaelyn convince Parker to help them, or was she just wasting her time? Time—that was something Gladamyr knew they didn't have enough of. It wouldn't take long for things to start changing in Dreams. The mortals were what kept Dreams alive. It was their imaginations, the human consciousness that held the world as he knew it together. And now here he was putting all his faith in two mortal children, one of whom wasn't even willing to listen. No, there had to be something else he could do, or someone else he could trust—but who?

Allyon suddenly came to mind, and Gladamyr slumped down onto the cold, black ground. He hadn't really had the time to think about what Cerulean said at the Crossing. Allyon is dead. The words stung now, biting at his heart. Although he did not want to accept it, he knew it had to be true. Allyon was gone, or else how could Fyren take over the council?

The Dream Keeper closed his dark eyes and fought back the urge to cry. He thought of his friend, who was more of a father; the reason he had become a dream keeper in the first place. Allyon had seen in Gladamyr something no one had ever tried to see: Light. He'd seen goodness—even in a Nightmare. Allyon told Gladamyr many times that it wasn't what you appeared on the outside that made someone who they were, but what reflected on the inside. Gladamyr was a Mare, created in one of the darkest parts of the realm, but even then Allyon saw the good in him.

"You always saw the good in me," Gladamyr whispered.

The memory of Allyon's voice penetrated his mind, "then see it too."

It was a memory. Allyon had said that very thing just after Gladamyr became a dream keeper. He had not thought he would make a good dream keeper, but Allyon insisted he would be one of the best.

"The council has obviously made a mistake," Gladamyr had argued.

"I am the head of the council and I do not make mistakes," Allyon replied. "Put aside your past, Gladamyr, and focus on a new future. Forget what you did as a Mare. Think of what you can do now as a dream keeper. You can accomplish anything because you have the power inside you to do it."

"Why is it that you can see what I cannot?"

"You have to look deeper than on the surface. Nothing of real importance lies at the top of the water. The treasure is found at the bottom. Look deeper, my boy, and see it too."

The image of Allyon faded from Gladamyr's thoughts as he wiped away the tears from his cheeks. He looked down at the two iridescent keys and the dreamstone in his hand. Gladamyr wasn't alone in this fight. He did have help. Somewhere deep inside him was the power to do anything. And although he couldn't see it himself, he knew that Allyon had seen it. Cerulean had said that he was their only hope, and he had to do something. Fyren mustn't destroy their world.

With a newfound determination, Gladamyr dropped the keys and dreamstone back in his pants pocket. Then, focusing all of his energy on his arms, he watched as they began to stretch and widen. The expanding bone in his forearms became thin and hollow and the muscle small yet strong. The light purple skin stretched out into wings that darkened to match the starless sky.

With conscious effort, Gladamyr raised and lowered the newly formed wings. The force of air pressed against his skin, and very slowly he lifted off the ground. He leaped up the trunk of a nearby tree and climbed to the topmost branch. Exerting all his energy, he raised his wings and swept them downward, lifting himself into the dark sky. Flying was not the ideal way to travel, but with the mortals back in Awake, he had no way to use the keys' powers to open doors. He'd fly back to Teorainn and see what the rebel shifter was up to. With luck, no one would be searching the Crossing for a fugitive dream keeper.

Parker had a headache. His head felt like someone had been screaming in his ears all night. He got up from his bed and looked moodily around his room. Shadows created by the early morning light stretched across the floor. They reminded him of something—oh yes, the dream he'd had. There was something different about it but he couldn't quite remember. He stood for a moment staring at a pile of dirty clothes, trying desperately to remember what the dream was about. It felt important, but it wasn't long before his headache made him stop. If it was that important, he'd remember it later. He had to get ready for school.

After showering and getting dressed, Parker felt a hundred times better. The headache was gone and he felt more awake. Looking down, he saw the case to his video game lying on the bedroom floor. He smiled.

Thanks to an internet search the night before, he didn't have to worry about what to tell his friends when they questioned him about Medieval Assassin. Luck had once again played into his hand. Parker learned from the website that the game had an optional ending, and that if you let the goblin general attack you first, you could use a defense charm that allowed you to steal the villain's powers. It was great! Parker had gained the defense charm early on in the game and never used it, so everything fit together perfectly. He knew just what to say.

Lying to your friends won't make them like you any better, the voice in Parker's head told him. Parker tried to ignore it. The little voice liked to pop up every now and then just to make him feel guilty. Normally it was the voice of his mother, or Dr. Gates—people he looked up to and knew would disapprove of his actions. But this time the voice was different, younger and high pitched—a girl's voice. *You can't even be yourself.* That last thought was different, like a memory. When had a girl told him that he couldn't be himself around his friends? The knowledge of the voice's owner kept coming and going too fast in his mind for him to take hold of. He hated it when he couldn't place two things together. It was like trying to remember something he knew but couldn't quite say.

"Parker, are you ready?"

Parker shook his head as if to pull himself from the tangled memory web he was fighting and turned to his mother. She looked terrible. It wasn't the clothes or the hairdo—no, they looked pretty much the same as every other day—all business. Even her makeup was perfectly applied like it always was. She looked sick or something. Her face was pale, and she had dark half circles under her eyes, which were bloodshot and glassy.

"Are you okay, Mom?"

"I have a headache, and I haven't slept all night. I've been stewing about this hearing I have this morning. My client has four children, and he wants to take them from their mother. I hate cases that have kids involved." She paused, then tried to smile, but it only made her look worse. The lines deepened under her eyes, making her look older. She let out a wide yawn and continued, "Anywhoo, I've got to drop you off early so I can review my notes. Are you about ready?"

Parker nodded and grabbed his backpack. What had he just been thinking about? Oh yeah, the voice in his head. Who did it belong to?

"What's wrong, honey?"

"Do you ever get stumped trying to remember something—like you know the answer to something, but it's just out of reach?"

"All the time, Parker. And just wait, as you get older, it only gets worse. One day someone will ask you a question, and you know you have the answer, but it's like trying to remember a dream."

CHAPTER FOUR
THE PROPHECY

Y ou're ready early," Zelda said, coming into the kitchen where Kaelyn sat at the table with a large bowl of Cocoa Puffs.

"I've got to get to school to do something," she said, through a mouthful of cereal.

"Not anything illegal, I hope."

"Well—I was planning on spray painting a pig on Tiffany's locker if that's okay."

"Fine by me—but please use environmentally safe paint. I'd hate to think of our world getting closer to its end because of that girl. Oh, and while you are doing that, can you run by Vice-Principal Larkin's office and tell him that I've just had a premonition that one of his students will be in detention for the next month."

"Will do." Kaelyn smiled.

"You seem like you slept pretty good last night."

"I did. Had a good dream. How about you?"

"I haven't slept yet. I got hooked on watching the Ghosts and Psychics marathon—it just got over. It was s-o-o creepy, I almost woke you up to watch it with me, but then I thought that wouldn't be very responsible of me."

"Maybe next time."

"If it's a weekend for sure. Oh, I forgot to tell you, my friend Tanis is coming over today for a reading, and she's bringing her cousin, Lena. You're about the same age. I thought you might hit it off. I think she goes to school on the reservation, so she's not going to be part of that Barbie club."

"Sounds cool, Zelly."

Kaelyn emptied her bowl and tossed it into the sink. She had to talk to Parker before their first class started, or she wouldn't get another chance until lunch period. She grabbed her coat and backpack and went to give Zelda a hug. She stopped short. Zelda's face twitched. Her eyes rolled up into her head. Kaelyn was just about to ask if she was okay when a guttural, unnatural voice escaped her aunt's lips. "Seek the web from the unknown friend. It will be the key to the shifter's end."

Kaelyn stood staring at her aunt. The words sent chills up and down her back. Without warning, Zelda pulled Kaelyn into a hug, then stepped back and looked behind her.

"What is it? Did you see something?" she asked, looking around the kitchen.

"Huh?"

"You look like you've just seen a ghost."

"I didn't see anything," Kaelyn lied. She'd heard plenty, and was sure it was an actual prophecy given by an actual psychic. "I have to go, Zelly."

"And I have got to go to bed. I'm tripping out. No more watching reality ghost shows for me."

Kaelyn shook her head and smiled. "You know, Zelly, you have got to be the only psychic around that's afraid of ghosts. I mean, isn't it your job to contact the dead or something?"

"I am not afraid of ghosts! As long as they don't bother me in the shower, I can handle them. On one of the episodes this one psychic had them—you know, ghosts—coming into her shower and telling her about how they died and stuff. Very creepy."

"Have you ever had ghosts bother you in the shower?"

Zelda thought for a moment then bobbed her head. "There was this one time when it felt like someone was watching me in the shower, but I think that was after watching Psycho. Yeah, I don't think I should watch shows like that anymore."

Kaelyn laughed and Zelda smiled. They both knew the moment another episode of Ghost Psychics was on she'd find Zelda in front of the TV. Kaelyn gave her aunt another hug, picked up her backpack, and patted her pocket—just to make sure she still had the stone.

"Remember what I said, Kae," Zelda said seriously.

Kaelyn immediately thought about the strange words her aunt had spoken about a web and the end of a shifter. It had to be some sort of prophecy or something.

"Kaelyn?"

"Huh?"

"About talking to Larkin if you go ahead and spray paint her locker," Zelda said, smiling. "Love you, kiddo."

"Love you, too," Kaelyn replied, closing the kitchen door. She took three steps into the damp morning air before coming to a dead stop. She had to write down Zelda's prophecy before she forgot it, so she pulled out her notebook, and wrote down the words her aunt had said. *Seek the web from the unknown friend. It will be the key to the shifter's end.*

Shifter—that word connected the prophecy with

Dreams. Fyren was a shifter. It was the only other time she had ever heard the word. Web—what was the web? A spider's web, the World Wide Web, webbed feet? And who was the person, the unknown friend? *Let it not be Tiffany*, Kaelyn prayed. She had enough to handle with one popular kid at school, let alone someone who hated her very presence. Kaelyn jogged down the street, her backpack flopping against her back; she had to get to Parker. He had to believe her.

Parker got out of the car and waved to his mom. He couldn't get over how tired she looked. He was used to the idea of his mother being invincible, nothing could harm her. He watched as she drove down the street and turned the corner. Then something else coming up the street caught his eye. It was the new girl, Kaelyn; running so hard that her pink backpack kept bouncing up and down behind her.

"Hola, Parker, buenos días."

Parker turned around. It was Mr. Martinez, and he looked haggard. His face was unshaven and his clothes messy. His shirt had been buttoned wrong, and it was half tucked into his pants. Despite his tired appearance the teacher smiled and stood looking at Parker as if waiting for a reply.

"Oh—¡hola, Mr. Martinez," Parker said in a flat, dry tone.

"Guess I'm not the only one who didn't get any sleep last night. You kids need to spend more time snoozing at home than in school. Got to be those video games."

Parker had no reply. His stomach felt as if it was doing somersaults. He'd forgotten to write his stupid paper for Mr. Martinez. The Spanish teacher waited for a moment before realizing he wasn't getting much of a conversation out of his student. "I'll see you in class, Parker. Adios!"

He watched as his Spanish teacher enter the school. Parker ran up the steps and through the front door. He had to get to the library, and fast. Why hadn't he written his stupid paper? It wasn't like it was that hard of an assignment. All he had to do was explain what he did in a day, and then write it out in Spanish. He had even promised himself he was going to proof-read it for Mr. Martinez saving his skin yesterday with Jason. *That stupid Medieval Assassin!*

Had he just told his friends the truth about not beating the game, he wouldn't have had to avoid them all yesterday, wasted his time searching the internet trying to find out the ending to the game, or have forgotten about doing his assignment. Kaelyn was right; he was so wrapped up in trying to be cool that he couldn't be himself around his friends. Wait a minute—when did he talk to Kaelyn about not being able to be himself?

"I knew you'd be back. Once kids find out how cool the library is, they keep coming back." The old librarian sat at her desk in the center of the room flipping through a massive book. Was it his imagination or did she look ten times older today than she did yesterday? Maybe, like his mom, and Mr. Martinez, she didn't get much sleep last night.

"I . . . I needed a place to finish a paper that's due today."

"Well, this is a great place to do it, but mind your time. You can't really hear the bell in here, and I don't think your mother would want you to be late to class."

"It shouldn't take me long."

The librarian smiled and the wrinkles on her face creased. Then she looked down and went about flipping through the large book.

Parker crossed over to one of the desks and quickly took out his Spanish book and a notebook. Trying to push the strange thoughts about Kaelyn and a man with purple skin out of his mind, he began to write his assignment.

Kaelyn could have sworn Parker had just seen her, yet he took off into the school. Was he running away from her? Maybe he did remember visiting Dreams last night, and he still didn't want any part of it. Or maybe she was jumping to conclusions. After all, she saw him talk to a teacher and go into the school. Kaelyn headed up the school steps and in through the front doors. The halls were filled with students, but she didn't see Parker among them. She did see the Spanish teacher that Parker had been talking to, but she didn't know him well enough to go and speak to him. She did notice, however, that he looked very tired. In fact, everyone looked really tired. Kids yawned or walked half-dizzy. One kid looked like he was crying and didn't want to be here.

Gladamyr had warned this would happen. The Crossing had been closed and no one was allowed to dream except her and Parker because Gladamyr had their keys. Kaelyn couldn't imagine what would happen to everyone if they didn't stop Fyren soon. Would people start to go crazy, and do bad things—or worse, would they just start to drop dead?

Practically running down the halls, Kaelyn peeked into each classroom trying to find Parker. The halls got more crowded by the minute and she could tell that most kids and teachers were not in pleasant moods.

"Hey, watch it!" one kid shouted.

"Mr. Wilson, keep your voice down and you, girl, stop running in the halls," a rotund teacher called out.

Kaelyn ignored them all. She had to find Parker. The first bell sounded and all the kids took off for their classes. Kaelyn got pushed and forced to go the wrong direction. She struggled for a moment then was past the unruly crowd. Suddenly, she crashed into Tiffany's band of Plastics.

"OMG, Freak Show!" Tiffany said, pushing Kaelyn back.

"Did she just touch you, Tiff?" Brianna asked in a high-pitched squawk.

"What's your problem?" Madison jabbed.

"Hey loser, you're going to make us late for class, now move." Tiffany shoved Kaelyn with her bejeweled hand and Kaelyn about fell over.

"What is your problem, Tiffany?" Kaelyn shouted, pushing her back.

The group of Plastics stared at Kaelyn in shock. It wasn't normal for anyone to stand up for themselves, especially to Tiffany, but Kaelyn had had enough of their taunts. She'd wanted to stand up for herself the moment the Plastics called her names and evicted her from her own locker. She didn't know what gave her the strength now. Was it her knowledge that the world was in jeopardy, or was it her determination to find Parker? Whichever the source was, Kaelyn liked the feeling of taking charge of her own life.

"You don't have to push people around like you

own the world, 'cause you don't," she said, breathing hard.

Tiffany's strawberry passion mouth dropped. "What. Did. You. Just. Say. *To. Me?*"

"What are you, deaf? Too much hairspray in your ears?" Kaelyn snapped. She looked around and noticed that a large circle of kids had formed around her and the Plastics. *Had any of them ever stood up to Tiffany? Was that why they were all staring?*

"Whatever, loser."

"That's it? That's your great comeback? Come on, Tiffany, I've seen old cows with better comebacks."

Kaelyn waited for Tiffany to say something. The seconds were like hours and soon the Plastics started to look at Tiffany like she was losing. Losing to a loser.

"Just shut up, Freak Show."

"Shut up is what people say when they can't think of anything else," Kaelyn argued.

"Just shut up—go have your crazy aunt voodoo you somewhere else."

"As if she is a witch or something, Tiffany? She's a psychic, a psychic, not a witch or voodoo mama or whatever you keep calling her. And she's pretty good at what she does. Your mother never complains when she's handing over her money—"

The crowd 'oohed' with excitement and some of the Plastics looked at Tiffany with worried expressions.

"Oh, you didn't tell your friends that your mom pays up to two hundred dollars a month to find out where her next true love is? Oh, don't look so shocked, Madison, you called the house once asking about your dead grandma. I should know—we have caller ID. You aren't any better than anyone else, so stop pretending you are. You're just silly girls who think you feel better when you put others down, but it will never make you any better, only look stupid for doing it. Why can't you let people just be themselves?"

Tiffany looked at Kaelyn red-eyed and furious, but she had no comeback. Most of the kids stood with their jaws dropped in surprise. The hall was silent and Kaelyn felt her heart pounding in her chest. The tardy bell rang and like an alarm, it ripped everyone from their trance. Kids ran to their classrooms, and the noise of shoes on floor and the swishing of backpacks filled the halls.

Kaelyn smiled at the Plastics before walking confidently past them.

Not even a full day had passed since Fyren ordered the Crossing to be shut down and Gladamyr already saw the change happening to his world. As the Dream Keeper flew over the border city of Teorainn, he noticed the lush color that accompanied the realm of Favor on the northern side of the wall fading. Gone were the endless fields of green grasses and spring flowers. Now the grass yellowed and the flowers withered. On the southern side, the wall seemed to have grown darker. The crags and creases in the ground had become sharper and deeper. Gladamyr saw that the only realm benefiting from the closing of the Crossing was Mares.

It was eerie to come into a city that had always been full of light and life. The streets were barren of dreamlings and the once constant blue sky was dark and bleak. All the windows in the high buildings that lined the vast wall were dark and motionless. It was as if every living thing had been removed from the city. Small fires could be spotted here and there, but there was no one around to put out the flames. The dark smoke just drifted up, melting into the thick greyness above. Gladamyr bent his shoulders, and his wings moved him closer to the Crossing.

This building was massive compared to any other in Teorainn, towering above the city like an imposing mountain. It had always been a thing of beauty, its outer walls carved with spells and symbols that were leafed in gold. The winding stairs that tangled themselves on either side of the wall were like braids of long silver hair. The platform was like a delicate mouth of ruby red that led to the gate to Awake. But now the Crossing stood like a stone gargoyle overshadowing a once beautiful city. Fyren had in hours practically destroyed what took centuries to build.

Gladamyr swooped down onto the border wall and in an instant, shifted his form. Gone were the wings; his arms were back but he was now smaller and darker, his color matching the stone wall perfectly. He quickly scanned the wall and saw no one. The wall was unnatural without the soft hum of the lullaby that was so familiar to this place, the silence haunting. Pushing dread from his mind, he moved quickly toward the looming building. As he ran, Gladamyr focused once more on his arms and hands. He urged the muscles in his arms to strengthen and grow; he pushed his fingers and palms to grow small needles. Once he was five feet from the façade, he stretched out his newly formed arms and with little effort climbed up the side of the building.

It took longer than Gladamyr anticipated, more of a struggle with his mind than his muscles. The closer he got to Fyren, the more he wanted to turn around and hide. It was the echoing voices of Allyon and Cerulean that kept him climbing. The ever changing world below pulled him closer to his foe. Gladamyr needed to know what Fyren was planning. He needed to get information and the only way he could do that was to sneak in and get it himself. The plan, of course, hadn't been well thought out. Gladamyr knew that the moment one of Fyren's dreamlings found him, any hope would be gone. *But how can I save the world if I don't know what I'm saving it from?* There was also the faint hope in the back of Gladamyr's mind that Allyon was here, hidden somewhere. Perhaps, by chance, he would find him.

The window that Gladamyr needed was set far back on the building and would have been impossible to reach while flapping large wings, so the climb, however wearisome, was worth it. Pressing himself against the glass, Gladamyr tried to clear his mind, but the memories of the last time he stood by this window would not leave him.

"Can you tell us about your birth, Gladamyr?" asked one of the council members.

"I can only remember that my creator was very young."

"And where in Mares were you created?"

"In Dorchadas. In the shadow of Draig."

At this, several of the council members murmured, and Gladamyr felt a flush break across his face. He knew what they all thought and heard what some said: That anything formed in the shadow of that mountain was nothing but pure evil. Dorchadas was a place filled with carrion and worms, and that was the best of it. No Mare had ever been born in the heart of Mares before. Gladamyr kept his eyes riveted on the highly polished floor, trying not to focus on the twelve dreamlings reflected there. Suddenly a loud knocking echoed through the room as Allyon hammered his gavel.

"Please—let's have order." Allyon's voice stopped all speech,

and the council members looked toward their leader. "Let not the dreamling's place of birth be what determines his fate as a keeper. We have no choice where mortals think us up. I know of a great many keepers created in the best of places who have amounted to very little. So be it, Gladamyr is the heart of Mares—do you look differently on me for being the heart of Favor? Our birthplace has nothing to do with what we've become. I will hear nothing more on the subject. Now then, Gladamyr, tell us why you want to be a keeper?"

The answer had been rehearsed so many times that Gladamyr could have said it backwards, but he could not get the images of his birth out of his mind. He saw the girl, the one who created him. He felt her fear, the horror she felt at the unnatural sight of him. He saw the pink nightgown that was soon stained red as he tore into it and ripped her mind back to Awake. He heard Allyon repeat the question again and returned his focus to the council members.

"I want to be a keeper to help the mortals; to be more than just a monster born to scare them."

"Thank you, Gladamyr," Allyon said. "Now if you will please wait outside in the antechamber while we discuss your request."

Gladamyr waited a full hour, staring out the window into the border city. He thought about the bad things he had done as a fully-fledged shifter. He thought about how Fyren had taught him to use the mortals' fear against them and how to shift his body to become what they feared most. He did not want to be that anymore. If he was not made a keeper, then he didn't know what he'd do with the rest of eternity. He couldn't go back to Mares, could not after what he had done to so many children. It was cold in the small room. A draft blew in from the window. It and his thoughts caused goose bumps to prickle his arms and legs.

"The decision was unanimous," Allyon said, pulling him from his thoughts.

Gladamyr turned from the window and looked into Allyon's face. The old dreamling had a smile that complemented his bright, blue eyes. There was no look of disappointment or shame, and Gladamyr felt instant relief. Even if the council was unanimous against him becoming a dream keeper, he knew that Allyon would still be his friend.

"Might I be the first to welcome you to the Crossing, Dream Keeper."

Gladamyr literally shook the memories from his head. He had to focus; he had only successfully done this shift once before and never through such a small gap. He knew the window had a gap somewhere. Gladamyr had felt the draft the day he awaited the council's decision. He just had to let himself feel it now. Closing his eyes, he tried to picture his body dissolving. Slowly, the figure of the Dream Keeper melted away in a haze of smoke. Like vapor, Gladamyr snaked in through the crack in the window seal. What seemed like eternity passed, and then with a smile, Gladamyr found himself in the small antechamber outside the Keeper Council's court. A familiar voice cried out in horror.

Gladamyr froze.

"I believe your first class has already started," the librarian said, pulling Parker out of a daydream. "I wrote you a note so your teacher will excuse you being tardy."

He looked up at the ancient woman, smiled a thank you, and took the note. Then he glanced down at his assignment. The only visible thing he'd written was his name in the upper right hand corner. *Great! Maybe I can get Mr. Martinez to let me turn it in late.*

Parker could have kicked himself. He was supposed to write that darn assignment, not daydream about a dream. *Was it a dream?* He thought he would remember a man with purple skin had he actually seen one. *And what about Kaelyn? Why did I dream about Kaelyn?* Hurriedly, he shoved his book and notebook into his bag and raced out the library door.

As if it were a sad rerun of the day before, Parker felt pain, then watched as papers and books sailed through the hallway. A familiar humph escaped his lungs as he collapsed on top of a girl. And not just any girl: Kaelyn Clarke.

"I'm so sorry," Parker said, pushing up.

"Please don't tell me you're planning on making this a habit?"

He felt his face burning and knew his cheeks were turning red. He tried desperately to hide his embarrassment by picking up papers and other fallen objects. He doubted he would feel so weird about the situation had he not been thinking about this girl only two seconds before.

"I'm glad I finally found you," she said.

Parker looked up. She smiled at him, her blue eyes twinkling. Parker felt a sudden flush in the pit of his stomach, a strange sensation.

An irritated voice sounded from up the hall. "Dude, what are you doing? Mrs. Coleson is, like, going crazy. You wouldn't believe what I had to tell her to get a hall pass."

It was Jason running toward him and Parker didn't know what to say. He didn't know what the heck he was doing. He shook his head and looked around for his backpack. Spotting it behind Kaelyn, he moved toward her. Jason finally took notice of Kaelyn.

"Hey freak-show, I heard you went all psycho on Tiffany. Weeoooh . . ." he sang in a high-pitched, melodramatic tune.

Parker looked at Kaelyn. Her smile dropped and her face began to go red.

"Come on, dude, let's go," Jason moaned.

"Parker, wait! I have to talk to you."

Parker didn't know what to do. He liked Kaelyn. She was a nice girl, but she was also a loser and being seen with her two days in a row wouldn't look good. Parker decided to pretend he didn't hear her. He quickly grabbed his backpack off the floor and turned toward Jason.

"Please—" she called out.

Man! Why couldn't she just take a hint? Parker turned and said in his most irritated voice, "What?"

Kaelyn's face fell even more. Then in a whisper she said, "I dreamed about you last night—"

Jason's bark-like laugh echoed down the hall and Parker felt sick. It was true! She had been in his dream. The strange man in purple, the weird shadowed land. It was all true—but how?

Jason snickered, pointing his finger at Kaelyn. "Girl, you're funny. Will you dream about me tonight?" He made obscene gestures at Kaelyn.

Parker couldn't take it anymore. "Jason, come on man, stop. Let's go."

"Yeah, okay," he said, still sniggering. "Dude, that girl is s-o-o weird. Have you ever looked at her wrist? Tiffany says she has scars from trying to ax herself."

Parker risked a glance behind him before they turned the corner. Kaelyn was standing motionless amongst the scattered pages and books, one hand in her pocket and tears snaking down her cheeks. Parker didn't know if he had ever felt so low.

Half of Kaelyn wanted to run into the girls' bathroom and cry hysterically, while the other half wanted to hit Parker upside the head. *Was being popular so important for him that he could just stand there and let someone humiliate another person?*

I dreamed about you? That was a lame thing to say, an annoying inner voice said. Kaelyn tried to ignore it. *He's popular, Kaelyn, and you're a loser. Try and remember your station.* Kaelyn wiped a tear from her eye. "Please just shut up," she told herself. *Why? It's true. You're a loser. A LOSER!*

Kaelyn threw her hands in the air and screamed an angry roar. She didn't know who she was more upset at, Parker or herself. She had the guts to stand up to Tiffany just minutes ago, but when it came to standing up to Parker and his cretin friend, she became weak. This was more important than popularity or embarrassment. She and Parker were the only ones who knew the truth about Dreams. They were the only two who could help—save the world.

"Did someone attack you?"

Kaelyn turned around to see the old librarian standing in the doorway to the library. She was holding a large rubber stamp in the air like a weapon. A smile betrayed Kaelyn's thoughts and she shook her head.

"No, I'm fine. Just dropped my stuff—having a bad day, I guess."

The old woman lowered her stamp and clutched her chest. "Was it you who screamed?"

"Sorry."

"At my age, dear, I'm just a few sudden jumps away from having teatime with worms, so keep it down."

"I will—and I'm sorry—"

"No worries. Now then, I can't help you pick all this up, still paying off the new hip, but I can write you a note so you won't get in trouble."

Kaelyn walked into her history class and nonchalantly tossed her note on her teacher's desk. Then she took the available seat by the window. She kept her eyes fixed on the desk so she didn't make eye contact with any of the other kids, especially Tiffany, or the other Plastics. Kaelyn knew that her face was flushed, and she couldn't allow them to see her broken, especially after what happened in the hallway that morning.

"Alright, Miss Clarke," Mr. Plattsburg said, eyeing the note, "we are discussing last night's homework on European powers. Maybe you could tell me the three major powers during the seventeenth century?"

Kaelyn scrabbled through her mind to try and remember her reading from last night, but she just couldn't. The horrible scene with Parker had still not left her, and all she could think about was him. She looked back and forth between her backpack—where the answer sat in her notebook—and Mr. Plattsburg's bloodshot eyes.

"Ummm—"

"No, sorry Miss Clarke, but 'Umm' was not part of Europe's powers during the seventeenth century."

Some of the kids in the room giggled.

"Why are you laughing?" Mr. Plattsburg raising his voice. "Miss Foster, perhaps you know the answer since you are so inclined to giggle at Miss Clarke?"

Brianna's Plastic face fell into an imitation of a scolded child. Eyes pinned on the floor, she shook her head and then slumped further into her chair. Mr. Plattsburg let out a growl and stomped over to his desk. Pushing papers aside, some of them floating to the floor, he grabbed their textbook and flipped angrily through its pages.

"Miss Clarke," he half shouted, "please read the opening sentence on page ninety-seven."

Kaelyn hurriedly dug through her bag. It was a complete mess. She pulled out papers, notebooks, broken pencils and a smashed sandwich before finally retrieving her textbook. The pages were all muddled, half of them sticking out at awkward angles. Some of the kids let out giggles, but Kaelyn tried to ignore them. She found page ninety-seven and quickly scanned the opening sentence.

"The major—" Kaelyn's voiced cracked. More kids giggled, but she cleared her throat and began again. "The major powers in seventeenth century Europe were France, England, and Spain."

"Yes!" Mr. Plattsburg shouted. "Read it again!"

"The major powers in seventeenth century Europe were France, England, and Spain," Kaelyn repeated.

"Yes! Now everyone read it!"

It took a moment for all the kids to open the right page, but Mr. Plattsburg didn't wait. Like a hysterical broken record he shouted the sentence over and over, looking at each and every student with his bloodshot eyes until every last voice in the room was in unison with his own.

"That's enough!" he shouted, silencing the classroom. "Why is it that no one can recall this information when it was written in the very first sentence of the chapter?"

"I'm really tired," a boy sitting next to Kaelyn mumbled. He said it quietly, but the elephant ears of Mr. Plattsburg pricked and the cross teacher turned on the complainer.

"Who isn't tired, Mr. Holland? Don't you think I am a little tired? Do you hear me complaining about being up all night with a colicky baby? Do you see me not doing my homework? I read the chapter last night, just like I asked *you* to read it. Why am I the *only one* paying attention IN THIS CLASS?"

The classroom was silent except for the echoing shout of the enraged history teacher. Most of the kids sat low in their seats, their eyes fixed to the floor, avoiding their teacher's glare. No one wanted to be his next target. Bryce Holland, who normally was one of Mr. Plattsburg's favorites in the class, being a history geek, was on the brink of tears. Kaelyn, like the others, kept her eyes down, but she forced a peek up at the teacher. He seemed to have given up on the class altogether and was now sitting at his desk, straightening the papers he had knocked over. Sensing her gaze he looked up and their eyes connected. A flush of panic raced through her stomach as Mr. Plattsburg smiled.

"Kaelyn," he said in a singsong voice, "do you have a question?"

The kids in the classroom all looked from Kaelyn to Mr. Plattsburg. No one had ever heard Mr. Plattsburg refer to any of them by their given names. Most were sure he didn't even know their first names. Kaelyn held her breath and shook her head. The history teacher leaned back in his chair and stretched his arms in the air, letting out a yawn. "Well, then. I suggest you and the rest of the class spend the remainder of the time re-reading the assigned chapter." And with that he closed his eyes and appeared to go to sleep.

CHAPTER FIVE
NAP TIME

Parker's stomach had knots in it ever since he left Kaelyn in the hallway. He couldn't get her last words to him out of his head: *"I dreamed about you last night."* At first he wanted to believe they had shared a dream, but that was impossible. Jason had to be right— she was a freak. Maybe what she said was the pure truth, she had dreamed about him. Parker was sure that a lot of people dreamed about other people, but it wasn't something one publically announced. After all, Parker had dreamed about her last night too. He thought back, trying to remember the events of his dream, but it wasn't so clear anymore. A stone wall, a purple-skinned man in a dark trench coat, Kaelyn in a car crash . . . screaming— they were all just fragments, like a conversation he'd somehow forgotten. *Dreams.* He remembered the word Dreams—not as in sleeping, but as a place.

"Dude," Jason whispered, snapping Parker out of his thoughts.

He looked up to see Mrs. Coleson staring him down like a hungry hawk after an exposed mouse. Parker looked from his red-eyed teacher to the white board, hoping there would be some clue as to what she had said, but it was blank. He glanced around the room, and all the students were staring at him. They were no help. Finally giving in, he asked the one question he absolutely knew Mrs. Coleson did not want to hear.

"What? I wasn't—"

"Get out," the teacher said in a cold flat tone.

Parker was confused. *Was she telling him to leave class? What had he done?* He looked back at her with a confused expression, hoping she would give a reason. But she just stared him down, her face tight and emotionless. Parker, after some hesitation, stood up and looked around. Jason, who was sitting behind him, was slumped in his seat and avoiding eye contact. *Nice friend*, thought Parker. He grabbed his bag and started moving for the door.

"Wait." Mrs. Coleson went to her desk and pulled a pink slip from the drawer. After frantically scratching something over it with her ballpoint pen, she handed it and the librarian's note to him. "Take both of these to the principal's office."

Parker took the two pieces of paper and quietly left the classroom. As soon as he shut the door behind him, he heard Mrs. Coleson start in on a lecture about the level of respect for teachers in their school. Parker walked a ways down the hall and then looked at the pink slip. At the top it read: Mrs. Coleson, Period 1, English. Date: 22 February. Student: Parker Bennett. Reason: Tardiness, and lack of respect to an educator. See attached drawing he tried to pass off as an *excuse*.

Parker turned over the pink slip and looked at the piece of paper he had given Mrs. Coleson. A crude drawing of what appeared to be a creature that was half donkey, half—was that supposed to be Mrs. Coleson? It could have been anyone except for the fact that the woman's face had buck teeth and horn rimmed glasses. Parker thought the drawing was comical, but had no idea why the librarian would give him a drawing of …Wait, he remembered crashing into Kaelyn and stuff falling out of his bag. He must have grabbed one of Kaelyn's drawings instead of his note.

This was just a horrible misunderstanding. Now he had to go to the principal's office. *Would they call his mom?* She would totally flip out. He would be grounded from gaming for a week, maybe two. This, he knew, was what people called karma. What goes around comes around, or something like that. He had lied to his friends about beating *Medieval Assassin* and was a total jerk-head to Kaelyn, now the cosmos was punishing him for it. He stuffed the pink slip and drawing in his pocket and marched down the hallway. Ten steps later the bell rang and the hall filled with students.

Immediately Jason was at his side, asking what had just happened with Mrs. Coleson.

"I didn't do it on purpose. The note got mixed up."

"It was so cool, man," Jason cooed. "I mean, she didn't even look at the note at first, ya know? She just tossed it on her desk and kept talking about homophones. Like, who cares if butt and but sound the same? Then you acted as if you didn't even hear her when she went off on you."

"She what?"

"Dude, you must've gotten less sleep than I did. 'Cause you're seriously tripping today."

"Yeah, I didn't . . ." Parker began, but then Jason saw Tiffany down the hall and started calling out for her.

"Yo! Tiff, you won't believe what Parker just did to Mrs. Coleson."

Jason headed off to get Tiffany and Parker took the

opportunity to run in the opposite direction. Parker was really ashamed of what had happened and didn't want to talk about it with everyone in school. Sometimes Jason acted like everything was just a game, but this wasn't a game. Parker was in serious trouble. He knew that the moment his mom heard about this, she would be on the phone to his father shouting about how gaming was corrupting their son and how a father figure, other than a therapist, would be nice for once. Parker walked fast and was outside in no time, ignoring Jason's voice calling after him.

As soon as he was out the door, Parker yelled, took off his backpack and threw it across the snow covered lawn. Soundlessly the backpack plopped down in a mound of snow and disappeared. The cold air stung Parker's nose, but it felt good to be outside in the silence.

"I find that screaming helps, too."

Parker turned his head to see Kaelyn leaning against the wall.

Parker's blank expression made Kaelyn feel as though he couldn't see her. His cheeks were red, and they clashed with his chocolate brown eyes. Kaelyn had forgotten what she was going to say. Maybe it was those brown eyes, or the fact that he was finally here with her. "Parker—"

"I know what you're going to say and I just don't know."

"You don't know, or you don't want to believe?"

He didn't answer right away. He first stared at the wet pavement and then the snowy lawn. For a moment

Kaelyn wanted to say something, but cautiously held back. She walked slowly forward until she stood beside him. Parker made a shy shuffle with his foot, kicking over some snow onto the pavement, then in almost a whisper he spoke.

"I remember talking to you but I can't remember when. I remember a man with—"

"Purple skin?"

"But that's impossible! It's not real. No one can share the same dream."

"Parker, that's because it wasn't a dream. It was real. We were there . . . together . . .we—" Kaelyn cut off, she didn't know what else to say. She turned her eyes toward the snow and mindlessly grabbed her arm, tracing her fingers over the scar on her wrist. It was cold and she didn't have her coat. She had only come out here to avoid some of the Plastics. She had stood up to Tiffany and that meant a war had been declared. It wasn't over until one of them fell; David or Goliath.

"I'm sorry about your dad."

His statement completely surprised her. *How did he—what did he—?*

"I saw what you dream about when you go to sleep. I saw the car accident. You got that scar on your wrist when the EMT pulled you out of the car. How was I able to see that?"

Kaelyn tried to ignore the memories of the accident. She had to focus on what she was trying to do here and it didn't involve crying.

"Parker, do you remember you took my hand and saved me from that nightmare?"

Parker nodded.

"Then you also remember talking to the dream keeper and what he said about Dreams?"

"He said it was another world, kind of like another dimension, I guess."

"Exactly! Dreams is connected to our world more than anyone knows. Haven't you noticed that everyone is really tired and moody? Gladamyr said this would happen. Our minds . . . our consciousness have to go there or we don't truly rest."

"Like REM."

"Yes! But no one can get REM 'cause no one can enter Dreams—"

"Except us."

His statement hung in the air like a declaration. *Finally*, Kaelyn thought, *Parker understands*. It was as if a weight had been lifted off her chest. She no longer had to do this on her own, she had Parker. Together they would help Gladamyr and—*save the world?*

"What are we going to do?" Parker asked, locking eyes with her. Kaelyn reached into her pocket and pulled out the dreamstone. In the sunlight it reflected brighter than the twinkling snow. Parker's eyes widened and a smile spread over his face.

"Parker Bennett, we're going to take a nap."

The scream ripped through Gladamyr's mind. In an instant, his body shifted to match the red drapes in front of the antechamber's window. With a flinch he matched the stone walls. His arms flittered into wings. He knew he was alone but the scream had startled him into shifting uncontrollably. He needed to calm down. He had to focus. *Deep breaths,* he told himself as he imagined his body shrinking smaller and smaller. He let his arms shift into wings and then he was no more than a small purple fly, hidden beneath the window.

The scream came again. Gladamyr tried to block it out. The need to save her was overwhelming. He wanted to shift into a bull and barrel past the doors, but he knew it would do nothing to help her. With silent wings, Gladamyr lifted his tiny body off the floor and flew toward the chamber door.

"Please, no more," Cerulean cried out. "Can't you see you're killing him?"

The sight that awaited Gladamyr behind the door was something out of the darkest parts of Mares. In the center of the chamber, surrounded by many high seats filled with dark creatures, a dreamling writhed. His face was covered with a large black widow spider that appeared to be sewing his mouth up with its webbing. Every few stabs the spider inflicted with its needle, the poor dreamling would cry out in agony. Gladamyr didn't recognize the victim, his face was so distorted by the toxic poison, but he recognized the voice—Felix, a dream keeper.

"Please, stop! Stop!"

Gladamyr turned to Cerulean. Her delicate blue form was wrapped in webbing and strapped to a thick wooden chair next to the convulsing Felix. A manic laugh sounded throughout the chamber. Gladamyr looked up to see those sitting on the council bench. Fyren was the first Mare that came into focus. With his long dark cloak hooding his pale skull face, he resembled what the mortals dreamed up as Death. He sat in the high seat, Allyon's seat. Fyren had no expression. He merely gazed down upon the spider and Felix, his bright, indigo eyes showing no sign that he heard the screaming, Cerulean's pleading, or the insane laughter.

Gladamyr inspected the Mare to Fyren's left, an

insane clown-faced dreamling named Mentia. His wide, painted grin and jagged, shark teeth went well with his sadistic laugh. The clown seemed to be enjoying the proceedings more than anyone. Along with his hysterical laughing, the circus Mare would clap his hands and even blow kisses to the spider. His red clown suit with yellow polka-dots seemed a strange contrast to such an awful nature. To Fyren's right was Minyon. The spider Mare was clicking nonsense with his mandibles, but like Fyren, seemed not to notice the endless cries and insane laughter. He looked much the same as Gladamyr remembered except for one change, a large cavity in the side of his head, which explained who controlled the black widow spider sewing Felix's mouth.

Gladamyr recognized many of the dreamlings sitting on the bench. There was Mab, a very beautiful Favor who had once ruled the council as a queen until she was banished by Allyon. Slither, a snake-faced Mare, was apparently shedding its skin while sitting next to an irritable Iniga, a Mare born in the fires of the black mountain. Her skin was onyx with cracks of glowing red that Gladamyr knew could break into open flame any second. There was Cato, a devilish fire pixie; Dorjan, a dwarf dragon; Somnus, an evil Mare who liked to eat his mortal victims back to Awake; and others. Fyren had transformed the keeper's council into a ruling body of monsters. There were twelve in all, with Fyren as their leader.

"Enough for now," Fyren hissed. "I will ask you once again, Felix. Where did you last see Gladamyr?"

The chamber went silent. Even the clicking from Minyon and Mentia's laughter stopped. Gladamyr fought his body's urge to shift, to change into a form more protective than a house fly. Felix cried and coughed at the same time.

"He's already told you—why can't you believe him? Gladamyr is in Dorchadas. He'd gone to the—"

"Silence the fairy!" With Fyren's order the black widow leaped over to Cerulean's face and began stabbing its needle into her upper lip. The blue dreamling let out an ear splitting cry as the spider stabbed repeatedly. Gladamyr couldn't think or concentrate on his shifting. He knew Felix and Cerulean were trying to protect him by telling Fyren he had gone to his birthplace, but Fyren knew that Dorchadas would be the last place Gladamyr would go. All urges to stay concealed left Gladamyr and with a split second decision, he shifted.

Gladamyr's body ballooned out, morphing into a monster. His hands became large pincers that quickly sliced the black widow in half. Black, inky blood and spider gore flew toward the council bench. Minyon let out a howl of clicks and screams as he clutched the cavity that would never be filled. Gladamyr shifted again, and a long sharp tail slipped down his back and slashed open the webs binding Cerulean and Felix. In seconds he had them in his arms, which had now shifted back to hands, and they ran for the chamber door.

Before they reached it, the Mares closest to the doorway threw themselves off the bench and slammed into the doorframe. The doorway crashed shut. Roars from the Mares on the council bench—mixed with Mentia's laughter, and Minyon' clicks—filled the chamber.

Gladamyr turned in time to see Dorjan swinging his horned tail. It pelted Gladamyr across the face and made him drop the two dreamlings. Then Cato soared down from his seat, throwing balls of fire at the Dream Keeper. Cerulean, who had managed to recover from the spider's venom, deflected the fireballs with conjured orbs of water. The two forms of realm magic collided, engulfing the chamber in red and blue smoke.

Other Mares advanced, leaping over the benches and each other to have a shot at the Dream Keeper. Mentia pulled rubber chickens from his pockets and threw them at Gladamyr. In midflight they came alive, gross terror in their faces and needle sharp fangs in their beaks. Gladamyr shifted again. His arms turned back into pincers and one by one he snapped the chickens in half, all the while fighting off Dorjan's tail with his own and trying not to get hit by one of Cato's fireballs.

A loud crack deafened Gladamyr as Cerulean shot a spinning orb at Cato. It was a direct hit, sending Cato into Iniga, who had just begun emitting flames. Both Mares fell back, crashing down on the balustrade and shattering the bench behind. Fire surrounded the room. Mentia let out a mix of terrified screams and panic-stricken laughter as the last few chickens turned back on him when they saw the fire. The clown Mare danced around hysterically, crashing down onto Fyren in a mess of polka-dots and chicken feathers.

Gladamyr was in full combat with Dorjan. The dwarf dragon abandoned his tail-attack and went straight for the Dream Keeper's neck. Gladamyr blocked his attack with his arm, but Dorjan clamped the arm in his mouth. Gladamyr shifted again, forcing his arm to grow. Dorjan's dragon teeth pierced his flesh, but he tried to ignore the pain. His arm continued to grow, eventually breaking through the dragon's clutch, shattering Dorjan's jaws. Painful cries filled the air. The dwarf dragon reared back in pain, then took to the air. The erratic flapping of his wings sent the fire up the walls, encasing the chamber in flames.

Two more Mares jumped at Gladamyr, but he was able to fight them off. As he sent the last Mare, a hairy beast with a monstrous face, crashing onto the council bench, Gladamyr could barely see the forms of Cerulean and Felix. The chamber was a chaotic mix of magic, smoke and flames. Both his friends were motionless heaps on the floor. The only way out of the chamber was blocked, and Gladamyr knew he only had moments to escape. He ran over to Cerulean. A small stream of silver blood flowed from a cut across her right eye but she shook off the pain and lifted herself up. Gladamyr turned to Felix, who hadn't moved since the doorway crashed in. He hunched down and lifted Felix onto his shoulder.

"What do we do?" Cerulean shouted over the mayhem.

Gladamyr looked around. He didn't know what to do. If it was just him, he could shift into something small enough to fit through a crack, but what about Cerulean and Felix? He was about to try actually shifting into a bull to crash through the rubble in front of the door when he felt a chilling terror begin to trickle down his neck. The Dream Keeper turned slowly around.

"You've been very naughty, Gladamyr," Fyren growled.

Fyren's hood had fallen back and his white skull face reflected red in the firelight. His evil, indigo eyes made Gladamyr's vision blurry, and he couldn't make out anything but the bright eyes slowly advancing before him.

"Nowhere to go, *Dream Keeper*," Fyren taunted. "No one to save you this time."

Gladamyr knew Fyren was using fear to paralyze him. He knew because Fyren had taught him to use it on others. *Close your eyes, Gladamyr, and don't look, just close them*, he told himself, but it wasn't working. Moisture formed in his eyes and the tears helped him focus on more than just the two glowing spheres. He saw that all Fyren's dreamlings were gathering behind the Mare, and Mab handed Fyren a sword. It was the deepest black Gladamyr had ever seen, as if all light had been extinguished with this one blade. Fyren took the sword by its hilt and lifted it as an executioner would a battle axe.

"Gladamyr, I'm sorry . . . I tried . . ." Cerulean whispered, holding the Dream Keeper closer.

Gladamyr knew this was it. His existence as a dreamling would be over. His life was ending at this very moment. It was cold; cold except for—the heat in his pocket. Gladamyr reached down into his pocket and snatched out the two glowing golden keys. He looked up and saw shock register across Fyren's skull face as Gladamyr turned the keys in the air. A doorway appeared, along with two children. Fyren roared and charged the closing door but he was too late to stop Gladamyr, Cerulean, Felix, Parker and Kaelyn from Crossing into Dreams.

It hadn't taken Parker as long as he thought to fall asleep. His first impression was that it wouldn't ever happen. He was, after all, on the floor of a girls' bathroom, locked in a stall holding hands with Kaelyn. She had assured him that she hid in that restroom all the time and no one ever came in, but still it was a weird place to take a nap. Parker closed his eyes and tried to clear his mind of all thoughts except a dark shade of purple. His mom taught him when he was little to try to picture a specific color in your mind and let it lead you to dreams. Unexpectedly, the color disappeared and Parker was no longer in the girls' bathroom at school but in Dreams.

Hundreds of images came into view all in a matter of seconds. The purple color was replaced by a large room filled with red, blue, and black smoke billowing out from a hot orange and yellow fire. The fire devoured everything and Parker felt the heat on his face and arms. He was scared of burning to death until he saw the really scary things coming at him; a hoard of dark monsters led by a wicked looking skeleton holding a black sword above his head. Panic flared up inside him and he didn't know what to do. Then something yanked at him and a strange, golden door appeared out of nowhere. A bizarre sensation spread over Parker as if he were flying through the air, and he opened his eyes to find he was in yet another fantastic place.

The landscape consisted of large, red sand dunes that went further than Parker could see. The sky was more orange than red and the sight made him feel like he had landed on Mars. It was hard to comprehend what he saw. Scattered around the dunes were ruins of old stone buildings, but instead of paint or wallpaper, the walls were covered with the sky. Some walls showed sunsets, others bright blue or dark starry skies, one even depicted the sky during a thunderstorm with lightning flashing and cracking across its surface.

"Where are we?" Kaelyn asked.

Parker had to look down to see he still held hands with her. Somehow he had forgotten everything in those few short seconds. He glanced at her and noticed she wasn't looking at him, or the strange world they had come to, but at three figures in the sand.

"You couldn't have come at a better time." It was the purple man, and he motioned them to come over.

"A better time?" Parker choked out. "We were just about killed by some zombie thing and his pack of monsters. Need I mention the inferno?"

"I admit it wasn't the best moment to enter Dreams, but it did have its merits. You just saved our lives."

Saved their lives? Parker hadn't done anything but fall asleep. If that was all it took to save someone's life then the title of hero was seriously overdone. He looked at Kaelyn, who shrugged, and then down at the creature they were all hovering over. Parker had to fight down the desire to puke. The man's face was gross, like something out of a horror movie. His eyes and cheeks were swollen to the point that his skin looked like it was going to pop, his nose looked like it had been stung by a killer bee and his lips—they were halfway sewn shut with a thick gooey string.

"What happened to him?" Parker managed to say.

"Minyon was sewing his mouth closed for not giving up information. The bloating is a reaction to the spider venom. It will go down shortly. He just needs to rest."

Parker looked at the woman who had spoken and saw that she too had a swollen lip and two stitches in the corner of her mouth. Then he noticed she was blue. Yes, blue! Not *Smurf* or *Avatar* blue, but a pale shade like the color of the morning sky.

"Is your color a reaction to the venom as well?" he asked. Kaelyn gave him a sharp elbow in his side, but the blue lady laughed and shook her head.

"You'll find that many dreamlings are different shades, just as mortals are in your world," the purple man said.

"We don't have any blue or purple people where I come from," Parker argued.

"Well, the color doesn't make the person, now does it?" Kaelyn said, glaring at Parker.

The purple man just smiled.

"So what happened to you?" Parker asked.

The purple man stood and glanced around. "Before we say too much, I need to make sure we are safe." He leaped atop one of the sky walls and stared out at the vast desert. Then he jumped off, landing in front of the small group. "We appear to be alone here, but I don't want to risk anything right now. Fyren has proven to have a wider reach than I thought. Everyone pull in close to this wall without touching it. Cerulean, help me move Felix. The children are bound by the dreamstone."

Parker found himself in a tight half-circle next to a wall with a dark and rainy scene. Everyone was told to face out toward the desert. Then the purple man, who Parker already thought looked cool with his long violet hair and chiseled features, transformed. It was the most bizarre thing Parker had ever seen. The man's body completely flattened and stretched out, creating an arched dome. His head somehow remained in the center of the dome unchanged, but the rest of his body had stretched into a thin tent of sorts, shielding them from the desert. Like a chameleon, the purple skin changed until it matched the wall behind them. It was as if Parker was staring at a head floating in the middle of a dark, rainy night.

"That was totally wicked!" Parker said. "Can you change into anything you want?"

"Really, Parker!" Kaelyn scolded.

"What? It might be a good thing to know later on. I mean, aren't we supposed to be saving the world or something?" Parker said it as a joke, but in the silence that followed he contemplated what he had just said.

Saving the world! *How on earth was he supposed to save the world?* His mom didn't even let him stay up on New Year's Eve because it was three hours past his bed time. She didn't let him have a pocket knife, something every fourteen-year-old boy in town had. *And who was here to help him? Kaelyn—oh, she'd be great—the school loser who hid in the bathroom during lunch period to avoid the popular girls. One dreamling whose face resembled something pulled out from under an elephant's butt, and a blue lady who looked like she was about to collapse. The morphing dude seemed like he could handle things, though.* Maybe Parker could get him to transform into a tank, and they could just blast the skeleton man and his goons into dust.

"Can you morph into say, a fighter jet with missiles, and we could just blow up this guy?"

"Sorry—I can't. And besides a fighter jet wouldn't do anything against Fyren. Mortal war machines are useless anywhere in Dreams."

"Before we talk about blowing things up," Kaelyn said, "shouldn't we actually see what's going on? Like, who this guy is and why he is so set on destroying our worlds."

Parker looked at her. *For a girl she was actually pretty smart. One of the first tricks in gaming was to know the objective of the game; what was the enemy doing that the hero needed to stop. Once you knew that, a plan could be laid out.*

"He's trying to restore Mares," the blue lady said.

The purple man frowned. "What'd you mean, Cerulean? By cutting mortals off from Dreams, he's only going to destroy it."

"I don't exactly know, Gladamyr. I overheard them. Not Fyren, but the others. By removing mortals, he weakens the border wall. It almost sounds like he wants to tear down the barrier, mixing the realms. They called it 'restoring Mares'."

"It doesn't sound like a bad idea," Kaelyn said quietly.

"What do you mean?" Parker asked.

"Gladamyr explained that when we first came to Dreams, he had to take me to Mares. It was my assigned realm for the night. You, Parker, got to go to Favor." Kaelyn turned to the purple man for confirmation. He nodded and she continued. "So if the wall is removed and the realms mix, then mortals won't be forced into one realm or the other. It could be more our choice how we spent our time in Dreams. Right?"

Everyone thought about what Kaelyn said. Then the purple man called Gladamyr spoke. "I understand that it might seem what Fyren is doing is right, but you must believe me when I say this dreamling has never done anything that did not benefit himself in the end. He may want to mix the realms and bring equality to Dreams, but there has to be more. Cerulean, you said they called it 'restoring Mares'? How can the mixing of the realms be restoring Mares? How can you restore something that's always been there?"

The blue lady shook her head.

"Maybe by mixing the realms one can overpower the other?" Parker tried.

"No. The power, as you call it, can only be achieved when the balance of the mortals' consciousness is too far given to one specific realm," Cerulean said, as if quoting text from a book. "For example, one of the dreamlings you saw very briefly is Mab, and she once successfully gave power over to one realm."

"How?" asked Parker.

"A little over four hundred years ago, your years mind you—our time is inconsistent here—Mab took control of the keeper's council. Not by force mind you, she was a Favor of the highest standing and very popular among most of the council members at that time. She started things off smoothly, making sure that the realms alternated hosting a mortal for their duration in Dreams. Then slowly she shifted the balance toward that of Mares."

"Why Mares?" Kaelyn asked. "Wouldn't she want it to be tipped toward Favor?"

"And give mortals the chance to dream bliss?" Cerulean laughed. "Mab has never been kind toward mortals. I believe she finds you inferior to her. She shifted the balance toward Mares to torture mankind. This happened about a hundred years ago, still your time. Our historians tell that Awake began to have a harsh outbreak of violent attacks, which led to a great war that covered your world."

"World War One," Kaelyn guessed.

"Yes. In our history it's called *Mab's First. Mab's Second* came just a short time after that. During her second outbreak, thousands of people, all wearing stars on their clothes, were immediately taken to endure Mares. I am afraid they had no rest in Dreams from the horrors they lived in Awake. They are called the *star-children* in our records."

"They are called the Jews of the Holocaust in ours," Kaelyn said bleakly.

"You see, Dreams affects Awake in every way. Mab merely tipped the balance slightly to one realm and it almost destroyed your world. The more mortals she sent to Mares, the stronger that realm became. Some say that dreamlings escaped into your world, bringing with them the power to wield good or evil."

Parker thought about Gladamyr coming into their world. Someone that could morph into anything they wanted at will. Gladamyr could be a superhero and save people from terrible things happening. No criminal or terrorist could stand up to him. If one bad guy was this huge thug with massive muscles, Gladamyr could just make himself bigger. Who could stop such a guy? *Who could stop such a guy?* If a dreamling were good, then they could wield good, but what about those who were bad? Parker thought of the skeleton man—Fyren—coming into Awake. He didn't even know what powers the dreamling possessed, but if they came anywhere close to Gladamyr's, no one would be safe. Not the President, the Pope—his mom—no one.

"How was Mab stopped?" Kaelyn asked.

"Allyon," Gladamyr answered.

"Yes," Cerulean agreed, "it was Allyon who removed the self-proclaimed queen. And he did it with the help of a mortal child. A young girl who used that very dreamstone you're holding."

CHAPTER SIX
CONFESSING

Kaelyn looked down at the dreamstone in her hand, its opaque surface reflecting the starry sky around her. This stone had once belonged to another girl; someone who had helped bring the reign of a wicked queen to an end. Perhaps it could once again help defeat Fyren and save Dreams and Awake. Kaelyn felt a glimmer of hope. They sort of knew what Fyren was planning. Now they needed to come up with a plan, but first Kaelyn thought they should at least get to know each other.

"Cerulean," Kaelyn began, "that's your name, right?"

"Yes."

"Like the color . . . so pretty . . . it matches you well."

"Yeah," Parker chimed in, "your hair is the same color as the crayon."

"As the what?" Cerulean had a gentle smile on her pale blue lips.

"The crayon—you know, to color with—markers, pens—paper—crayons?"

Kaelyn gave Parker yet another glare, and she saw his eyebrows furl.

"Sorry," he said. "When I get nervous I start to say really stupid things. I mean, who cares if your name comes from a Crayola box, or that you're blue or he's purple . . . I mean . . .sorry . . . "

"Parker, it's okay," Kaelyn said. "We have every right to be nervous. I think for starters we should at least introduce ourselves. My name is Kaelyn Clarke, and I'll be fifteen in a few weeks." *Who cares about your age?* Kaelyn thought, turning a little red. "I guess you don't need to know my age."

"No, I think knowing your age is very helpful— especially in the dream world. You see, the older you mortals become, the less imagination you have within you. The world of Dreams is created and sustained by your imagination. I am blue because the child who imagined me saw me as a blue fairy. To know that you, Kaelyn, are only fourteen tells me you still have a few more years left of wonderful things to create. You have heard my name spoken, but now I am going to reveal my name to you . . . I am sure Gladamyr has told you about the law I am about to break?"

Kaelyn nodded and then looked at Parker. *That's right, he doesn't know.* "I know but Parker doesn't."

"Then let me explain, Parker," Cerulean spoke quietly. "The greatest power a mortal can have over a dreamling is to know their name. It cannot be given by another, only the one it belongs to. There are many mysteries involved in the divulging of one's name. I do not fully know them all myself, however, I do know that if I give you my name you are free to call on me anytime and anyplace within Dreams. Your knowing my name means we're connected, it creates a bond between us.

This bond is solid and will remain for eternity. This is why the giving of my name is so extraordinary. Now then, my name is Cerulean, and I'm one hundred and eighty years old—that is your time, of course."

"A hundred and eighty?" Parker blurted. "Wow, you look amazing for such an old lady."

"Parker!" Kaelyn scolded. "She's not an old lady!"

Cerulean and Gladamyr laughed.

"What's so funny?" Parker asked.

"I am very young according to our time; Gladamyr is even younger than I. Remember I said once before that our time is inconsistent? Time changes in Dreams as the winds change in Awake."

The dreamling on the ground let out a moan, and Cerulean turned her attention to the poor thing, who was now beginning to shake. Gladamyr shifted slightly and his starry surface blinked out for a moment. He craned his neck down lower so he could better look at his comrade.

"Is he going to be okay?" Kaelyn asked, worry creeping into her voice.

"The venom is affecting him more than I first feared," said Cerulean. "Fyren has been tampering with the darkest of magic."

"We need help. Like, a doctor or healer," Parker pointed out. "In gaming there's always a healer to help the heroes recover when injured, or a magic plant or potion. Do you have anything like that in this world?"

"I know of nothing like that," Gladamyr said.

"Children," Cerulean said, "you must understand that in our world, we do not get sick or even—" She stopped, and Kaelyn noted the look that crossed her face.

"What is it?" she asked.

"It's just that what I was going to say is not true anymore. I mean, look at Felix. He is sick and all the other dream keepers are . . ." Cerulean's face turned pale as she stared hard at Gladamyr.

"Go on Cerulean, what about the others?"

"I only saw a few of them . . . but it was terrible. Fyren has Minyon seeing to the punishment of all dream keepers who do not swear allegiance to the new council. Some of the things that Mare has done to them are unspeakable. They are unrecognizable . . . I only knew one of them was Martinia because she had that green shawl she always wears tied around her head to stop the bleeding. Gladamyr, she was missing half her face! As if Minyon's spiders chewed it right off. I've never seen such darkness as this."

"Do you know what Fyren wants with the dream keepers?" Parker asked.

Cerulean shook her head. "Only that he is more interested in finding you than any of them." She directed this to Gladamyr and Kaelyn saw his form briefly shift and retighten.

"So how do we stop him?" Parker asked. "I mean, this guy and his followers have to have a weakness . . . something."

Everyone was quiet for a moment and Kaelyn realized that the time had come for her to share what she knew. They had to be told about Zelda's prophecy. She bravely took a deep breath and then cleared her throat.

"This might sound a little crazy, but I think I know how to defeat Fyren—"

BOOM!

Everything was a blur of light and images. Gladamyr's body contracted like a rubber band that had suddenly snapped. The starry sky disappeared and the red desert sand blew into Kaelyn's face, stinging her eyes. Cerulean screamed, or was it Felix—Kaelyn didn't know. Her head ached with every pelting grain of sand. She felt Parker's hand in hers, but it was sweaty and losing its grip. She tightened her fingers and tried to shield her eyes. She could make out three forms coming toward them, but the blowing sand made things look funny—one person looked like he was dressed as a clown and another looked like she was on fire. The figure in the center was the hardest to see because that's where the sand was blowing from.

"We need to get out of here," she heard Gladamyr call. "They found us too quickly. We can use your keys to—oh, NO!"

Before Kaelyn could say anything, the image of Gladamyr, Cerulean, Felix, and the red sandy world whipped around so fast that she couldn't pick out any one thing. There was a flash of purple and then she saw a white fluorescent light above her head. An angry voice was screaming, "GET UP! WAKE UP!"

"What are you two doing?"

"Are either of you on drugs?"

"Eloise, go call their parents."

"Do we need to call an ambulance?"

Kaelyn heard the clicking of heeled shoes on tile and then the sound of lots of kids' voices as a door opened and closed. She focused her eyes to see three people standing over her and Parker. They were Ms. Coleson, the old librarian, and the Vice Principal, Mr. Larkin. Kaelyn turned to look at Parker, who had gone completely ash-faced. Then the door to the girls' restroom burst open and Kaelyn felt her stomach flip over—twice. Tiffany and Brianna's perfect Plastic faces broke into triumphant smiles.

Gladamyr tackled Cerulean and they fell onto Felix, narrowly missing the burst of fire issuing from Iniga. Red sand swirled everywhere. Gladamyr could barely make out the wall beside them catching alight. The children had returned to Awake and there was nowhere to go. The crazed sound of Mentia's laughter echoed off the wall, and Gladamyr knew they only had seconds to escape. Shifting his arms into two large scoops, he picked up Cerulean and Felix and did the only thing he could think of. He ran and jumped into the wall covered with the night sky.

It was as if he had stepped straight into a black pool of diamond studded water. He was weightless and floating amongst the Milky Way. Brilliant stars and planets in all colors surrounded him. The star-filled heavens were spectacular. He looked down to see an equally stunned Cerulean, gazing in wonder at the sight. Felix, in his other arm, was motionless, his limbs lazily drifting in the space.

There was sound, but faint as if heard through water. Gladamyr could still make out the sand storm striking against the stone surface of the wall but there was no sand in sight, no connection at all to that part of Favor. He heard the whooshing of the fire too and the sound of Mentia's laughing.

"What are you doing, fool?" It was the voice of Iniga, harsh like her flames. The only response was hysterical giggling. Gladamyr looked about, trying to find where the voices were coming from, but there was nothing—just space and stars everywhere.

"Don't do that, you idiot, you could kill them in there and then what would we do?"

"Fyren wants him dead," replied a deep, hushed voice.

"That's Twister," whispered Cerulean. "He is the reason for the sand storm."

Gladamyr hadn't seen Twister in the council chambers, but the Dream Keeper knew the Mare well enough. Twister could move air with brutal force. Not many dreamlings could stand up to Twister, literally. If he didn't like a dreamling, all he had to do was push them over with a jet of air—and Twister liked few dreamlings.

"Mentia, you idiot, I said stop!" Iniga shouted.

"You're not in charge," roared Twister.

There was a loud, yet disturbingly muffled crash and then a whirlwind of whooshes and thuds. Gladamyr strained his ears trying to make out something. There was the sound of sand and fire and—*if only Mentia would stop his psychotic laughing.*

"He needs to die by the sword, you fool!" Iniga snapped.

"I—hee hee—know how—hee hee—to get them— hee—out—"

"NO!"

Stars fell in fragments of broken glass. Gladamyr watched as one solar system after another pulled away from the black space and fell into nothing. He turned every which way, trying to see how to escape, some way back to the world of red sand. He knew he shouldn't have jumped into the wall. It was a stupid thing to do. He had seen dreamlings enter the walls but never return. Hadn't he warned the others not to touch the wall? And yet he deliberately jumped into it. He wasn't even sure there was a way back to Favor once you entered, or even where this starry world existed. Panic took him. His shifting was happening uncontrollably again. Legs stretched and shrank, and his neck twisted in odd directions. He lost his hold on Cerulean and Felix. They both floated up and away from his ever shifting body.

Focus, Gladamyr, focus, he told himself. He was panicking—that's all. There was a way out. He just had to focus on one shape. Gladamyr's tailbone stretched out into the dragon tail he'd fought Dorjan with, then suddenly it shrank back into him, inverting his spine with a stab of pain. His hands puffed in and out, turning to smoke then back to flesh. A piece of razor sharp sky cut across his forearm. Gladamyr threw back his neck and cried out from the pain. Again he shifted.

Cerulean called out to him, pleading with him to focus his mind. Her voice was all it took. The shifting stopped and Gladamyr readjusted his body to that of the flying creature he had been hours before. He flapped his wings and soared up to the others, barely grabbing Felix before he got beheaded by a sharp blade of starry sky. Cerulean, who had pulled off her robe to unfurl her wings, flew into Gladamyr with the force of a falling boulder. Gladamyr caught her and pulled her in close to him and Felix just as a large piece of the Milky Way came crashing into them. Instantly, the shattered starry night vanished.

Parker tried to ignore the glares and shocked faces as he was escorted out of the girls' bathroom down the hall toward Principal Newton's office. He tried not to look at Jason, who was pointing and joking with Nick and Tyler. He disregarded Principal Newton's irritating lecture about breaking school rules—*yadda yadda yadda*—

and how your middle school report can—*yadda yadda yadda*. He tried to ignore hearing his mother arguing with the secretary about Parker being suspended for the day. He tried to ignore the thoughts in his head that said over and over, *Parker Bennett, you are such a loser!* Obviously he hadn't thought things through very clearly. *You can't just beat a video game in an hour—it takes time, why didn't you wait? You are such a loser. . . What about Gladamyr and Cerulean? They're in trouble. You are such a loser . . . There isn't much time left. Parker you are such a loser . . . Kaelyn, we have to get back there! Parker, you are such a loser. . .*

"Parker Ryan Bennett, what *were* you doing in the girls' bathroom?"

He had never seen his mom so mad in all his life. She still looked tired, but worse than ever. Her eyes were red and her face looked puffy—*had she been crying?* "Do you have any idea how hard it is to reschedule a hearing, not to mention having to come here and be told that my son has been caught napping with some strange girl in a restroom?"

"Mom, we—"

"I don't what to hear it, I really don't. I heard enough excuses when your father was around. I don't need this right now, Parker. I'm not ready to take on a troubled teenager. Now get in the car!"

Parker got into the back seat and slumped into the corner. In seconds, his mother slammed the driver's door and was peeling away from the school, cell phone in hand.

"Yes Estelle, this is Elisabeth Bennett—Parker's mom. I know that Dr. Gates doesn't have Parker for another few hours, but I was hoping as it's lunch time . . . well, I've had to pull Parker from school and . . . yes . . .

yes, of course . . . thank you, Estelle."

Oh no, your son is turning into a troubled teenager, better call a psychiatrist. Maybe we can pump him full of medicine or better yet, electroshock therapy. Parker watched as his mother tossed her phone on the seat next to her and glared at him through the rearview mirror. She didn't say another word to him, just kept sending that squinted glower through the mirror. It was silent all the way to the door of Dr. Gates' clinic.

"Ms. Bennett," the receptionist greeted his mom. "And hello to you too, Parker. Just have a seat, and Dr. Gates will be right with you."

"Thank you," Mom said curtly, and they sat down on the closest bench to Dr. Gates' office. Within a few minutes a girl and her mother came out of the office, followed by Dr. Gates.

"Estelle, will you schedule a follow up visit? I'd like to see you two in about a month."

"Thank you, Doctor," the woman said as she turned toward the receptionist.

"Ah, Parker, it's good to see you."

"Hey," Parker whispered back. This got him another hot glare from his mom, and she stood up and charged into the office.

"Ms. Bennett," Dr. Gates began, "I'd like to talk with Parker alone for a little while." She stood for a moment as if contemplating whether she wanted to listen or not, then nodded in agreement.

"I will be back in an hour then. This is actually better for me. I'll have time to rearrange my schedule. Thank you, Dr. Gates—Parker, behave yourself." And with that she was out the clinic door without so much as looking at Parker.

"Come inside, buddy, let's talk."

Zelda showed up to school a little after Kaelyn watched Parker and his mom leave the principal's office. Her aunt came bundled up in a crocheted blanket and wearing her pajamas and snow boots. From her red cheeks, Kaelyn saw that she'd walked rather than drove. Her aunt's appearance received lots of laughs and jokes from the on-looking kids, who the teachers were trying to get to return to the cafeteria. Kaelyn ignored them. She loved her aunt no matter what she looked like—Zelda knew who she was and didn't try to hide it. The first thing Zelda did was give Kaelyn a hug. Then she turned toward the secretary.

"I understand there was some trouble this morning involving a locker and some paint," she said. The secretary's eyes bulged and darted back and forth between Zelda, Kaelyn, and the principal's office door. She shook her head and eyed Zelda's clothes. Her nostrils flared and a scowl reshaped her face as if she had just smelled dog poop.

"I-I beg your pardon," she stammered. "I explained on the telephone that your child was caught just minutes ago taking a nap in the ladies lavatory."

"Oh, is that all?" Zelda laughed as she turned toward Kaelyn, who gave a small smile. "I couldn't understand a thing you said on the phone. You should really try speaking a little louder into the receiver. I could have sworn, Kae, you did that little thing you said you were going to do this morning."

The secretary's eyebrows went up and Kaelyn thought the woman's face resembled a vulture the more the conversation went on.

"You don't seem to understand, Miss—"

"Creighton."

"Excuse me?"

"What? You asked my name, didn't you? It's Creighton, Zelda Creighton. Surely you've heard my commercials? That's right, I'm Madam Zelda, psychic extraordinaire."

Zelda waved her arms flamboyantly. The secretary stared blank-faced.

"Oh, you must have thought I was calling you a *cretin*." Zelda laughed. "I get that a lot. In fact, my sister and I were teased so much when we were little about our name, I almost thought about changing it . . . ah . . . anywhoo, you were saying?"

"I was saying that your child was caught during her lunch hour in the girls' bathroom sleeping—"

"She can't take a quick nap during lunch period?"

"With a boy!"

Zelda went quiet and then looked down at Kaelyn, who tried to give her best expression that related to Zelda how sorry she was.

"As such, our principal has suspended her for the rest of the day. She is to also serve detention on Mondays after school for two weeks."

"For taking a nap in the bathroom?"

"She was with a boy!"

"I still don't see how this deserves suspension and detention. For crying out loud, I know my niece and she isn't the type of girl to fool around with boys in bathrooms, so unless they were found doing something other than napping, I will not permit her to attend detentions on Mondays. That's ludicrous, how many times did you nod off during school?"

"I was a model student!"

"I'm sure you were. Come on, Kaelyn, let's go spend your suspension at home eating ice cream and watching bad television."

Dr. Gates looked down at the carpet as if lost in the pattern. Parker knew he wouldn't believe him. Why did he tell a psychiatrist of all people that he traveled to a dream world in his sleep? *Get ready to pull out your prescription pad, let's see, two sessions of electroshock therapy combined with seven pills a day of this new anti-hallucination medication.*

"I knew I shouldn't have told you. It's just that I know my mom would never believe me if I tried. She wouldn't even let me explain."

"Parker, first of all I want you to know that you can tell me anything you feel you need to. I am not going to judge you or scold you for sharing what you feel you are experiencing. Now, you said that both you and this girl Kaelyn visit a world called Dreams in your sleep?"

Parker nodded.

"Kaelyn, isn't she the new girl?"

Again Parker nodded.

"I see," he sighed. "Do you want a candy bar?"

"What? A candy bar? I get kicked out of school and you offer me a candy bar?"

"Well, did you get lunch or anything? I'm going to have a candy bar—I'm hungry, so do you want one? I got Snickers or Butterfingers."

"Snickers," Parker said with a grin.

"Good to see you finally smiling."

"It's good to have a reason to."

"I think your mom is under a lot of stress right now,

so give her a break and I'll try to see if she can give you one. Now, if what you're saying is true, it would explain why I've been downing caffeine and sugar all day. I slept absolutely horrible last night." Dr. Gates laughed, then turned a serious expression on Parker. "Parker, as a professional, I have to say that I'm not sure I fully believe that what you're experiencing is real."

"But—"

"It's real to you, I know. Our minds are the most incredible things in the world. There's nothing like the human imagination."

"I didn't imagine it!" Parker shouted. "I didn't. Come on, Greg! Of all people, do you think I'd risk everyone catching me snoozing in the girls' bathroom with the biggest loser in school? My friends all saw me coming out of there with her. My life is over at school. Do you think I just made up something in my head?"

"As your friend, I believe you."

"But as my shrink you think I'm a quack job."

"I didn't say that."

Parker got off the couch and walked over to the window.

"Look. I'm not making this up. There's a world that our minds go to when we're asleep. It's called Dreams. A bad guy took over and that's why no one has gotten a good night's sleep lately. Now, the only people who can get into Dreams are me and Kaelyn. It's because Gladamyr accidentally took our keys—"

"Who?"

"Gladamyr, he's a dream keeper. A big purple dude who can change into whatever he wants. He took our keys from what's called the Crossing; that's where we, people, are supposed to enter Dreams. If I don't help him stop this bad guy then things could start looking really bad in Awake—our world."

Dr. Gates stared at the pattern in the carpet. Parker was frustrated and threw his hands in the air, yelling for the second time that day. Dr. Gates' head shot up and Estelle rushed into the office.

"Is everything okay?" she asked, looking from Dr. Gates to Parker.

Parker's mom pushed in past Estelle. Her eyes looked like they were about to catch on fire. Parker put his arms down and felt the heat of his cheeks blushing. Dr. Gates jumped up from his chair and motioned that everything was okay.

"Don't worry, ladies," he said. "I was just trying something out with Parker. I've found that when you have built up aggression, it's good to let it out by shouting. It works better than breaking things."

"I'm sorry for the interruption, Doctor."

"That's fine, Estelle, you can go back to your desk. Ms. Bennett, if you could come inside for a moment. Parker, if you could just wait outside, I'd like a word with your mom."

Parker slumped his shoulders and stole a glance at his mom, who now had a worried look on her face. He tried to say something but no words would come out, so he gave up. Then he looked at Dr. Gates, who was attempting a reassuring smile. Parker was not reassured. He had just told a shrink that he visited a dream world, and followed that by screaming like a mad man. He shut the office door and crumpled into a bench. Who cared if the world was coming to an end because his life was already over.

"All right Kae, it's time for me to be the responsible guardian," Zelda said a few minutes after leaving the school grounds. "What were you doing in the bathroom with a boy?"

Kaelyn stopped walking and stared at the snow-covered ground twinkling in the afternoon light. She tried to decide whether she should tell Zelda the truth or make something up. She could say that she didn't sleep well and sort of fell asleep—*Zelly wouldn't buy that. You told her this morning you slept great.* Maybe she should claim she had amnesia and didn't remember anything from first period to the moment she woke up. Other fantastical stories entered her mind, but Zelda was too good a person to lie to.

"Zelly," she began, still staring at the snow, "if I tell you something that sounds really—I mean *really*—out there, will you believe me?"

Zelda looked Kaelyn straight in the eyes. They were crystal blue with a white ring around the center, *just like mom's used to be.* Kaelyn felt the smallest of pains in her chest. She'd never seen her mom in Zelda at all. Zelda was a loud dresser and had a mop of red curls always up in a half-done bun. But when Zelda turned and looked at Kaelyn, the sun touched on her red curls turning them golden, and for just an instant, Zelda looked like her mom.

"You listen here, Kae," Zelda said seriously. "You can tell me anything. I will believe it."

Kaelyn smiled. "I know."

"So what is so really, really out there that you need to tell me?"

Kaelyn cleared her throat and began. She told Zelda about falling asleep and watching the car accident that killed her father, and how it played over and over in her head. She explained the pain she felt as she was thrown forward in her seat, the lap belt striking across her neck and the glass cutting into her wrist. She spoke of the man with purple skin, the Dream Keeper—Gladamyr—who saved her from the nightmare she'd been having for months. She told her all about Dreams and the world that could only be visited in sleep and how it was very real. Then she reached into her pocket and pulled out the opaque stone, and handed it to Zelda.

"The dreamstone," she said.

Zelda held the stone in her hand. She rotated it round and round. The afternoon sun caught on it, reflecting tiny rainbows all over her face. Then she closed her hand over the stone and looked at Kaelyn with that serious face that reminded Kaelyn of her mom.

"How are we going to do this, Kae?"

Gladamyr knew he was falling. Wind raced all around him, and his stomach churned with vertigo. He felt sick. He could faintly make out the light blue glow of Cerulean next to him, and he could feel her body tighten with the fear of impacting with the ground. Felix was still motionless except for the occasional gust of wind that moved his limbs in odd motions. The sensation of falling was continuous, and Gladamyr thought they would never stop. Then it hit him.

"I know where we are!"

Of course he knew where they were. He was a dream keeper. He had seen many mortals caught in the fall pits before. Mortals just wandered about in their imagined dream and would suddenly step onto a fall pit and start to scream and thrash as if they were falling to their deaths. The fall for them lasted only as long as the dream keeper wanted, for all he had to do was pull them off the pit and they no longer felt like they were falling.

"We're in a fall pit," Gladamyr shouted above the wind. "One of us has to separate and try to escape it. Then it's just a case of pulling us out the pit and we're free."

"Why does it sound like I'm the one getting separated here?" Cerulean shouted back.

"I need to hold onto Felix. If you can unfurl your wings it should be enough to—"

Cerulean didn't wait for Gladamyr to give her the order. She pushed out of his embrace and stretched her wings out, catching the wind. She let out a pained cry as she flew away, her faint blue glow vanishing.

Gladamyr waited with nothing but the sensation of falling. It was just him and Felix now in a world of dark, never ending abyss. Felix groaned, and Gladamyr tried to reassure the dreamling that he would be okay. Just then, a faint glow of blue light in the shape of a hand reached toward him. He took it. Instantly the wind holding him in flight died, and he crashed to the stony ground along with Felix. There was light now, a dim yellow light, but enough to see by. He glanced at Cerulean, who was smiling in spite of the awkward way her wings hung. He looked down at Felix and something strange caught Gladamyr's eye. The bloated section just above Felix's swollen cheek moved. It was a slight shift in the skin, but it looked as if something, just for a moment, had forgotten to be still.

Gladamyr cast around the ground for something sharp. He saw a jagged, arrow-shaped rock a few steps off and motioned silently for Cerulean to get it for him.

With a questioning look, she picked up the rock and handed it to him. Gladamyr stabbed the pointed side of the rock into Felix's face.

"What are you doing?" Cerulean shouted, pulling back on Gladamyr's arm. Felix let out a cry of pain, but Gladamyr paid no attention to either dreamling. He dug the rock around in a circular motion inside Felix's cheek, and then twisted his wrist in an arc. Something dark and wet with Felix's blood shot out from the dreamling's cheek, plopping onto the ground. It was one of Minyon's black widows. Gladamyr wasted no time; he shifted his fist into a large brick and brought it down, smashing the spider into oblivion.

"How did you—?" Cerulean began.

"I saw his skin move unnaturally and guessed."

"That's Minyon's creature, which is how they must have found us in the wasteland."

"And most likely the reason that Felix isn't healing of his own accord."

As if freed from an eternal silence, Felix cleared his throat and tried to say something, but neither Gladamyr nor Cerulean could make it out.

"Try not to talk, Felix. Give your body time to heal," Cerulean said, combing back his dark curls. She looked up at Gladamyr and her faced changed from concern to business. "Are there more fall pits in Dreams other than in this place?"

Understanding dawned on him, and he shifted his arms once more, scooping up his two companions. Then he began to run. It wouldn't be long before Fyren sent out another small army to find them. They had to get away from the fall pits fast.

CHAPTER SEVEN
WANTING MORE

"You're grounded."

"But Mom, I've already got detention."

"You're lucky that's not all you've got. Parker, I don't have time to argue with you about this. I have a lot to do now that I had to be pulled out of court. Just go to your room and do your homework, and I don't want to hear that game of yours at all."

Parker turned and was planning on stomping off, but he needed his mom to listen for once in her life. He needed her help. Dr. Gates wasn't any help. The second Parker told him, the guy kicked him out of his office and called his mother in. The only lucky thing was they didn't stop off at a pharmacy on the way home. Parker bravely turned around and tried his best to look innocent.

"Mom, can I just explain to you what I was doing?"

She looked at him and he could tell she was fighting a battle in her head of whether to just brush him off again or actually be a mother. She put down a handful of papers and sat down on the sofa.

"Parker, I understand that I haven't been a very good mother lately. And I'm very grateful that you have been patient with my work—"

"Mom, it has nothing to do with you, honest," Parker said, coming to her defense. "It was totally my fault that I got suspended. I screwed up and I'm sorry, but I really need to tell you why I was in the bathroom with Kaelyn."

"Okay then, tell me," she said with a small smile. "I'm listening."

"Well, it all started last night when I was sleeping. I had a dream that I was in the middle of playing my game—yeah, yeah, I know you don't like that game, but I've been trying to beat the last big boss guy, and so I was dreaming about it when—"

BUZZ BUZZ BUZZ

"Oh, Parker, honey, hold on a second," she said, picking up her phone. "Oh great, it's your father. Hello, Jeff . . .what . . . hold on . . . who told . . . oh I see . . . that's not . . . what do you mean I'm to blame—you're *never* around . . . don't even . . . I have responsibilities at work too, Jeff . . ."

Parker's heart-to-heart with his mother was over. She jumped up from the couch, grabbed her papers, and phone in hand went into her room arguing with his father. *The school must have called Dad.* Now his parents would fight about who to blame for Parker becoming a troubled teenager. He hated this. He hated the fact that his parents were more concerned about their careers than their family.

He knew a long time ago the divorce was coming. Dad spent more and more time away from home on business trips, and Mom spent more and more time at the office. Parker was fine with it at first. His dad bought him any game he wanted, and he had lots of time to play them, but he was also a kid alone in a big house—a kid that still needed the attention of two adults. Maybe they were to blame; both of them.

Parker went to his room and grabbed his backpack. A buzzing sound from the small pocket at the top reminded him that his friends had seen him being escorted out of the girls' bathroom with Kaelyn. He unzipped the pocket and pulled out his cell phone. There were six different text messages.

Dude WTH, in the GBR? ALOL! –Jason
[Dude what the heck, in the girls' bathroom?
Actually laughing out loud!]

TXT ME ASAP –Jason
[Text me, as soon as possible.]

OMGYG2BK, U & Kaelyn Clarke? –Tiffany
[Oh my God you have got to be kidding, you and Kaelyn Clarke?]

PCM –Connor
[Please call me.]

TMOT U <u>need</u> 2 TMB.
Tiff is saying U & Kaelyn are BFGF –Jason
[Trust me on this, you need to text me back.
Tiff is saying you and Kaelyn are boyfriend and girlfriend.]

URAL-Tiffany
[You are a loser!]

Parker didn't know what to say to any of them. They didn't understand. He wasn't a loser. He was trying to save the freaking world, and they didn't know what was going on. He quickly texted Jason a short response:

HHIS TTYL

[Head hung in shame, talk to you later.]

He ignored the other two. Tiffany needed to mind her own business and stop trying to run the school like she was the warden of her own prison, and Connor—he—he was just trying to be nice. Parker had no qualms about Connor; he was a nice kid, a borderline loser with his weight problem.

He went to turn off his cell phone when it buzzed again. Parker saw it was from a number he didn't recognize. It read:

Parker, let's go back to Dreams.
My aunt believes me.
She wants to help.
Call or text me back, ASAP. –Kaelyn.

A cloud of fire singed the hair on Gladamyr's head as it exploded above. He'd been running with Cerulean and Felix in his arms for hours and he was getting weak. Now he had Cato and Dorjan to worry about. The fire pixie and dwarf dragon spotted the three dreamlings just moments before leaving the fall pits, and had been relentless in their pursuit.

"If you'd put me down, I can try to—"

"You can't fly. Your wing is broken," Gladamyr said, cutting her off.

"Well, I can't draw on magic from the Earth when I'm not touching it, and it's ridiculous for you to keep running."

"I agree, Gladamyr," said Felix. "We need to make a

stand against them."

Gladamyr knew they were right. He couldn't keep running like this. He felt the strength leaving his arms and legs. The three of them needed to make a stand against Cato and Dorjan, but where? They had entered a part of Mares called the Chasm. It was as hostile and unfriendly as any part of Mares. The ground was scarred with large cracks that fell into endless ravines. Mountainous tumors of razor sharp stones were everywhere, and running through them was like running through a maze of broken glass. Several times Gladamyr leaped over a gorge only to stop and reverse to avoid colliding with a jutting rock formation; added to that, he now had to dodge fireballs.

"Where can we go?" he asked, hoping they saw something ahead that he hadn't.

"They are too high above," Felix called back. "We need to get up at their level."

"Gladamyr, up ahead. Can you climb up that?"

Gladamyr looked to where Cerulean pointed. It was the largest rock formation they had yet come across. It reached high into the inky sky and seemed flat on top. In a desperate situation it was perfect, but the climb looked like it could kill a man. The side of the mountain was covered in millions of horizontal stalactites sticking out like large, black, shark teeth.

"That will have to do," Gladamyr said unenthusiastically. "On the count of three I'm going to need to you two to climb onto my back. I can't stop, I need the momentum, so just try to do it."

"How are we supposed—?"

"One . . . two . . . three . . ."

In a split second Gladamyr dropped Cerulean and Felix. His arms stretched out and reshaped into long posts. His legs shifted and grew longer and stronger. He felt the slightest of stings as both Cerulean and Felix dug their fingers into his shoulders and neck, but that was it. He dove forward a few feet from the thorny side of the mountain and his post-like arms hit the ground. With great force from his strengthened legs, he pushed upward, flipping over several times in the air. He shifted again and his arms stretched further, hands bending into hooks as he caught two of the stalactites. Gladamyr swung out in a half-arc and flung his body upward, carrying the two dreamlings to the top of the mountain. They landed as another ball of fire careened into Gladamyr's chest.

He fell back, crashing onto the jagged surface of the mountain. Cerulean doused the fire with her blue magic and it misted around Gladamyr until even the painful burns on his chest ebbed away. Soon he was on his feet, facing Cato and Dorjan. Both were high in the air with their massive wings flapping wildly.

Dorjan was the first to attack. He flew down at Gladamyr like a targeted missile, teeth and talons exposed. Gladamyr shifted his body and collided with Dorjan midflight. Dorjan's tail whipped around, cutting deep into Gladamyr's back. The Dream Keeper let out a cry of pain and the uncontrollable shifting transformed him again. The fury inside him brought a monstrous being to the surface of his consciousness; a monster he had locked away deep in his soul. Gladamyr's focus blurred and all he saw was red, the color of hate.

His body flexed two or three times, shifting while still wrapped around the dwarf dragon. Sharp, black horns jutted from Gladamyr's body, stabbing Dorjan's thick, scaly hide. Dorjan tried to scream but his lungs had been pierced. In a rage, Gladamyr lengthened his razor sharp finger nails and dug them into Dorjan's scales. Pieces of the dwarf dragon scattered everywhere as Gladamyr tore at the dreamling. Still nothing but red. The color of hate; the color of mortal blood.

Shock brought Gladamyr back to focus, and he was only just able to shift his form back into a flying creature before getting impaled on the thorny surface of the ground.

He hovered in the air, taking in the scene before him. The first thing he registered was the horrified expressions on Cerulean's, Felix's, and even Cato's faces. Dorjan was nowhere. Only a cloud of dark colored dust spilling down from the sky. Gladamyr looked down at his hands and saw them covered in silvery blood, blood that had once belonged to the dwarf dragon. Pain dug at his heart, and he almost heard the voice of Fyren telling him, as he had so many times before: "Good job, my pet. You do know how to kill, don't you?"

"Zelly, it's been over an hour and he hasn't responded."

"Give him a little time, honey. He probably hasn't even seen his phone yet."

"You're right!" Kaelyn exclaimed, jumping up from the couch. "I should call his house phone, right? His mom probably took his phone away for getting suspended."

"That sounds kind of harsh," Zelda said, following Kaelyn into the kitchen. "I mean, he is already getting detention and all."

"I hear kids talk at school, and they say Parker's mom is one of the strictest moms in town."

"Yeah . . . still I feel that you catch more flies with honey than vinegar."

"What does that mean?"

"It means that if you treat others with respect, you'll get more out of them than if you are strict all the time. Oh, look at me, I don't know how to raise a teenager. I shouldn't be the one to cast stones."

"Now you're really confusing me," Kaelyn said, with a smile. She reached for the phone and it rang. Thinking it had to be Parker, she picked it up.

"It's about time you called me, we need to get back to . . . oh . . . um . . . hold on, please."

She handed the receiver to Zelda.

"Hello? Oh, yes, this is Madam Zelda, but I'm not taking calls to—what? . . . Who are you? . . . I see . . . Well . . . you'll have to be here within the hour and you can't stay long . . . Yes, that's the right address . . . you too."

"What was that all about?" Kaelyn said, eyeing her aunt.

"Some guy named Dr. Gates or something. Said it was urgent that he speak with us about you and Parker visiting Dreams."

Kaelyn didn't know what to say. Who was this Dr. Gates and how on earth did he know about Parker and her visiting Dreams? *And why hadn't Parker called her yet? Boys!* Kaelyn huffed out of the room and picked up her aunt's cell phone, punching in a message to Parker.

SOME GUY NAMED DR. GATES IS COMING OVER TO TALK TO US ABOUT DREAMS, KNOW ANYTHING ABOUT IT? CALL ME NOW! –Kaelyn.

There was a knock at the door and Kaelyn jumped. Having someone other than Parker and Zelda know about Dreams worried her. She thought of all those sci-fi movies she watched with her dad. The evil mastermind behind every scenario was a doctor such-and-such. Who knew whether this Dr. Gates wasn't some evil mastermind working with Fyren, and this was his way of getting at them? Zelda gave Kaelyn's shoulder a reassuring squeeze as she went to the door. Kaelyn punched 911 into the cell phone. Her thumb hovered over the send key, if the Doc tried anything funny she'd get the police.

"Tanis!" Zelda half shouted. "Oh, I completely forgot you were coming over today."

"Well now, Zelda, you aren't one for forgetting."

"To be honest, Tanis, I'm not myself today at all. I haven't slept yet—watched a marathon all night. Oh, this must be Lena! Hi, I'm Zelda, and this is my niece, Kaelyn."

Kaelyn hit the end key and set the phone down on the end table. Then she went to the door. Zelda's friend Tanis was a large Native American woman with dark skin, thick black hair, and purple lips. Lena shared some of her cousin's traits, but she was really skinny and instead of brown eyes, like Tanis', she had bright green.

"Hi," Kaelyn said shyly.

"Hey," Lena replied.

"Kaelyn, why don't you show Lena around the house?" Zelda asked, beckoning everyone in. "I won't waste your time, Tanis, let's get right to your card reading. Oh, and Kae, honey, listen for the door and when Dr. Gates gets here just have him wait in the front room."

Kaelyn nodded in agreement and then awkwardly

led Lena through the house.

Parker did exactly what his mom had told him to do. He switched his cell phone to silent and worked on his homework. It didn't take long to write Mr. Martinez's essay in Spanish. The subject was 'what you did this weekend' and Parker hadn't done much of anything but play *Medieval Assassin*. He did really well with the translation, but got hung up on words like troll and swamp demon; he didn't know the Spanish for them.

About an hour after his heart-to-heart with his mom abruptly ended, Parker's mom came in with an overheated TV dinner. The peas in one of the portioned off trays had popped and spewed steam. Parker hated peas. The meatloaf, if that's what it was, had cooked so much that the sauce had hardened around the edges of the tray. However unappetizing the meal looked though, it was welcoming. Parker had skipped lunch and he was starving. He was kind of surprised that his mom brought food to his room at all. She hated it when he ate anything in his room.

"Sorry I left it in too long," she said warmly, "but I got a phone call. Will you be okay if I leave you alone for a while? I need to go back to the firm."

"Sure, Mom, I'll be fine."

"I've thought a lot about what happened this afternoon at school, and I've thought a lot about what Dr. Gates told me, and I am going to let you off the hook this once."

"You mean I'm not grounded anymore?" Parker asked with a smile.

"No, you're not grounded. But Parker, I don't want

you doing anything like that again, you understand? You're still going to have to do detention after school on Monday, but once you've finished your homework, you can go ahead and play that video game you are so keen on beating."

"Thanks, Mom."

There was an awkward silence as Parker eyed his TV dinner and his mom stared off into space. She shook her head and went for the door.

"Mom, when you get back I'd still really like to talk to you about what happened today."

"I'd like that," she said, smiling.

"I love you."

"Love you too." She closed the door behind her.

Parker felt a whole lot better. He'd no idea what made his mom do a complete 180, but he wasn't going to complain. Well, the TV dinner was terrible, so he might complain about that. Parker figured in a few minutes when his mom was gone, he'd make something more fitting for a troubled teenager to eat. He picked up his cell phone and saw that he had a new message from Kaelyn. He shouldn't have ignored her text, but he needed a break to think things through.

She had said that her aunt believed her and wanted to help. The help of an adult would be great, but wasn't Kaelyn's aunt a quack job who told fortunes for a living? He thought briefly about Dr. Gates again. If there was a way to convince him and bring Dr. Gates to Dreams with them, they might be able to figure out how to beat Fyren. Suddenly, Jason came to mind. He was just as good a gamer as Parker and a really good strategist. If he got Jason to enter Dreams and got him to believe what was going on, he'd accomplish two things at once. The first was he would save his reputation at school, and the second, he could help save Dreams.

As Parker read the new text message, all sorts of strange emotions flowed through him. The first was surprise at what he was actually reading, followed by the sense of betrayal from Dr. Gates—wasn't patient-doctor stuff confidential? The third emotion was fear. What was Dr. Gates up to and why was he planning on meeting with Kaelyn and her aunt? Parker jumped up from his bed and ran into the office. He quickly brought the computer to life and pulled up the internet. Within a few seconds he had the address for *Madam Zelda's*. Without closing the screen, Parker charged out the door and headed down the street toward Kaelyn's house.

Cato flew away moments after Gladamyr had finished off Dorjan. The fire pixie didn't even bother turning around to see which direction the party headed and without Minyon's spy, Fyren would lose Gladamyr in Dreams. Gladamyr sat slumped atop a rock face that hung out over a vast ravine. The pit was so deep Gladamyr couldn't make out the bottom. It went on forever, like the melancholy feeling he always felt.

He asked Cerulean and Felix to give him a few minutes to collect himself before they went on. He said this for two reasons; one was because he was tired, and the other was the looks he kept getting from the others. Since the encounter with Dorjan neither of the dreamlings had said a word to Gladamyr; just gave him strange glances—strange glances that Gladamyr had received before, when he had asked to be a dream keeper and the council heard of his birth place.

He had no control over where he was created! Yes,

he was of Mares, and yes, he had done horrible things, but could a dreamling not change? Did the condition of someone's birth limit them in everything? Allyon had not thought so. Time and time again he had told Gladamyr that it was his choices that made him who he was, not anything else. *Yet why do his words seem so wrong when I look into their faces? Why do I still feel as though I'm a monster?*

"Gladamyr?"

The Dream Keeper looked over his shoulder to see Cerulean's pale blue face smiling back at him. Gladamyr nodded and then turned back to the chasm below.

"I know you probably don't want to talk, but I think you would feel better if you did."

"What is there to talk about?" he snapped.

"Now that's no way to address your superior . . . or your friend." Cerulean sighed and sat down next to him. "I'm sorry I acted strange, but to be honest, Gladamyr, I was frightened. I've never seen your true form—"

"This is my true form! I don't know what it was that I turned into back there, but that wasn't me, that's not who I am. I'm not a monster! I'm not!"

"No, Gladamyr, you're not a monster . . . I'm . . . I'm sorry . . . I just—"

"When I get really scared or upset or hurt . . . I can't control my shifting. It's really only happened a few times, but since Fyren shut down the Crossing, it's been happening a great deal. Now I don't expect you to understand, but I don't want to be a Mare. I want to be . . . I want to be . . ."

"Human?"

"I didn't say that."

"No." Cerulean nodded. "You didn't have to. You show it enough, Gladamyr. Apart from having purple skin, you look exactly like a human to me."

"Looking like something doesn't make you it."

"No, it doesn't. But I must ask you, Gladamyr, what exactly is a human . . . other than being mortal? What is it about them that has you so fixed on wanting to be one?"

Gladamyr had thought this question out in his mind a hundred times and always the same answer came to him. "Humans are not bad."

"Plenty of them are. Kaelyn spoke about wars in her world, and people that hurt other people just because they believed different things. Is that not bad? There are plenty of bad ones."

"They're not one hundred percent good either."

"Again, I have to disagree. Parker and Kaelyn are good. They risk a lot helping us."

"Still wrong, Cerulean," Gladamyr said, tossing a small pebble down the deep chasm. "Humans are neither one hundred percent good nor bad, they are both. Within them is the ability to do good or evil. It is their will that makes them human—their ability to choose to be one or the other. That is what I want—the will that humans have. I want the choice to be good if I so desire it, instead of being naturally evil."

"But you do have a choice. Look at yourself—you're willfully defying Fyren. You're choosing to save our world. You're choosing to be good."

"There has to be more to it, though. If I was truly changed I would not shift into evil. I would not have—" Gladamyr couldn't finish. He was so ashamed of what he had done; and not just to Dorjan, to all the many humans and dreamlings alike whom he had hurt.

"Gladamyr." Cerulean hesitated. "What happened with Dorjan? How did you kill him? I've never seen another dreamling die. I've seen the horrors that Fyren has inflicted on the dream keepers, but never so far as to erase them from existence. How did you—"

"I don't know."

This is bad timing! I finally meet a girl who could possibly be my friend, and I can't focus because I'm trying to save the world. Kaelyn smiled at the joke Lena had just made, but she wasn't really listening. *It was a joke, right? Great Kaelyn, what if she just told you her grandmother died and you just smiled at it? Subjects change fast—*

"My aunt says you go to school on a reservation?"

"Yeah, it's about an hour from here. It's okay, I guess. It's kind of small, but we do have a basketball team, and we just might have a shot at winning regionals if Riana would get off me. She's our team captain and she thinks she's all that. Girl, does she need to clue in. She lets no one touch the ball but her."

"Oh, you have one at your school too, eh?"

"A prissy princess that acts like she owns the school—yeah, we got one. She keeps telling the coach to bench me so I stop hogging her ball—did you hear me say 'her' ball? She practically has the whole team and the coach wrapped around her finger. But honestly, she can't touch me 'cause I've got talent."

"I've never been very good at basketball," Kaelyn said, finally focusing on Lena instead of the annoying panic in her head. "I used to play with my dad, but I'd always miss."

"You should give it a go sometime. I can give you a few pointers."

"I'd like that."

"I like your room," Lena said, looking at the bare

yellow walls and clashing pink-flowered curtains. Now Kaelyn knew Lena was just trying to be nice. Heck, there wasn't a thing that had personality. Nothing but a worn out quilt her mom had sewn.

"Oh, I haven't really done anything to it . . ."

"You should . . . you could paint a bright accent wall there, and put up a big poster of a boy band right here." Lena danced around the room for a moment mumbling something about an ooh-ooh baby, and then sat on the bed. "Oh, and of course you need a dream catcher above your bed."

"What's a dream catcher?" Kaelyn was intrigued. Her mind jumped at anything with 'dream' in it.

"Like this," Lena said, pulling out a chain from around her neck. A tiny gold loop with strings all tangled around the middle hung from the chain. Below the loop were three tiny gold feathers that twinkled as Lena held out her keepsake.

"Oh, it's beautiful."

"Thanks, my grandmother gave it to me when I turned thirteen. She said I was a woman now so I earned a special one. I still keep the dream catcher she made for me when I was little above my bed."

"Is it like a special symbol to your people?"

Lena laughed.

"You're funny, 'my people.' Not really. It's a tradition, I guess. White people make them too, you know. In fact I know a white lady in Colorado who makes them for a living. She's my mom's friend. She does a really good job. She ties little stones in the strings too, you know to make them prettier, but I like my grandmother's."

"What's it for?"

"To catch bad dreams. See the strings? They're like a

spider's web and they catch all the bad dreams in the net. The small hole in the middle is for the good dreams to pass through."

Kaelyn was just about to ask if she could touch the dream catcher when the doorbell rang. A feeling of dread came over her. That would be Dr. Gates. Who was this man, and what did he have to do with her and Parker visiting Dreams? Kaelyn looked at Lena for a split second, wishing they'd met another time, because if this doctor started discussing a place Kaelyn visited in her sleep, all hopes of a friendship would be out the door.

CHAPTER EIGHT
NIGHTMARES

The door opened just a crack and Parker saw Kaelyn's blue eyes staring quizzically at him. Then it flew open and she came tumbling into his arms for a hug. His feet were not securely planted on the icy steps, and they both toppled over into the snow.

"I'm so glad you came over!"

"I can see that," he said, pushing Kaelyn off.

"I'm sorry. I just got so excited when I saw it was you and not some crazy doctor."

"Is Gates here?"

"No, he called and said—hey, wait a minute! You know about him knowing?" Kaelyn pushed Parker down and quickly stood up, marching inside. He hurriedly followed.

"I had to tell someone, and he was the only person I thought I could confide in. After all, he's my shrink. I should be able to tell him anything, and he's supposed to keep it a secret, something about patient confidentiality or whatever. And you told your aunt, so don't go sounding all . . ."

Parker just noticed the other girl in the room. She was Native American and very pretty. She had silky black hair and brilliant green eyes. For a moment Parker lost his train of thought while he tried to fix his disheveled appearance. Then he clued in to what he had just said. *Dude, you really know how to look like a loser without even trying. You don't even know her and you fess up to seeing a shrink—puh-leeze!*

"Parker, this is Lena," Kaelyn began, noticing Parker's sudden interest in Lena. "She's here with her cousin to meet with Zelda."

"Hi," Parker said, feeling his cheeks burn. He moved in toward Kaelyn and whispered, "Why is your aunt doing a fortune-telling right now? I thought she wanted to help us?"

"She does, but she forgot that they were coming over. And then Doctor-what's-his-face called and—well, there you have it."

"I'm sorry, do you two want to be alone?" Lena asked, eyeing Parker suspiciously.

"Ahh no," Parker said, dramatically. "We were just um. . . a—"

"Rehearsing . . . for the school play," Kaelyn said, not very convincingly.

"What?" Parker blurted.

"Homework."

"Oh, yeah," he laughed. "Homework—we're supposed to study for this big test tomorrow."

"You didn't say you had a test, Kaelyn. What class?"

"Spanish," Parker coughed, just as Kaelyn said, "History."

Lena smiled warmly at the two of them and Parker's cheeks flared with heat. Luckily, just at that moment Kaelyn's aunt and Lena's cousin came into the front room. They both looked tired. Lena's cousin had dark circles under her eyes, but Kaelyn's aunt looked like she hadn't slept in weeks. She had a nest of red hair all tied up in a bun that wasn't really keeping the hair out of her face. She was wearing pajamas and—yes—fuzzy bunny slippers. *This is supposed to be our big help? No wonder her aunt believed her. The lady is a complete whack job.*

"You must be Parker," Zelda said, going straight over and giving him a hug. Parker stood awkwardly and lifted his arms but he didn't know whether he was to hug back or just stand there. He sort of did both. "Kae has told me all about you. Wow, he does have a good aura."

Parker looked at Kaelyn, who too was turning red. She gave him an apologetic shrug.

"Thank you, Zelda," Lena's cousin said. "You know, you should stay awake more often. You're much more in tune when you're sleepy."

"Oh, you're just being nice."

"Yes, I am. That reading was the worst yet. Please, I don't gamble on anything, so how do you expect me to come into money?"

"I just say what's in the cards."

"I know." She laughed. "It was good seeing you, though. Call me and we'll chat. Nice to meet you Kaelyn—and you too . . ." she said, eyeing Parker conspiratorially.

"Bye, Lena," Kaelyn said quickly before they opened the door.

"Bye, Kaelyn. Bye, Parker. Sweet dreams."

They opened the door and standing on the porch with his arm raised ready to knock, was Dr. Gates. He looked at the mass of people before him until his eyes fell on Parker, who tried to send back the harshest mental message he could think of.

The trek through the Chasm took longer than Gladamyr thought it would. It was very different traveling through Dreams when you didn't have a mortal to help you create doorways. This was how it must be in the real world. As far as Gladamyr knew, mortals did not have doorways that took you directly from one place to another. He had seen the big, boxy things called cars appear often in mortal dreams and even the large, bird-shaped things called air planes, but none of those things were needed in a world where they could travel to faraway lands in the blink of an eye. This got Gladamyr thinking about Fyren's dreamlings—no sooner had Gladamyr said they were trapped in a fall pit than Cato and Dorjan showed up. It was the same when they were at the sky walls. Fyren's cronies had shown up out of nowhere.

"Fyren has got to be using mortals to help him," Gladamyr blurted out. This was the first time anyone had said anything in hours, and Cerulean and Felix looked puzzled at his declaration. "Think about it, Felix. Hasn't all this walking been making you wish you had a mortal to open a doorway for you? Cerulean, I know that the fairykind like to fly around, but dream keepers use doorways more than anyone in Dreams. We have to in order to do our job. There is no way any of us could walk all the mortals through all the different realms."

Cerulean looked shocked. "And you're suggesting Fyren has mortals working for him because . . . ?"

"Think about it. We weren't even at the sky walls half an hour before Iniga and Twister came out of nowhere. Back at the fall pits I barely said out loud where we were, and not ten minutes later Cato and Dorjan showed up. There is—"

"No way they could have traveled that distance without the help of a mortal," Felix jumped in. "Cerulean, he's right! They have to be using doorways to travel, and they can only be opened with the help of a mortal. Which means—"

"Fyren hasn't stopped all activity at the Crossing!"

There was silence as they all processed this information. Fyren was still allowing mortals to visit Dreams, but how many and where was he taking them when they visited? Gladamyr studied the land before him. They were close to the border wall now and yet the paling of the darkness that normally happened the closer you got to the wall wasn't visible. In fact, it looked as though Mares was gaining more and more influence over Dreams. Truly, this could only be tested by seeing the realm of Favor; it was hard to tell if such a dark and creepy place was getting any better or worse.

"Where do we go now?" Felix asked, seeing the border wall ahead.

"Favor, of course," answered Cerulean. "I need to draw magic from its soil to heal my wing and Felix. You too, could be healed faster once there; although you're making great improvements since the spider."

"Yes, I agree." Felix nodded. "What do you say, Gladamyr?"

Gladamyr, still lost in his thoughts, didn't answer. He just kept walking briskly toward the border wall. If Fyren was using mortals to help him in this conquest of Dreams, then that gave the Mare even more power. How was it possible to defeat a being so powerful? Gladamyr thought back to Dorjan and how he had been torn apart by Gladamyr's own dark power. Would he have to revert back into a monster in order to save Dreams? The thought of doing that again brought even more pain and guilt to his soul. But wait, he was forgetting something! Gladamyr too had the help of mortals. Parker and Kaelyn! They would be the key in all of this. They were the ones who would save Dreams from Fyren. But where were they?

Parker had wanted to give Dr. Gates an earful the minute he saw him, but it took some time before Lena and her cousin got in their car, and even more time before Zelda let the doctor into her house. She was hesitant at first until Parker said that he knew the doctor and that for the most part he was harmless. Now, all the fire that Parker had built up at first seeing the shrink was dwindling to ash. Dr. Gates sat motionless on the couch, and Parker had to wonder if the Doc himself knew what he was doing there.

"And just what is it that you're doing here?" demanded Zelda, taking a seat opposite Dr. Gates.

"I told you on the phone it was about Parker and Kaelyn visiting Dreams."

Zelda folded her arms. "I have no idea what you're talking about. My niece hasn't been anywhere today except for school."

"Zelly," Kaelyn laughed. "It's okay. Parker said he tried to tell Dr. Gates about Dreams, but he didn't believe him."

"I never said I didn't believe you, Parker."

"No, you just kicked me out of your office the minute I told you and then had my mom come in—and by the way, aren't you breaking some doctor-patient rule by telling people what I talked to you about? Whatever happened to confidentiality? I could have you disbarred or debunked, or whatever it is they do to shrinks that blab their mouths off."

"I understand how you can be upset with me but, Parker, I'm here to help. I've told you before that you could tell me anything and that I would only try to help you. I hope that you consider me a friend."

"Friends don't go blabbing about things they share in secret. The next thing I know, you could be telling Kaelyn everything else we've talked about."

"Oh, really?" Kaelyn said. "Do tell, Doc."

Parker glared at her. Why was she trying to make light of the situation? Dr. Gates just said he was Parker's friend. If he was a friend then he wouldn't have said anything without asking Parker first. It was wrong, and Kaelyn's joke wasn't quenching the fire that flared up once again.

"What exactly did you come over here for? What were you going to tell them that you weren't going to let me in on? Why come here and not to me?"

"Parker, honey," Zelda said sweetly, "you need to sit down and have some tea or something. Your aura is getting cloudy."

What? My aura is getting cloudy? Parker was once again taken aback. Two days ago he would never have dreamed that he'd be standing in the front room of the town's most crackpot psychic along with his traitorous psychiatrist and the biggest loser in school. This was just too much. He was about to scream, like he'd done twice already that day, when Kaelyn took his hand. Instantly, all the hate welling up in him left. His mind became less, to use Zelda's word, cloudy. Screaming and barking question after question was getting him nowhere. Parker sat down next to Kaelyn, who kept a firm grip on his hand. He looked down at their entwined fingers. Kaelyn held the dreamstone in her other hand. *Another use for the dreamstone—it relaxes troubled teenage boys.*

"Oh, now that's better," Zelda said, smiling. Parker just shook his head at the psychic and glared once again at Gates.

"Parker, I do owe you an apology—I should never have come over here to discuss your session today without your permission, but I guess I was bending the rules a bit. I was hoping Kaelyn would've just shared her experience and then I wouldn't have to say anything."

"Have you ever thought about doing psychic work?" Zelda asked, seemingly interested in Dr. Gates. "A lot of times people are not open to readings, so I just get them talking about their lives. Before you know it they've predicted they had new love or lots of money was coming their way."

"Zelly . . ." Kaelyn sighed. "Can we stay on subject please?"

"That was on subject! He's talking about mind manipulation and so was I."

"I wasn't going to try and manipulate anyone..."

"That's what it sounded like to me."

"I was just going to try and get her to—"

"Tell you stuff without her realizing she was saying it. Yes, that is mind manipulation."

"I wasn't trying to—"

"Okay!" Parker and Kaelyn shouted in unison.

The two adults finally shut up and looked at Parker and Kaelyn. Kaelyn gave Parker's hand a little squeeze, and he took that as a sign to lead the conversation.

"Alright, Doc, so you came over to get Kaelyn to talk about her experience. We get that. Now just tell us why?"

Dr. Gates didn't answer right away. Instead, he reached into the breast pocket of his coat and pulled out a handful of folded papers. He laid them out on the coffee table and held one of the pages close to his chest. Parker looked down at the rest. They showed poorly sketched drawings of purple shaped things. Some looked like a child's interpretation of a dragon or hairy beast or bat thing. He and Kaelyn looked at Dr. Gates questioningly.

"These are all drawings that a young patient being treated for childhood schizophrenia did. This particular boy was only nine at the time, but he had been telling his parents for months how he was plagued in his sleep by a monster that could take on different shapes. The boy was so terrified of sleeping that he would go days without rest, and suffered small bouts of hallucinations at odd times. His parents ended up hospitalizing him under the direction of a harsh doctor who tried all sorts of medicine to cure the boy. A year or so later, the doctor suffered a mild heart attack and the boy transferred to another clinic where he received better care that resulted in a diagnosis of insomnia. Once given the proper medication and attention, the boy was cured. When I decided to go into practice for myself, it was to help children like this boy. You see, all he wanted was someone to believe what he was telling them—and no one would.

"When you told me, Parker, about your story, my first impression as a psychiatrist was to treat you for insomnia or some sort of sleep deprivation—it's what the clinical books tell me to do. But I went in to child psychiatry to help children, not just pump them full of pharmaceuticals. Thinking as Greg Gates and not as Dr.

Gates, I had to believe you. Just before you left my office, you said a name that shocked me back to when I was a nine year-old boy being plagued by a nightmare. You said a name that gave me goose bumps and refreshed my mind with memories of terror."

Dr. Gates turned around the page he held close to his chest, and Parker could make out another of the crude purple drawings. Below the monstrous form was the name *Gladamyr.* Kaelyn gasped and let go of Parker's hand to cover her mouth.

"Yes, the little boy who drew these pictures was me," Dr. Gates said solemnly. "When I dreamed about this creature, I could sometimes hear someone egging the monster on. I heard his name, and today was the first time in twenty plus years that I heard it again. This is a drawing of Gladamyr—the same being you call a dream keeper."

Kaelyn flashbacked to her first conversation with Gladamyr, and how he'd told her that he was a monster. She had reassured him that he wasn't, that a monster wouldn't care if she was suffering in a nightmare or not. She sensed that Gladamyr had gone through some hard times and that perhaps even now he was still on a journey of self-discovery, but she had no idea he was capable of tormenting children. She looked at the vicious drawings the child Gates had produced. They were indeed nightmares brought to life. Some images had rows of killer teeth, others sharp talon hands, or even a spiked body; all different except the color. They were still purple, just like Gladamyr's skin.

She shook her head and closed her eyes, shutting out

the evil images of her friend. She thought of Gladamyr as she knew him—her dream keeper—her bond in Dreams. He was not a monster. He had compassion for mortals and he had compassion for his world. Kaelyn was sure she even saw that he loved Cerulean. She could see it in the way he looked at her when they spoke. It was the way Kaelyn's father looked at her mother when she'd say something funny, a reassuring gesture showing love. Whatever Dr. Gates had suffered as a child, Gladamyr was no longer that creature. Kaelyn knew Gladamyr had a dark past. After all, he knew a great deal about Fyren and Fyren was as bad as they came in Mares. But everyone should be given the benefit of the doubt; everyone should be given a second chance.

"Gladamyr is no longer that way," Kaelyn said, still shaking her head. "He might have once been a Mare, but he is now a dream keeper and all dream keepers are good. If you are showing us this to try and convince us not to help him then you have—"

"No, that's not it at all!" Dr. Gates cut in. "No, I was showing you these to tell you that I believe you. I mean, how can I not believe you when so much happened to me when I was little? I . . . I want to help you."

"What?" Parker asked.

"Even after sharing that Gladamoo tortured you as a child, you want to help him?" Zelda asked. No one corrected her for mispronouncing Gladamyr's name.

"I tell my patients all the time that you have to face your fears in order to overcome them. I am ready to face mine."

"You're in?" Parker said, smiling. "You're really in? This is great! I can't wait to tell Gladamyr—this will be great."

"So how do we start this?" Zelda asked. "I mean, do I need to go get us some pillows and blankets and, we just have a big session of astral projection?"

"Astral what?" they all asked at once.

"You know, astral projection. Come on, Doc, you've never heard of astral projection? You do understand hypnosis, don't you?"

"Well yes, now that you mention it. In hypnosis one leaves the present time and goes back in the memories. I guess you're saying astral projection is our consciousness leaving our bodies and going to Dreams."

"Wow, you're pretty smart," Zelda said flirtatiously.

"Alright then," Kaelyn cut across the weird, adult bonding session. "Pillows would be great, but you two can't come yet."

"That's right; we have to get your keys," Parker said.

"Why do you need my keys?" Zelda asked, looking confused. "Do I need drive us somewhere 'cause that car of mine is going nowhere in its condition. Come on, Doc, we'll take yours."

"No, your keys," Parker said.

"Your dream keys, remember?" Kaelyn prompted. "It's the way Gladamyr unlocks the doorway to our world—I guess."

"That's a lot of keys." Zelda sighed. "I mean, aren't there like seven billion people in the world? Where on earth would you store seven billon keys?"

Kaelyn hadn't thought of that, but Zelly was right. Where in Dreams were the keys kept? And surely they would be guarded. This was not going to be an easy task. *I sure hope Gladamyr is up for a challenge*, she thought to herself.

"You know what this means, don't you?" Parker asked, with a grin.

"Yep, it's time for us to take a nap."

"So you want us to go back to the Crossing and get keys?" Felix asked, dumbfounded.

"If that's where you keep 'em, then yes!" Parker said.

Gladamyr looked down at the two keys in his hands. They had dulled in color and would remain an antique gold until the mortals returned to Awake. He knew the place at the Crossing where millions of other keys, the clear iridescent ones that belonged to the mortals in Awake, were stored. Surely Fyren had his best guards protecting the vaults; they would be nearly impossible to get into without a fight. And then there was finding the keys they wanted. Gladamyr figured they could do that easy enough; the hard part would be not getting caught.

"I believe it can be done," he said, looking from Felix to the children. A smile spread across Parker and Kaelyn's faces just as frowns fell on Cerulean's and Felix's.

"And just how do you expect us to accomplish this task, Gladamyr?" Cerulean barked. It had been a long time since he had seen Cerulean's face change shade, and the red color now filling her cheeks was most welcoming. It made him feel at home.

"We know where they are," he said, nodding toward the children.

"And that's supposed to make a difference in the matter? The vaults are in the lower levels of the Crossing and are protected by enchantments. And let's not even mention the stihl—"

"She can be calmed by the lullaby—"

"And who do you think is just going to stand

142

around and sing it to her?"

Cerulean stared at Gladamyr with her hard blue eyes, and he stared right back, but he added a smile.

"I most assuredly won't sing to that creature!"

"I don't sing," chimed in Felix.

"It would take a dreamling with magic from Favor to calm such a creature," Gladamyr added.

"No! I refuse!" Cerulean spat. "Get some other fairy to sing to that thing. It will eat me the second I look at it."

"You would just need to distract it long enough for us to sneak by. Then you can follow behind. It doesn't go down further than the atrium."

"What exactly is a stihl?" asked Kaelyn.

"It's foul is what it is!" Cerulean blurted out.

"It's a type of dragon," Felix answered. "They are horribly fond of treasure, so they are great guards. Stihls can breathe fire like most dragons and are rare in their own right. They have this sort of smell about them that—"

"Stinks to high heaven, is what it does! Even the idea of breathing in the fumes around that thing makes me want to vomit. And just the sight of it . . . aww!" Cerulean sighed and Gladamyr couldn't help but laugh. The stihl was unusually hideous and did exert a pungent aroma that was hard to bear for most, but wasn't that the point? The keeper's council couldn't have just any old dreamling going down into the vaults. Most of the keys were brought up to the main gate and then rotated as the shifts went on. Normally there were only a few hundred haulers that ventured past the stihl, and the lullaby that sounded continuously at the Crossing kept the creature calm enough for them to go about their work.

"So we just have to get past this stihl thing and we

can go straight to the keys?" Kaelyn asked.

"It's not as easy as that," Gladamyr answered.

"I was worried about that." Parker sighed. "Okay, give us the low down."

"Once we are past the stihl, we need to make our way into the lower levels, get the keys, and then get out of there."

"That's it?" Parker asked.

"That's it."

"You make it sound as though we are just going to stroll in and take whatever we want," Cerulean said.

"That is the general plan, yes." Gladamyr smiled back.

Cerulean harrumphed. "When it all goes south, Gladamyr, don't say I didn't warn you."

There was a momentary flash of purple light, and then Kaelyn and the others were standing below a large stone wall that towered above them. They were in what appeared to be a city. There were tall sky scrapers all around, but instead of the cities at home, where they were made of steel and concrete and covered in glass, these buildings were all stone. What made the scene even stranger still was that the whole world around Kaelyn, except for her, Parker and the other three dreamlings, was without color; nothing but a world of black, white, and gray. A few buildings appeared to be on fire, but the fire wasn't orange and red like most fires. It was gray. It was like watching an old movie that had been filmed before the invention of colored pictures.

One building stood out from the rest. Not because it had color – no, this was still dark and gray as the others

— but it was enormous. The thing had to be larger than the Empire State Building, and that was a hundred and twenty stories high! It was beautiful—even without color. It had massive archways, and windows that were decorated with stained glass that would have been even more exquisite had they been tainted with reds, blues and yellows. The stone walls were carved with what looked to Kaelyn like ancient runes. There were all sorts of different writings, some even looked Egyptian. Kaelyn had been taken by her father to the British Museum, where she had seen something similar called the Rosetta Stone. It too had markings like this building's all over its surface. Markings her father said helped unlock the ancient language of the Egyptians.

"What's that?" Kaelyn whispered, pointing toward the building covered in runes.

"The Crossing," Gladamyr whispered back. "That's where the vaults are."

"That's where Fyren is," Felix mumbled.

"Shhh!" Cerulean stopped Felix. "I swear that Mare knows when someone says his name. Oh, my—"

Kaelyn looked back at Cerulean, who was on the verge of crying.

"Oh, just look at our home!"

It was then that Kaelyn realized that the absence of color was not originally how the city they had called Teorainn looked. Gladamyr had told Kaelyn that Dreams was changing more and more as time went by without any mortals visiting. It was just the first time she had seen something that looked like it had actually changed. The land of Mares was always dark and unwelcoming, but this city looked like it had once been the most beautiful thing created. It was being slowly washed away.

"We should get moving before someone notices a bunch of people hanging out in a deserted city," Parker suggested.

"Good idea," Gladamyr said. "I hope this works. Please don't walk too fast. I need time to memorize the space in front of me."

With that, Gladamyr's body shifted. His lower body became very thin and tall. His stomach hovered higher than Felix's head, who was the tallest in the group. Then Gladamyr's upper body opened out like an umbrella and shielded them from above as Kaelyn and the others closed in tight together. They walked slowly toward a door at the rear of the Crossing, and Gladamyr's upper body changed color to match the ground beneath them, almost as if he were a chameleon hiding from a hungry predator.

"I don't see anyone guarding this entrance," Felix muttered.

"That doesn't mean there isn't someone on the other side of the door," Parker said.

Kaelyn's stomach tightened. She knew that getting the keys was important. Zelda and Dr. Gates would be a huge help, but was it worth the risk? Gladamyr had said there were several Mares out hunting for him and that coming directly to the Crossing was something even Fyren would never anticipate. Yet the nervousness wouldn't leave her.

As they approached the large, old fashioned, oak door with black iron hinges, Kaelyn noticed that it didn't have a handle; it merely had a small key hole in its center. Gladamyr shifted his body once more until he was his normal self. He placed an ear to the door and listened intently, his hand up as a signal to remain silent. A few minutes passed before he nodded toward Felix.

The dark-haired dreamling stepped up to the center of the door and muttered under his breath. Kaelyn couldn't see around Felix, but she heard the strangest sound as if something was pushing up out of the ground. Then the lock clicked like it was being picked. Within seconds the door opened and Kaelyn saw a green vine hanging from the key hole. She didn't have time to ask any questions.

Gladamyr pulled them all into the Crossing and the door closed behind them.

Brilliant color! The hallway was full of color. The walls were shiny blue granite, and the floors were covered in a dark cranberry carpet. Everything was rich in design, and Kaelyn felt as though she had stepped into a palace rather than a gray stone building. They moved quickly down hallway after hallway and up and down several flights of stairs, Gladamyr and Cerulean at their head with Felix following behind. Kaelyn still held hands with Parker but every minute or so she had to switch hands because Parker's were very sweaty and it felt gross. Kaelyn found it odd that the Crossing would be so deserted, but she reassured herself that Fyren had stopped all activity and most of Fyren's Mares were out trying to find Gladamyr.

They entered a large open atrium, and Kaelyn about dropped Parker's hand so she could cover an escaped gasp. The hall was breathtaking. There were huge statues in perfect white marble, of all sorts of different creatures. Kaelyn recognized a few like fairies, dragons, griffins, unicorns, and others she'd seen in mythology books. Yet there were many more that she'd never imagined. They were all placed around the great circular room, all facing the center of the atrium and looking up at the ceiling, which was a dome with a large pool of shimmering liquid that somehow defied gravity. Kaelyn wanted to ask what the pool was, but she knew they had to stay quiet. Was the pool something magical, like the fountain of youth, or perhaps the source of Dreams' powers? Question after question entered her mind as she gazed up at the shimmering surface.

Kaelyn couldn't take her eyes off the pool above and suddenly found herself going down a flight of large marble stairs that led deep into the building, far away from the hall of statues and the shimmering pool. For the first time she noticed there was no source of light anywhere. No light bulbs or torches on the walls. The rooms just naturally glowed somehow. *Great! Even more questions to ask.* Kaelyn hated it when she wanted to know something and wasn't able to ask. She drove Zelda crazy all the time when they watched a movie that was familiar to Zelda, but new to Kaelyn. *What happens next? Does he end up with her in the end? They don't die, do they?* She'd ask these questions but Zelda always said, "I'm not telling. Just watch."

Just then, there was a shuffling sound up ahead and Kaelyn felt her legs shake in fear. *Was it Fyren? I don't want to see him and his skeleton face . . . maybe the clown . . . or the stihl . . . something worse—don't think that way. Get a hold of yourself. Gladamyr will protect you, Parker . . .*

As if he was reading her thoughts, Parker tightened his grip on her hand and she felt for the moment safe; still scared, but safe.

Whoosh! Crash! Smack! BOOM!

CHAPTER NINE
THE VAULTS

Parker and Kaelyn fell back onto Felix as Gladamyr and Cerulean were scooped from the stairs and thrown up against the granite walls. Cerulean's body peeled away from the wall and slapped to the floor. Gladamyr shifted mid-flight into a creature the size of a rhinoceros and crashed hard into the wall, shattering the stonework. Parker smelled the stihl before he saw it. The odor of sewage and sulfur burned his nose, and he instantly retched. His eyes were watering so badly, he couldn't see. It was as if someone had just shot onion juice in his eyes.

Forgetting the dreamstone and having to hold onto Kaelyn's hand, he let go and covered his eyes. He moved away from Kaelyn and Felix and threw up on the last few steps of the staircase. He heard the stihl in the room but it seemed to be over by Gladamyr who, fortunately, was on the opposite side of the atrium. Parker could get to safety, but the only problem was he couldn't see. His eyes would not stop watering, and the smell was so noxious that he was continually dry heaving. He heard Kaelyn too, coughing and spilling out the contents of her stomach, and for the briefest moment he wondered if their bodies were throwing up as well back in Awake.

"Parker, over here," Felix said, and Parker followed the sound of his voice.

There was some sort of fight going on now between Gladamyr and the stihl, but without sight it was hard to know what was going on.

"Here," Felix said, handing him something that felt like a fuzzy leaf, "put this on your eyes, and it will help. We need to get to the doorway just beyond. It will take us into the vaults."

"Parker . . . Parker . . ." Kaelyn moaned, coughing once more.

Parker put the leaves on his eyes and they plastered themselves to his eyelids. With no need to hold them there, he reached out and found Kaelyn's hand. She squeezed it lightly and tapped it with her other hand. They followed Felix blindly, one hand clutching the back of the dreamling's trench coat, and holding hands with the other. The sound of Gladamyr and the stihl fighting got louder and louder, and Parker was sure that anyone else in the Crossing would hear and soon be on their way. Felix understood this too. The dreamling moved faster, only pausing for a brief moment when something large crashed in front of them.

Then something unexpected happened; a magical, beautiful voice began to sing. The music echoed around the room and Parker had a sudden urge to close his eyes and sleep. This, Parker thought, was the most ironic thing he'd ever thought; to dream of sleeping when he was already asleep. The lullaby continued and miraculously, the sounds of the battle between Gladamyr and the stihl stopped. Parker heard a loud gurgling yawn that he assumed came from the stihl and, without warning, a trumpeting snore. Parker wished more than anything that he could open his eyes, but they were sealed shut with some sort of paste that ebbed from the leaves Felix had given him.

"Is that Cerulean?" Kaelyn whispered.

"Yes," Felix said, in reverent response.

Wow, Parker thought, *that chick can really sing.* Wasting no time, Felix moved them once more across the atrium. Soon, Gladamyr joined them and Parker felt Felix drop down and mumble something about stairs. The light shifted. Although Parker couldn't see the room they had entered, he could tell it wasn't as bright as the rest of the Crossing. It seemed to be—

"Here, I'll help take those off," Felix said. "They should have done their job by now."

Felix pulled at the edges of the leaves and soon Parker was able to open his eyes. Only then did he really look into Felix's face, noticing that his eyes were bright green, sort of looked like a cat's with a very large iris. Then he gazed at the place they had just entered. It was breathtaking.

It was a vast dark room, with a maze of shelves that ran as far as Parker could see. It was a library of sorts, with rows upon rows of shelves filled with shimmering iridescent keys. Some keys glowed brighter than others and set against a black sky, they were like billons of stars twinkling in a wide universe. Following Felix, Parker continued to walk down the wide steps that led to the base of the vaults.

Parker inspected a shelf that had hundreds of pegs with just one key on each peg, a gold insignia shining above it. He wondered what the words meant until he realized they were names, although not names he'd ever heard. There was Kama Kaothai, and Kanya

Kongsangchai, and Mali Kunakorn—*names from another country maybe?* Each key, like the names themselves, was uniquely different, and Parker could almost swear that if he looked close enough at the keys, he could see faces in their opaque surfaces, like a seer sees future events in a crystal ball. He turned toward Gladamyr, who started off down what seemed an endless aisle of keys. And the thought hit Parker, *how on Earth are we going to find three keys out of so many?*

"Where do we start?" whispered Kaelyn. "There are so many."

"The vaults are separated into what are called dream zones, then providences, then townships, then names—alphabetically, of course." Felix pointed to the section of keys Parker was staring at just moments before. Kaelyn saw a gold plate just at the top of the long shelf, and she read as Felix said aloud, "Dream zone 535, Thailand, Bangkok, Ka-Le."

"What dream zone is the United States?" she asked.

"It actually has about two thousand dream zones."

"What?" Parker sounded shocked. Kaelyn was shocked too, but there were around 300 million people in the U.S. That equaled out to well over one hundred fifty thousand people per zone, and that was still a lot of people.

Cerulean came running down the stairs. "We don't have much time, Gladamyr. What're you waiting around here for? There is no way they didn't hear that ruckus you created up there."

"She's right—this way!" Gladamyr said, running.

He turned down the aisle to Kaelyn's left, and she

and Parker followed behind, Felix and Cerulean in the rear. She tried to read the insignias on the shelves as they ran down aisle after aisle, but the words were unfamiliar. All she could make out was the dream zone. It was an endless maze and Kaelyn had no idea how Gladamyr knew where to go. They turned three more corners and skipped about a dozen rows, and then places started to look familiar. A sign read: *Portland, Maine, Ya-Z;* then *Westbrook, Maine, Aa-Ac.*

"We're in the U.S. now," she shouted.

"Yeah, on the east coast. We live on the west!" Parker said, trying to catch his breath.

Why did Parker have to burst her bubble? But he was right. Maine was a long way away from the brown beaches of the west coast. They passed by several more aisles before Gladamyr came to an abrupt stop and Kaelyn and Parker crashed into his back. The horrible smell of the stihl pierced her nose before anything else. Suddenly the dark room was lit from above by spectacular orange flames, and the stihl soared down upon them.

Gladamyr pushed the children back toward Cerulean, and Felix jumped high into the air, shifting his arms into large bat-like wings. He once again flew into the stinking beast. They collided and crashed into the shelves below. Hooks, brackets, and keys flew everywhere. Gladamyr rolled over and over, trying to pin down the stihl. He managed to pull one of the beast's wings back, which kept it from turning over, but the creature was too strong. He soon lost his control over it. It kicked him square in the chest and he fell back onto a shelf, its contents crashing down upon him.

He was up again in a flash, charging after the stihl. The beast climbed over the tops of the shelves, trying to expand its massive wings. Gladamyr was just about to tackle the thing once more when something grabbed hold of the side of his neck and a stabbing pain pounded from his ear to his elbow. He pulled the thing off his neck. It was an evil black chicken with bloody teeth, like a piranha's, snapping at his hands. With one twist of his wrist he broke the little monster's neck and threw it down. A hysterical, yet sad laugh snickered behind him, and a feeling of dread came over Gladamyr.

He turned around, trying to keep his balance atop the teetering shelf, to see a hoard of Fyren's Mares entering the vaults. Minyon, Slither, and the crazed clown Mentia, led the party. Several others followed behind, growling and shouting as they ran into the maze of keys. Gladamyr forgot about the stinking stihl and leaped from shelf to shelf, trying to get back to the children. This mission was over. They had to get to safety now. This wasn't the place to fight. There just wasn't room.

More chickens followed Gladamyr's trail, and the stihl made a turnaround, blowing jets of fire that didn't seem to catch on the shelves but caught on a chicken. The fiery thing fell off the wall and ran madly through the maze. Under better circumstances, Gladamyr would have found the sight funny. He spotted Parker and Kaelyn running along with Felix and Cerulean. They were making good headway; if everything timed right, they just might get the keys and be able to doorway out of this place.

"Gladamyr, look out!" Parker cried.

The stihl torpedoed into Gladamyr. The Dream

Keeper sailed through the air and crashed down onto the hard, glassy floor. The beast's tail wrapped around his neck and squeezed so tight Gladamyr thought his head would pop off. He saw flashes of red as evil began to overtake the Dream Keeper. The monster within was breaking free once more. Gladamyr tried to fight it. He pushed all hateful emotions down deep inside, but it was too much while trying to fight off the stihl.

Once more, wicked, black spikes shot out from his body, and the stihl roared in pain. Its tail loosened from around his neck, and Gladamyr took hold of his emotions. He thought of Cerulean having to see him kill another dreamling. He thought of Kaelyn and how she saw him as good. He thought of the first mortal he'd ever met, and her pink nightgown. The evil was suppressed, but the fight wasn't over.

With Gladamyr's spikes gone, the stihl made a comeback. It knocked him back against a wall of keys. Its talons tore at his flesh and silvery blood soon covered his purple skin. There was horrible pain. He shifted again, his arms doubling their length, his hands growing to the size of large chairs. He slammed his hands down tight on the stihl. It writhed back and Gladamyr shifted again. He flipped the thing over and brought its head down to the ground with a loud smack. Using all the strength he could find, Gladamyr hoisted the thing over his head. He threw the creature over the shelf, and the stihl's body slapped the floor.

"Well done, Gladamyr," a cruel voice said from behind him. "But it takes more than that to kill a stihl. I know you have it in you, so why not try?"

Gladamyr turned to see the shining white skull face of Fyren. He stood in his long black robes, holding a deep black blade across his arms. Gladamyr had a flash of what the mortals visualized as Death, or what some called the Grim Reaper—Fyren seemed to have taken the form as his permanent shift.

Gladamyr spat in disgust. "I'm *not* a killer!".

"Oh, no?" Fyren laughed. "What of Dorjan? Cato told me what you did to him, Gladamyr. I couldn't be more proud of you for that. Dorjan was a disappointment."

"Like I was a disappointment?"

Fyren's bone jaw tightened. "You could've been better than I, Gladamyr, more powerful than any Mare that lived—yet you can't see things the way they really are, the way they *should* be. You're evil, Gladamyr, evil! Why not accept it? I saw your birth in Dorchadas—the heart of Mares. I alone saw you tear your mortal back to Awake so she could die from the wounds you inflicted. I was there Gladamyr . . . I know you better than you know yourself . . . I know—"

"You know nothing!" Gladamyr shouted as he ran toward Fyren. Death lifted his sword and brought it down.

"Get down!" Felix shouted as the wall of keys in front of them crashed to the floor. Kaelyn was pulled under Parker as if he could somehow protect her from the massive blow. Keys, brackets, and shelving clattered to the floor, cracking the glassy surface. Kaelyn cried out in fright, and Parker held her tighter under him. *Had he been hit—what happens if you die in your sleep?* Kaelyn thought. She looked up and, above them, a strange archway of stone had magically sprung out of the floor, protecting them from the brunt of the wreckage. She was just about to ask how it got there when Felix pulled both her and Parker up, and they charged down another aisle.

"Gladamyr needs our help," Parker shouted from beside her.

"He can handle the stihl on his own. We need to get the keys," Cerulean called back.

"Up ahead!" Felix cried. "I see your section. Quick, what are their names again?"

"Zelda Creighton—with a 'C'," Kaelyn answered.

The shelves were neatly organized by alphabet, so it only took seconds for Kaelyn to find Zelda's key. It hung on its own peg with a golden insignia above it. Kaelyn shoved it in her pocket.

"Got it!" she said. "Now Gates, Dr. Gates."

"Greg!" Parker added.

Kaelyn was the first to find Dr. Gates' key as well, and she grabbed it and shoved it next to Zelda's. She turned around to look for Gladamyr. *Where is he?* Kaelyn remembered seeing the dragon-like thing crashing into his body and then the howling scream. *Please let him be okay, please.* Hysterical laughter sounded and Kaelyn's heart raced even faster.

Coming down the hall was a group of Mares, led by the crazy clown she'd seen earlier that day. His bright red, polka-dot outfit and orange hair rippled. He held two vicious looking chickens in each hand. Kaelyn could think of nothing but screaming and running. Yet even as she turned to run she saw another group coming up the other direction. A snake-thing with protruding fangs was in the lead. She turned to Cerulean and Felix, who both had worried expressions. She turned toward Parker—but he wasn't even looking at the things coming to kill them. He was looking at the blasted keys, as if searching for something!

"Parker!" Kaelyn shouted. "Can't you see we have company?"

The clown threw one of the chickens and it came to life midflight. Its mouth opened, exposing rows of sharp, pointy teeth. Kaelyn jumped back but Parker stooped forward, letting go of her hand. She tried to grab it again but his hand wasn't there. Instead he had reached out, grabbing for one of the keys.

She tried to scream his name but the sound was cut from her. Overbalancing, she landed hard on the floor, the dreamstone flying from her hand and skittering away. Kaelyn quickly regained her feet and chased after the stone. She couldn't lose it—it was the only way for her to see into Dreams. *Or was it?* She wasn't holding the stone and yet she could still see perfectly fine. The Mares were still charging down the aisle and the stone lay feet away. She jumped for it, skidding on the floor just as a rock or boulder—something large – rushed overhead. It narrowly missed Felix, who turned round and round as if trying to decide something.

"Get Kaelyn," Felix yelled. "I'll take care of Parker."

Cerulean hurried to Kaelyn and lifted her into the air. They soared above the crazy clown and his band of monsters, and Kaelyn saw Felix lift himself and Parker over the top of one of the shelves. The two groups of Mares collided. Cerulean circled round, and Kaelyn was about to breathe a sigh of relief when a cloud of flames engulfed them.

Parker stuffed the key into his pocket. He and Felix ran, twisting and turning down the maze of endless shelves, trying to avoid the monsters behind them. The stihl roared overhead and every now and then the corridors between the key shelves lit up in orange flames. Felix yanked on Parker's shoulders, slamming his back into the brackets along one shelf. Keys clanged, spilling out onto the glassy floor as an angry, carnivorous chicken flew past his face. The clown let out a cackle of crazed laugher, and Parker knew he would never look at a chicken the same way again.

"Parker, this way!" Felix yelled, pulling on his shoulder once more.

Parker needed no invitation. He saw Mentia and what looked like four other Mares heading down the corridor of keys. And the lunatic clown was the least of their problems. Something resembling a half-snake-half-man thing whipped past the polka-dotted dreamling, wide fangs bared. Parker turned and bolted behind Felix as fast as he could. They turned corners and doubled back down different aisles, but their pursuers could not be shaken off.

Assault after assault of fire bombs, torn up sections of glassy floor, and vicious chickens made Parker's heart beat so fast he could literally feel it pounding in his ears. There was nothing he could do to avoid the attacks. All he could do was dodge them—*or was there something?*

"Felix," he called. "Isn't there *anything* we can do?"

As if in response Felix abruptly turned around, and Parker skidded past him, sliding on the glassy floor. Felix lifted his hands straight out, and a small green light seemed to mist its way out from his palms. The snake-like Mare was the first around the corner, its scaled body moving fast over the floor. It reared up, facing Felix, a smile clashing with its fanged mouth.

"Oh, it'ssss jussst you," the thing hissed. "What you

going to do, Felixssss? Bore me with flowerssss—? I like daffodilssss, or perhapssss you could jussst ssssing me a sssong?"

"Not today," Felix replied as he stretched his hands out.

Thick vines burst out of the floor and grabbed hold of the snake-thing. Tendrils shot out everywhere and spiraled up the snake-creature, entangling it in a large net of thick, leafy ropes. The vines formed a barricade, blocking off that part of the hallway.

"Move Parker, it won't hold them long," Felix shouted, barreling past.

"That was cool!" Parker puffed out, panting behind the dreamling. Yet within seconds the sound of the Mares crashing through the makeshift barrier echoed behind them. They turned yet another corner and ran down the endless rows of shelves, twinkling with iridescent keys. The sight of them made Parker think of the key he had grabbed—Jason's key—and he reached into his pocket to make sure it was still there. He pulled it out and smiled at it. If they ever got through this, it would be great to have Jason by his side.

A wall of keys crashed down in front of them. The aisle lit up with orange flames. The familiar, horrible smell of sewage and sulfur stung Parker's nose, and then the stihl came swooping down in front of them. In a split second, Felix conjured vines. They ripped from the floor and tangled around the beast. It snarled and puffed out clouds of ash as it tried to get away from the torrent of greenery engulfing it. A loose chunk of flooring punched Parker in the center of his back and he pitched forward. As he crashed to the floor, Jason's key flew off into the inferno of flames created by the stihl.

"No!" he groaned. He rolled, narrowly missing

another chunk of flooring, and looked back to see Felix pulling vines out of the floor, once again trying to barricade the Mares while still fighting off the stihl. Parker achingly got to his knees and searched for Jason's key. He found it yards away. *If I can reach it, Felix and I can...*

"Parker, go!" Felix roared.

Parker looked back at the dreamling. Felix's face dripped sweat as he turned around and around, calling forth vines and roots from the floor. The stihl was breaking through the ties that bound it and Parker knew it wouldn't take long before the creature burst through. The snake-thing and the crowd of others behind it chomped through the barrier Felix continued to build, but Parker knew the fight was over. The aisle right behind Felix was clear, and Felix was telling him to go. To leave him and let him deal with the nightmares. But Parker couldn't leave. He couldn't abandon Felix. And Jason's key! Parker could get the key if he —

"Go now!" Felix shouted.

Parker dove for Jason's key, but a vine shot out of the floor and wrapped itself around his ankle. He was pulled away from the key, away from Felix, away from the horrors breaking through the vines. He was thrown so hard down the empty hall, he skidded along the glassy floor. He looked up to see vines tangling around the walls of keys. Within seconds he was closed off from Felix, and the sound of snapping and the rushing of monsters filled his ears. The roar of the stihl and the howls of the Mares thankfully drowned out any cry from Felix. With more pain than he'd ever felt in his heart before, Parker turned and ran down the corridor.

With a quick shift of his shoulder, Gladamyr parried the first swing of Fyren's sword. It narrowly missed, cutting clean through the sleeve of his purple duster. Gladamyr shifted his arm to twice its normal size and swung, aiming for the skeleton face. Fyren shifted too and Gladamyr's arm plowed through a cloud of mist that reshaped itself into a monster with the mouth of a shark. Fyren chomped down, teeth sinking deep into Gladamyr's arm.

Gladamyr screamed, and the flash of red anger blurred his vision. He forced himself to focus and instantly his arm was as hard as stone. Fyren spit out the Dream Keeper's arm and tried another swing of the sword. Gladamyr parried once more, crashing back into a shelf of keys. The hooks dug into his back but Gladamyr didn't want to be anywhere near Fyren's sword. The look of it alone frightened him more than anything he'd ever seen—even more than himself.

A large spider leaped up Gladamyr's leg, stabbing its tiny needle over and over into his calf. It was trying to tie his legs together. Gladamyr turned his head to see Minyon and a few other dreamlings coming down the long corridor. Panic rose inside him. He could barely hold off Fyren, and now there were more to deal with. Gladamyr pushed off the shelf and rolled once again, dodging a blow from Fyren. He grabbed hold of the nasty spider and squished it. Black goo ran between his fingers and a satisfying cry of anguish burst from Minyon.

Gladamyr ran at Fyren once more. He crashed into the demon with such force, they both tumbled through the shelf into another aisle. Fyren turned into mist and

Gladamyr hit the ground face down. Fyren cried out a call of victory, lifting the black blade, bringing it swiftly down. Gladamyr couldn't move quickly enough. Searing pain shot throughout his body.

He fell back on the glassy floor, convulsing and uncontrollably shifting. He rolled and flipped. He felt the ground shaking. A deep angry groan rumbled from beneath the earth. Then all was red—nothing but red, red and the pain. Gladamyr tried to focus. He tried to tell himself to move, to flee before Fyren had another chance to use his sword, but his strength was gone. The sword, whatever it was, had more power over darkness than Gladamyr ever had. Horrible flashbacks of the cruel things he'd done in his past infected his mind over and over. He saw mortals screaming, running, hiding hopelessly from him. He saw them plead for mercy, yet he gave none. He saw himself as a nightmare.

"Not here, fool," a shrill voice cried out.

The voice sounded distant, but it helped Gladamyr bring his mind back, helped him see through the red and focus on controlling the shifting.

"How dare you address him in such a manner?" clicked another voice.

"Off me beast! I am a *queen*!"

"Leave her be, Minyon. She is right," Fyren hissed. "He cannot be finished here. It must be done in Éadrom. Bind him with the light of Favor. It will force him to stay in one shift."

Bind him—no, Gladamyr knew he mustn't allow himself to be taken prisoner. He had to get control. He had to focus—he had to fight. What had helped him last time? Cerulean and Kaelyn . . . he thought of them. He thought of Cerulean's face after he killed Dorjan, and Kaelyn's tear-filled eyes as she told him that he was not a monster. He saw their faces and the red was gone.

The sting of an enchanted rope snaked its way around his right ankle. It had to be Mab conjuring the rope. Gladamyr felt the power of Favor ebbing through it. He focused his efforts once more and shifted. His arms were once again wings and his legs shrank, making the rope lose its grip. With every last bit of strength he could muster the Dream Keeper launched himself into the air, leaving Mab, Minyon, and a furious Fyren behind him.

Cerulean managed to drop them down below the cloud of fire, but Kaelyn still felt the heat of it on her face. As they flew around the vaults, she found the source of the fire. A red-winged fairy was shooting fireballs at them! Cerulean dove again, and Kaelyn wondered if they had a better chance back in the maze of shelves.

Another ball of fire shot past, and Cerulean dove down so fast she lost hold of Kaelyn. Kaelyn only let out a small cry. *This is it—this is how you are going to die.* She'd had many dreams where she had fallen down deep caverns and never hit the ground. But here the ground got closer and closer. Its shiny surface was just asking for something to smash into it—like a windshield longs for a bug.

"Gotcha!" Cerulean said, as she caught Kaelyn just feet from the ground.

"I didn't even worry," Kaelyn lied. Cerulean didn't answer. They lifted higher and higher into the room. Kaelyn began to worry. Wouldn't they hit the ceiling? As the thought entered her mind, Cerulean shot them downward, right toward the oncoming fireball.

"I've had enough of that blasted pixie!" she shouted. "Kaelyn, I need you to focus on something for me. Can you do that?"

Kaelyn nodded. "Yes."

"Think of something really cold—like the coldest you've ever been in your life. Try to send that image to me through your thoughts."

Is she crazy? How on Earth am I supposed to think of something cold when we're was flying towards a ball of fire? Kaelyn shook the pessimist from her mind and thought about her last winter she had spent in Scotland with her dad. The temperature dropped so low that the loch near their flat turned to ice. She remembered the surface of the water had an old shoe sticking out of the ice as if someone had thrown it in just before the water froze. She thought of building a snowman with her dad, and how she lost her gloves and her hands were so cold. *How do I send images?* she thought, but Cerulean laughed.

"Perfect!"

Cerulean shifted Kaelyn from her arms to her hip, holding her with one strong arm. Then she stuck the other one straight out and Kaelyn laughed, thinking that she was flying with a super hero. *Blue Fairy to the rescue!*

"Keep focusing!" Cerulean shouted, and Kaelyn instantly thought once again of the frozen lake and her dad tossing a snowball that accidentally hit her right in the face; it stung in two ways.

A shield of blue formed around Cerulean's fist, and they flew through the ball of fire without so much as a singed hair. Kaelyn saw the red pixie again. He darted around like a jittery bug. Kaelyn again thought of that snowball and how it hurt when it hit her—the sting of cold snow. A huge blue ball of ice shot from Cerulean's fist and slammed into the legs of the pixie like a cannonball. The pixie did somersaults in the air, his fire shooting off target.

"How did you do that?" Cerulean asked, excited.

"I didn't do anything!"

"Focus your thoughts. You must have thought that up or it wouldn't have happened. Think instant freeze."

Instant freeze? Kaelyn thought about what froze instantly. *Liquid nitrogen.* Could it somehow be formed into a ball? Some sort of weapon? Wouldn't it turn to gas—*no, not in my dream world.* Kaelyn focused her thoughts and a rapid fire of small balls of liquid nitrogen shot out of Cerulean's fist. They pelted into shelves and keys, freezing instantly anything they touched. One hit the fleeing pixie's wings, and he dropped mid-beat, plummeting to the glassy floor. His wings shattered in a million pieces.

"Serves you right!" Cerulean spat, slowing to a hover.

Kaelyn was proud of what they had accomplished but it was pathetic the way the pixie tried to collect his shattered wings. He would probably never fly again and it was her fault. She had removed a bird's wings.

"Don't pity that creature," Cerulean said softly. "He would have seen you burn just for the mere pleasure of it. Cato is not worthy of your thoughts."

Before Kaelyn could stop herself, a strange thing happened. She thought of the snowman that she and her dad made together. Her dad gave it wings; he said it was an angel, and if they asked could it say 'hi' to her mom for her. It was a great idea. Blue light exploded out of Cerulean's hand and shot down, slamming into Cato's back. He fell forward, his body slapping on the floor. Something white and glittery popped from his back.

Wings! Wings made of snow, just as her dad had made.

Cerulean breathed in deep. Kaelyn didn't know what to say. Had she just given a fire pixie wings made of snow? Cato stood and turned this way and that, trying to look at his new wings. He reached back and touched the tips of them with his fingers, and then put his fingers in his mouth as if they got burnt.

"It seems the mortal has given you a gift, Cato," Cerulean laughed. "Wings of snow for a fire pixie! I guess you will have to decide which you like better: flying or fire."

A roar rumbled through the cavernous room, and the floor beneath Parker's feet cracked and split. Shelves shook as if there was an earthquake, and keys clattered to the floor. Parker halted, not knowing what was going on. *Was it some monstrous Mare, or were the vaults falling apart? And who was that screaming? Gladamyr? No, it couldn't—*

Something rounded the corner of the aisle up ahead, and Parker's insides froze. The figure hobbled toward him, dragging its left leg behind it. It was human, or had been human once. It was tall and bone thin with a collection of muscle, skin, and a few torn rags covering its form. Parker played lots of video games involving zombies, and the figure before him was nowhere close to the lame computer generated things that gave him nightmares before. This zombie was something out of the blackest imagination. Parker tried to back away, tried to get his legs to obey, but the zombie had him transfixed with horror.

Three more stumbling figures rounded the corner and Parker was able to look away from the zombie, only to lock his gaze onto the messy group of corpses lumbering toward him. Something above his head flashed orange, and the zombies lit in a way that made every wet thing glimmer. Parker's stomach churned and the light faded once again, dimming the rotted flesh before him. Alarms sounded in Parker's head, trying desperately to get him to close his eyes, to look away and run, but it was as if magic was controlling him. The flesh peeling off bone and the fluid plopping onto the floor was something he simply could not look away from.

The zombie closest to him let out a gurgle, and Parker's eyes snapped from the three behind to the one inches from his face. That split second glance from one zombie to another allowed Parker to stumble back a few steps before being frozen again. He was disgusted by the sight before him. The thing had been trying to eat him. The zombie had literally snapped at his cheek as he backed away—and now he was frozen again! Parker tried to close his eyes but they were glued open. They itched and stung and leaked tears down his face, but he couldn't close them.

The zombie smiled, if the horror of broken teeth and a sawed off lip could be called a smile. It gurgled an excited call. The others gurgled out replies, and Parker tensed from his neck to his knees. They sounded like cows mooing through water, and it would have been funny if it hadn't come from cannibalistic corpses. The zombie was again inches away, and it opened a misshaped mouth and leaned in toward Parker for a bite.

The tension in Parker's legs released and he toppled back onto the hard floor, just as a stone figure of a knight with a sword and shield erupted from the floor, impaling the corpse on the end of its saber. Parker had the use of his eyes once more, and he did everything he could not to look at the moaning zombies trying to get past the stone figure. Within seconds he was on his feet and running. He wiped away the mass of tears wetting his cheeks. The aisle lit up orange once more, then bright blue, and Parker looked up to see a red fairy-like thing get hit with a stream of blue light. It seemed to be frozen as it fell. Parker's eyes followed it down until he registered that he'd just run himself into a dead end.

He didn't turn around—he knew what was behind him. He could hear the horrible sound of muscles squelching and bones scraping on the glass floor. He couldn't look again. He couldn't let the last thing he ever saw be a rotting corpse.

He searched around for something to climb up on, but the shelves were too small and the hooks gave way when he tried to pull up on them. What was he going to do? He had no idea where the stone knight had come from, and waiting around for the zombies to be inches away from eating his face was not something he wanted to do.

Parker ripped keys off the wall. Turning around with his eyes closed, he chucked the keys as hard as he could at the creatures. He couldn't tell if the keys hurt as they hit the zombies. They made no sound other than their gurgling moo. Parker kept turning in circles, pulling keys off the shelf behind him and then hurling them at the zombies. What else could he to do? *Any time, Gladamyr . . . any time you can come—*

"Wait a minute!" Parker thought out loud. He had a way to save himself! He was linked with Gladamyr. All he had to do was call out Gladamyr's name and the Dream Keeper had to come—it was part of their binding!

"Gladamyr! Gladamyr, I need you . . . Gladamyr . . .

Cerulean . . . Kaelyn!" Parker looked around him, expecting Gladamyr to pop out of nowhere and carry him through another magic door, but there was no one. Just walls of keys and hooks and—

The zombies were just feet away. Parker couldn't help but notice how they walked. One was in the lead while two others flanked behind. The fourth, who was coming along slowly with only the use of his arms, having left half of himself on the stone knight's sword, was a few feet behind them. This was it! This was going to be the last thing Parker Bennett ever saw. And for the millionth time the thought of whether or not he could die in his dreams entered his mind.

CHAPTER TEN
ESCAPE

W hat the heck is he doing? Just run past them!"
Kaelyn shouted into the wind as Cerulean flew
down toward Parker and the three and a half
zombies surrounding him. She wondered if Dreams was
having an effect on Parker's attention span. First it was
the keys and now zombies. *Come on, Parker, just—*
Suddenly, three stone statues shot out from the floor,
shattering the glassy surface around them. They were
large knights with hefty shields and she couldn't work
out whether they were blocking the zombies from
getting at Parker, or trapping him. The statues left just
inches between Parker, the zombies, and the wall of keys
behind him.

"Kaelyn," called Cerulean, "close your eyes and
don't look at them."

"At what? The statues or the zombies?"

"Just close your eyes."

Kaelyn obediently shut her eyes and tried to tune
into the other senses she had available. She felt them
swooping down. That was clear with the lurching in her
stomach. And the sound—the sound was awful. The

zombies moaned like animals. There were other strange sounds too, wet sucking and slapping sounds, and Kaelyn was thankful she didn't have her eyes open. The sound was enough.

"Parker," Cerulean shouted, "Parker, it's Cerulean. Take my hand. Parker!"

"Why isn't he listening?" Kaelyn shouted. The zombies got more and more excited, their moaning calls almost like a sick chorus of dying carolers.

"It's the Carrion; they have a paralyzing effect on mortals. We need to get his eyes off them."

"MAAAHH MAAAHH!" the zombies called.

"We need to hurry! They're climbing the statues!"

"Parker! Parker!" Kaelyn shouted. "Cerulean, can you land next to him?"

"Not enough room for my wings."

"Then drop me!"

"I can't, Kaelyn—the Carrion are almost over—"

"Drop me now!"

"Okay . . . just don't open your eyes. You've only got seconds."

Kaelyn took Cerulean's arm and held on tightly to her hand. She was hanging down in the air, trying to feel the ground beneath her feet; nothing there. She was tempted to open her eyes but she knew the threat the zombies posed. She just had to hope she was close enough to the ground not to break her legs. Kaelyn took a deep breath and let go. Thankfully the ground was not too far off.

She squatted with her arms out in front of her, trying to feel for Parker. In a second she found his pant leg and stood, pulling on him while calling out his name. He was like a stone statue too, fixed and unmovable. She grabbed his arm and pulled, but still nothing. *His eyes, you idiot, cover his eyes,* she shouted to herself.

She moved her hands up his arm to his neck, then over his wet face till she found his eyes. She placed her hand over them and tried again to move him, but nothing happened. His eyes were still open, she could tell because she felt the wet eyeball on her hand. Panic took hold as the zombies groaned louder and louder. The sound of snapping and cracking filled her ears.

"It's not working!" she called out.

"It's too late! The Carrion are too close, and he's over exposed. Give me your hand. I can try to reach his."

Kaelyn lifted her arm into the air along with Parker's, but it was no use. She couldn't get his arm to stretch far enough, and Cerulean wasn't able to reach. *Think of something, quick! Hurry or you're zombie food . . . Really, would they eat us . . .? Stop thinking about the zombies! Think of a way to get out of there! A way to wake up Parker . . . no, that's a dumb idea . . . or maybe not, at least it's an idea!*

Mentally telling herself to shut up for once, Kaelyn moved in front of Parker so she was face to face with him. Then she did the one thing fairytales and nursery rhymes said to do when someone was under a spell. She kissed him.

The first thought for Kaelyn was that his lips were very wet. She tasted tears trickling into her mouth. Taking a risk, she opened her eyes. She momentarily saw the big brown puppy dog eyes that she loved so much, and then they closed. They closed! Instantly she shut her own eyes, and stepped back.

"Parker, keep your eyes shut! Give me your hand."

He obeyed and Kaelyn stretched her arm up for Cerulean to take hold of. Parker stretched too, and then they lifted up off the cracked floor and into the air.

Kaelyn sneaked another chance to open her eyes. She and Parker were in a hug of sorts, one arm wrapped around each other and the other pulling them up and away from the zombies. Parker had his eyes tightly closed, and Kaelyn couldn't help but smile. He looked cute with his face all scrunched up . . . *reality check, Kaelyn—that's Parker Bennett, one of the most popular guys in school and guess what, he's not that into you . . . you may have just kissed him, but get over yourself. You're no Tiffany!*

Kaelyn tried to get the always rude, put you down, nauseating, inner voice to shut up. She didn't know why, but whenever she got excited for something, her inner voice would try to make her feel bad about it. It was like fighting a war with herself, between the girl she wanted to be and the girl she kept telling herself she was. Kaelyn looked away from Parker and down at the shelves below them. The zombies had successfully climbed over the statues but were now pinned behind them. She was about to look back at Parker when something dark and purple caught her eye.

"Cerulean, turn back!"

"What is it?"

"I think it's Gladamyr."

Parker didn't want to open his eyes even though he knew they were safely away from the zombies. He had never been more scared in all his life. He hated the fact that he just stood there as death came to eat his face off. It was horrible and the disgusting images of zombies kept blinking over and over in his mind. *Just open your eyes and you will see something better.* Parker struggled for a second longer, then opened his eyes.

The image was Kaelyn, and she was a welcoming sight. Her blonde hair was blowing wildly in the wind as they flew above the room of shelves and keys. She wasn't looking at him, though, but something down below. He hesitated to follow her gaze. He didn't want to see the zombies again, but wait, hadn't she said Gladamyr was down there?

Just his name helped Parker to be brave, and he followed Kaelyn's line of sight. If it was Gladamyr, then what the heck had happened to him? Cerulean came in fast and tried to steady herself as Parker and Kaelyn let go of her hands. Then she slowly set down and ran toward the Dream Keeper.

"Gladamyr, what happened? Oh . . . my . . . my . . . oh . . ."

Kaelyn crouched down, trying to pull Cerulean off Gladamyr's body. Tears were running down her face and Parker felt that he was going to cry too. Was Gladamyr dead? It couldn't be so. It just couldn't be, but was that why he never came when Parker called?

Parker crouched down and helped Kaelyn pull Cerulean away from Gladamyr's body. Silver blood stained her blue skin, and Parker knew Gladamyr was gone. Somehow the Dream Keeper had been killed. He hardly knew the dreamling, yet sorrow won out, and Parker felt tears he didn't know he had left leaking out. Kaelyn turned to him and he held her tightly in his arms. They both cried for the loss of their bond—their connection to the world of Dreams.

A groan, muffled by Cerulean's body, sounded, and the three grief-stricken companions looked at their fallen hero. Cerulean said his name over and over, and little wisps of blue light flitted from her fingers onto Gladamyr's face.

"Gladamyr . . . Gladamyr . . . Gladamyr . . ."

"Yes, Boss, I'm listening," was the whispered reply.

"Oh!" Cerulean sobbed, holding him tighter.

Parker's face broke out in a wide grin, and he even laughed. Kaelyn laughed too. They all circled around the Dream Keeper.

"Now, this is touching," said a cold, high-pitched voice.

Parker's blood froze. He realized they hadn't bothered looking around to see what dangers awaited them. This was a trap! They turned to see a regal woman wearing a large crown, flanked by the crazy clown and at least ten other wild and monstrous characters. The absence of the skeleton was at the forefront of Parker's thoughts, and he turned his head to see where the Mare might be hiding.

"Oh, he's not here . . . yet," the woman said.

"Who asked you?" Parker sneered at the woman.

Kaelyn squeezed Parker's hand, warning him to be careful. He didn't heed her. He stood up and stared back at the woman just as coldly. There was something about her he didn't like.

"Well, well, a mortal with a backbone," she said, stretching her neck so she appeared to be taller. "Now, peasant, hand over the keys you stole and we might let you return to Awake unscarred."

"Bite me!" Parker spat. Again Kaelyn squeezed his hand, but the glittering woman only laughed.

"Oh, I am sure I can arrange for someone to do that. Somnus, perhaps you would like to *bite* the peasant?"

An enormous Mare, part-wolf, part-man, stepped out from the ranks. He was clearly a werewolf. He was everything the horror stories said about them; tall, disfigured, sharp teeth, and red, glowing eyes. He looked like he would enjoy taking a bite out of anything: Parker, Kaelyn, some little girl in a red cloak. Yet Parker didn't back down. Humiliated by the control the zombies had exerted over him, he was tired of running. He thought of Felix and how he'd not backed down when the snake Mare mocked him. Mares wanted mortals to fear them, but Parker was tired of being afraid. These monsters chased them all over the vaults, and he was sick of it.

"Tell us what you really want, *troll*, and we'll think about giving it to you." *A troll, had he actually called that beautiful woman in glittery jewels a troll*—? Yeah, he was mad.

"How dare you! I shall have your head—"

"Oh, going to wear it around your neck? It would fit in quite nicely with the oversized hunks of plastic. Tell me, did you raid some old lady's jewelry box for those?"

"Easy, Parker," Kaelyn whispered. "There are more of them than us."

"Listen to the little lady, Parker, and settle down," the woman cooed.

"Drop dead," Kaelyn spat. "Just who do you think you are to start ordering people around like they're your slaves?"

Parker was somewhat surprised and at the same time excited. Kaelyn didn't like the woman either. In fact, it seemed no one in the room particularly cared for her. None of the other Mares came to her defense; they just let the two mortal kids have a go at her.

"Let me guess, you must be Mab?" Kaelyn went on. "Self-proclaimed queen of Dreams. We have self-proclaimed rulers in our world too. We call them *delusional* and they end up in little rooms with padded walls."

"How dare you speak to me in such a—"

"Blah, blah, blah . . . stop trying to scare us. We're not scared, and tell us what you want," Parker snapped. "Quick now—we're getting bored."

Kaelyn squeezed his hand and Parker almost heard her thoughts in his mind. *Just what is it you are planning on doing besides getting them riled up?* The answer was that he didn't know. Call it nature or something, but that woman, Mab, made Parker's blood boil. He hated people like that, people who thought they owned everything and the whole world was in their debt somehow. Tiffany was like that and Tiffany was a dog. Her attitude took away every last good look she ever owned and made her ugly. But Kaelyn was right. What were they going to do? The keys, that was it!

Parker tried to block Cerulean from the others, and hoped she would take the hint. They were hopelessly outnumbered; it would be a losing battle. Parker knew they had to get away from here, and the only way was for Cerulean to get their keys from Gladamyr's pocket. Then they could do that door thing and get the heck out of Dodge. He had to keep the Mares distracted; keep their eyes off the blue fairy behind him.

"So who does your hair? That guy?" Parker motioned toward the wolf thing. The Mares turned to look at Somnus, who was clearly having a bad hair day. Kaelyn laughed and Parker smiled to himself. She had apparently gotten his idea.

"Please, Parker, don't insult the wolf," she said. "He obviously has more talent than that. A baby orangutan could've done a better job using its feet. Anyway, it's no match for that dress. I mean, look at it. Are corsets and hoop skirts still in fashion in Dreams? Is anyone else walking around looking like an upside down wine glass?"

At this, the clown Mare laughed hysterically. Mab

turned to him and slapped him across the face, which only made him laugh harder.

"It's true, it's true," the clown blurted out between cackles. "You do resemble that . . . she even has the whine to go with the glass—whine, whine, whine—"

"Wow, and that's coming from the best dressed among you," Kaelyn laughed.

Parker couldn't help but laugh and even a few of the other Mares began to let out giggles, none compared to the wild hysterics coming from the clown. "Yes, yes!" he said as he rolled on the ground. Mab, who was clearly irate from the clown's outrageous remarks about her, beat him with one of his own rubber chickens. The wolf thing barked, which Parker guessed was a laugh, but he couldn't tell.

"All hail her majesty!" Kaelyn cheered.

"She'll buy us all drinks," the clown giggled. "Plenty of whine to spare."

"ENOUGH!" Mab screamed, and the floor shook. "I'll not tolerate such insubordination. And I'm through with *your* foolishness."

She pulled out something small and black from the lace at her chest. She held it up like a dagger and drove it into the back of the clown. The Mare let out the most horrific sound Parker had ever heard. Gone were the crazed cackles, gone the jaunts and plain goofiness. The clown was in agony. Mab tore down his shoulder and arced her wrist in a triumphant motion; the clown's arm dropped to the floor and vanished in a cloud of black dust before even hitting the glossy surface.

Mab stood up straight and eyed the group of Mares around her. Parker didn't think she looked beautiful anymore. Mab looked evil. She had a psycho look in her eye that made him think she'd start killing babies any minute.

"NOW, I WILL HAVE ORDER HERE!" she demanded. "I AM THE QUEEN, AND I WILL BE OBEYED!"

The unruly Mares all bowed their heads in respect for their vicious queen. Parker stared, wondering what the heck she had in her hand and how was it able to cut the arm off a dreamling? He hoped Cerulean had enough time because taunting the queen again was out of the question.

"GIVE ME THE KEYS NOW!" Mab barked, holding out her hand.

Her order was so powerful that Parker would have handed over the keys if he had them. But he didn't, and he looked to Kaelyn, who clearly was not going to let Mab tell her what to do. For some reason Kaelyn looked like she was about to rip a limb off Mab.

"No!" she hissed.

"NOW!"

"Get over yourself. *I said no!*"

"Kaelyn, honey, give her the keys you took. It'll be okay." The voice was calm and sweet, and Parker and Kaelyn both looked round to see who the voice belonged to. A man stepped out from behind the ranks of Mares. He was of average height and had sandy blond hair that was a little messy. Parker recognized him at once. He was the man in Kaelyn's dream, the car crash nightmare.

"Daddy!" Kaelyn moved forward, about to run for him. Parker held her tightly and grabbed her other arm just in case.

"No Kae, that's not your dad," he said, holding her back.

"Just give the keys to us, Kaelyn, and this will have

all been just a bad dream," her dad said softly. Parker looked at him closely. He looked real but he had to be a fake. Was the dreamstone not working? Were they not able to see the way things were? But then Parker saw it, the black sword. It hung at the waist of the Mare pretending to be Kaelyn's dad. It was the same sword the skeleton had—it was Fyren!

"Kae, Kaelyn," Parker said, holding her now in a backwards bear hug. "He is not your dad. Your dad died. I'm sorry, but he died and that is Fyren. See the sword? He can't shift the sword. He can only shift himself and remember, he can read thoughts. He can see your dad in his mind."

Kaelyn looked at the sword, at her dad, and Parker felt her relax against him. Fyren roared out a terrible cry and morphed into another figure—Parker's mom.

"Hand over the keys now, Parker, or you'll be grounded for life!"

Parker was amazed at the transformation. Fyren looked just like his mom. Her dark brown hair fell perfectly around her lightly tanned face. But the dreamstone helped show Parker the flaws in Fyren's shifting. The sword still hung at his waist, and the evil glare was still visible in his mother's eyes.

"Nice try, Skeletor, but that doesn't even work for my mom."

Mab let out an angry cry. She lifted her hand with the black thing and ran at Parker and Kaelyn. Fyren morphed back into the skeleton shape and held Mab back.

"It's her! He belongs to her! I will make her pay!" Mab screamed.

"They are bonded," hissed Fyren. "Remember that."

Fyren dropped Mab's wrist and she stood there, eyes

fixed on Parker with a look of contempt. Fyren glared too, but the fiery, glowing eyes were more hypnotic than scary once Parker thought about it. What had Fyren meant by 'they are bonded'? It was as if the Mares were afraid of Parker and Kaelyn, as if being connected—bonded—with Gladamyr made them dangerous.

"What do you want from us?" Parker asked.

"The keys you took," Fyren replied, and just for a second Parker thought how weird it was to watch Fyren's skull jaw lift up and down as he spoke.

"Come on, you were chasing us long before we got keys," he said.

Fyren's skull face lifted and Parker could swear he looked like a skeleton smiling.

"They know nothing, Mab. They cannot harm us in any way." The expressions on the group of Mares' faces turned from puzzled to murderous. Parker suddenly became very scared that he and Kaelyn were about to die.

"Get their keys!" Fyren roared.

The Mares ran at Parker and Kaelyn with fangs, claws, and weapons poised to kill. Parker turned to Kaelyn and held her tight in his arms. He felt a pull from behind and the world before him vanished in a spinning cloud of purple mist. The door shut on the group of angry Mares. Parker turned to Cerulean, who had a smile on her face.

"Freaking leave it to the last second, why don't you!"

Kaelyn dropped to the ground and let out the breath she was holding. The sight of Death and monsters charging after her with murder in their eyes was too much for her. She started to breathe heavily and Parker crouched down beside her, putting a shaky hand on her shoulder. She looked up at him and he gave her a concerned smile. She smiled back, but she was still trying to calm her breathing.

"You okay?" he asked.

"Ya . . . Yah," Kaelyn sighed. "It was just . . . so . . ."

"I know."

"What do they want? And why were they scared one minute of touching us and the next second about to tear us to shreds?"

"What's up with that?" Parker asked, turning to Cerulean, who was busy looking in the folds of Gladamyr's trench coat.

"What are you doing?"

"Checking for Minyon's spies," she replied, now checking herself over. "I don't want to be followed again. I suggest you check each other."

Kaelyn looked over Parker's back and neck. He was sweaty and kind of smelled bad, but she ignored that— all boys smelled bad when they were sweaty. It was just weird to think that things like sweat and tears acted the same way even in a dream world. She also noticed he had a few cuts on his neck and arms.

"Parker, you're bleeding!"

"What? Where?"

He looked at the rip in his shirt and the cut underneath, and felt for the marks on his neck. "Awesome!"

"You're not serious—you're excited to be hurt?"

"It's cool, you know, like battle wounds. I'm a real warrior now," he said, with a triumphant grin.

"Really? Are you telling me guys go off to war hoping to get hurt?"

"Not like seriously hurt, but yeah. It's like a badge of honor—to show you actually fought something. Ya know, to impress the girls back home."

"I'm not impressed," Kaelyn blurted, and she wished she hadn't. Parker's face fell. *There you go, Johnny Rain Cloud, say goodbye to ever kissing those lips again.* Kaelyn tried to backpedal. "I mean, I don't think girls get impressed. I think it makes them worry you came so close to getting even more hurt—like him."

Kaelyn pointed at Gladamyr, who was not looking good at all. He was alive but that was it. He seemed to go in and out of consciousness, and for a moment Kaelyn wondered where dreamlings went to when they slept.

"Kaelyn is right, Parker," Cerulean said softly. "I am not impressed at all with this."

"What can we do for him?" Parker asked, looking worried again for his bond.

"Are we free of spies?" Cerulean asked. Kaelyn and Parker nodded. Cerulean cradled Gladamyr under one arm and reached out her hand for them to take. Kaelyn grabbed Parker's, and then together they took Cerulean's. Once again they spun through a vortex of purple mist and came out standing in a new world.

The scene was odd. It was nighttime and the moon gleamed brightly overhead. Not just one moon, but three. They stood on a small platform that reached from a land of craggy dark rocks to a vast expanse of ocean. Next to the platform, in the water, was a pirate ship. An actual pirate ship! The thing was massive with huge sails, enough rope to tie up a giant, and even a Jolly Roger flag atop the mast. Kaelyn immediately thought of the *Pirates of the Caribbean* movie, and she could tell Parker was thinking the same. He had the world's biggest smile on his face. Then Kaelyn noticed the ship was vacant of pirates or sailors, and she turned to Cerulean.

"Where are all the pirates?"

"This ship only has one crewmember, and he could be anywhere." The blue dreamling gazed around the boat, trying to find someone who clearly wasn't there.

"Are we getting on the ship to go somewhere?"

"That's the plan."

"No person, mortal, or dreamling is getting on me ship without me consent, arr!"

Kaelyn turned to see the most pirate-looking man she'd ever laid eyes on. *Eat your heart out, Captain Hook. This guy has you beat!* The dreamling stood about five feet tall and walked upon two wooden stilts which were attached to his black and red striped trousers with what appeared to be a hundred safety pins at each knee. Around his waist hung four ancient ball pistols, one overly large wooden sword, and five small cherry bombs. He wore a brown vest over his yellowed shirt, which opened at the chest revealing a tattoo of an overweight mermaid. Trailing behind him was a cape of sorts, the black and white Jolly Roger waving frantically in the wind. His beard consisted of three thick, orange braids that stretched down to his chest, and he had an eye patch over his right eye. Atop his head was a large, fuchsia colored tricorne hat adorned with plumes of purple ostrich feathers.

"Captain Loofyn Bootie at your service, arr," growled the dreamling, holding out a hook. Kaelyn and Parker looked down at the hook. It was polished silver and it was attached to the dreamling's wrist. Then they noticed that both of Captain Bootie's hands had been replaced by hooks.

"I see ye noticed me hardware—lost 'em buggers in an onslaught o' sea witches. Ye see, I was manning me ship in the sea south o' the deserted isle when not a hundred sea witches surrounded me ship. It took every last bit o' strength I had to fight them off. They took me hands and legs but I kept me ship."

"Permission to come aboard your ship, Captain, and a request of passage," Cerulean said with a respectful bow. Kaelyn did the same and, after a moment of hesitation, Parker too bowed his head respectfully.

"Well, well, never been shown such respect. Permission granted, me fine blue lady."

"Thank you, Captain. Is there any way you could help bring Gladamyr aboard? He has been terribly wounded and—"

"Gladamyr!"

Kaelyn was worried that Captain Bootie might be in ranks with Fyren, and every muscle in her body tensed. She could tell that Parker thought the same because he grabbed her protectively by the shoulders. Then the pirate's voice turned deep and somber.

"Cerulean, what trouble has me friend gotten himself into this time?"

"I'll tell you when we are safely aboard and heading for the No More Islands."

"To No More, is it then? Oh my, we are in trouble, aren't we?"

CHAPTER ELEVEN
BEING BRAVE

Parker watched in awe as, with a small nod of the pirate's head, his ship came to life. It was eerie and spectacular all at once. Things were moving about on board with no one controlling them. Ropes flung themselves from the side of the craft and wrapped protectively around Gladamyr, and soon the Dream Keeper was hoisted aboard the ship. A large plank carried by invisible men lowered down from the ship and Captain Bootie quickly hobbled up it. Cerulean followed and, with a little help from Kaelyn yanking on Parker's arm, they were soon standing on a plank of wood lifting high above the platform and out over the rolling water. Parker's stomach churned just a little, but then he remembered this was the coolest thing he had ever done. Any thought of sickness left immediately.

"Welcome aboard the Dreamer, arr," Captain Bootie said as the plank touched down on the ship's deck. As if the ship knew its name, everything at once shifted: the boards, the ropes, the canons, and even the mop buckets. They all seemed to salute the new arrivals. Parker hopped off the plank and peered around wide-eyed.

"Never been on a ship, have ye, lad?" Captain Bootie asked.

"No, Sir . . . er, Captain."

"Call me Loofyn or Bootie, no formal dealings today, arr. 'Twill take ye a moment to get yer sea legs, but ye'll get them soon enough."

"Loofyn," Cerulean interrupted. "Where can I find Gladamyr?"

The pirate leaned his head to one side as if listening to something and Parker thought he heard a whisper, or perhaps it was just the rustle of the sails. A second later, Captain Bootie nodded toward the large ornate door at the rear of the deck.

"Dreamer had him laid in the Captain's quarters, arr."

"Well, if you will please excuse me, I need to see if there is anything I can do for him. Kaelyn, will you please come with me? I might need your assistance."

Kaelyn looked at Cerulean, and then at Parker and their locked hands. Parker had been wondering the same thing: Did they even need the dreamstone anymore? It seemed as if the thing had become useless to them. Parker was able to see Dreams as it was without touching the dreamstone or Kaelyn.

"I guess I'll be right back," Kaelyn said with a smile, letting go of his hand.

Parker had to admit that it was kind of weird to hold a girl's hand all the time, but when Kaelyn let go he felt as though something left him. Call it the dreamstone's power, or just the fact that Parker had grown to like Kaelyn, but it was something, and it wasn't just the warmth of another person.

"If ye want, lad, we could paint a picture of her. It

would last longer."

Parker shook his gaze away from the door he had been staring at for who knows how long, and looked at the pirate. A wide and toothless mouth barked out chuckles of laughter. The dreamling reached out and put his over-large fuchsia colored hat on top of Parker's head. The brim fell down and smacked the bridge of Parker's nose.

"First lesson: look the part. We're goin' to the No More, lad, and the way don't smile upon cheeky boys. 'Tis time to become a man. Come up to the crow's nest for a bit and it'll make a man outa ya."

Before Parker knew it, he was in a small barrel-like thing atop the highest mast on the ship. Loofyn crowded in next to him, and the large feathers in the hat Parker wore were apparently tickling the pirate because he kept chuckling.

"Quite the sight lad, ain't it?"

It was! The wonder and beauty of the scene before Parker was one he would always remember. The three moons danced next to the stars on the surface of the dark ocean before them, and it seemed to go on for eternity. Parker had a sudden urge to throw his arms out and shout that he was the king of the world, but that made him feel silly for thinking it. Honestly though, high up above the ship and looking out on a deep ocean of moons and stars, Parker did feel like the king of the world.

"Ah! I see ye got yer sea legs, lad. Look at the water, feel the wind in yer hair, breathe the ocean, and it'll give ye life. 'Tis a pirate's spirit, the ocean; our life, our love . . . our soul mate."

"How long have you been a pirate?"

"O, as long as I remember. I was born a pirate, arr."

"Does it ever get lonely?"

"What, out here in the blackness with nothin' but me ship? Na! She keeps me company, and I see a few fellows here and there."

"Like Gladamyr? He's your friend, right?"

"Aye, that he is. Did me a few favors back when, arr."

"Is he going to be okay?" Parker was hoping Captain Bootie would tell him that everything would be fine, and they would get to wherever it was they were going, and Gladamyr would recover.

"I don't know what ails him so."

"I think Fyren stabbed him with his sword."

"Fyren, ye say?" Captain Bootie looked worried.

"You know him?"

"Had a few mishaps with the Mare, aye."

"Yeah, we had one too many mishaps with the guy. I just wish we knew what the heck he was trying to do. I mean, why stop mortals from entering Dreams, and why try to kill Gladamyr, and what does he want from me and Kaelyn?"

Parker knew he asked the wrong person, but he had to ask. He needed answers. He felt like he was stuck in a dream that just seemed to repeat itself over and over with no meaning to it. He almost laughed out loud. He felt like he was stuck in a dream—and he was.

"I suppose Madam Blue knows where to find the answers, arr."

"Cerulean? Yeah, she told us a little but—"

"We're heading for No More, lad. If there are answers to be found, they'll be found in No More."

"What exactly is No More?" Parker asked. "It sounds like a place that doesn't even exist: No More— you know, like it's no longer there."

"Aye lad, but it is, arr. The islands get the name from the fact that no one ever returns from them . . . ah, ye got it then. We are heading for No More, arr."

Captain Bootie laughed and lowered himself down the ladder by latching his hooks to each rung. Parker took one last look at the beauty around him and followed the pirate down the mast.

Cerulean led Kaelyn into the ornately decorated room. The blue fairy marched past the large table and sitting area and went straight into the bed chamber. On the large, four-poster bed lay the Dream Keeper Gladamyr. The silver blood that had stained his purple duster also stained the crimson sheets on the bed. Kaelyn couldn't help it. She let out a gasp.

"Do not lose hope, Kaelyn," Cerulean whispered as she lifted Gladamyr's head and placed it on her lap. She then turned toward Gladamyr's wound and placed her hand on his back. Blue light shone from the tips of her fingers, and Gladamyr let out a groan.

Memories flashed in Kaelyn's mind. The scene reminded her of the car accident. She thought of the medics going to work on her father; placing hands on his chest and trying to shock him back to life. But it didn't work. Her father died. Kaelyn had little hope that it would work on Gladamyr. There was so much blood, and he wasn't even moving.

"It's not helping him . . ." Cerulean began to cry and Kaelyn could feel the tears coming too.

"Can you try again?" she asked.

"I have very little magic left . . . I need to recharge."

Cerulean sobbed and Kaelyn wondered if there

wasn't something other than a boss and employee thing going on with Gladamyr and Cerulean. It was obvious they were friends, but were they more? Did love exist in Dreams and could it exist between a Mare and a Favor?

Kaelyn touched Cerulean's shoulder. "You love him, don't you?"

Cerulean nodded and Kaelyn's tears fell. She knew what it was like to lose someone you loved. She thought of seeing her mother for the final time in the hospital. How weak she looked, her golden hair somehow white—matching her pale skin. Kaelyn was little, but she remembered her mom kissing her on the forehead and telling her to take care of Daddy. Kaelyn got to say goodbye to her mother, but she never said goodbye to her father. Sometimes, she wondered if that was why she dreamed about the accident every night. Perhaps she wished she could change the way things happened so she could at least let him kiss her on the forehead and say goodbye.

Now she watched Gladamyr slip away too. Another loved one leaving life without so much as a goodbye. *No!* She couldn't let him leave them. It was strange that she cared for him so much when she'd barely met him, but he had saved her. Kaelyn truly believed that with Gladamyr's help they could fix Dreams, defeat Fyren, and save their world, but he couldn't go away—he couldn't die. *Not today and not without a goodbye!*

She thought of Cato and how she had somehow given wings back to the fire pixie. She healed him without knowing how, but she did it. Gladamyr was bleeding and had a slash two feet long down his back, created by the blackest thing she had ever seen. How was she supposed to heal that? She searched her memory, trying to remember things she'd been taught in

her health classes—first aid and how to stop a severe cut
. . . *Pressure, you need pressure.*

Kaelyn climbed up onto the bed and placed her
hands against the wound. Gladamyr didn't cry out or
moan as she expected, and she wondered if he even had
the strength left to do so. She pressed in harder, willing
her hands to stop the blood, for the cells to coagulate
and form a barrier. *A barrier*—something she could
create! She thought of the gauze bandages that doctors
used to wrap patients. She thought of the long white
ones she saw wrapped around soldiers in old war
movies. She closed her eyes and willed the bandages to
appear, to stop the bleeding and bring life back to her
dream keeper.

"Gladamyr, please!" she cried out. "Please. I need
your help too. You have to want to live. You have to
want to fight back. Help me, please."

Light touched Kaelyn's eyes and she opened them to
see that Cerulean was using the last of her magic to help
heal him. The blue fairy cried out orders, commanding
Gladamyr to fight to stay alive. Kaelyn did the same and
suddenly, she felt it. Her hands were no longer wet, and
they were no longer touching Gladamyr's purple skin.
She looked down, and it had happened—a bright white
bandage had formed around Gladamyr's back, and the
blood had vanished! Every last drop was gone. It was no
longer on the sheets or the duster.

"Cerulean!" Kaelyn gasped.

The blue fairy looked shocked. A smile spread
across her tear-streaked face and she gazed down at
Gladamyr. His eyes were opening, and he smiled.
Cerulean pulled his head up and poured kisses all over
his face.

"Oh, Gladamyr, you worried me so much!" she said,

still sobbing.

Gladamyr coughed, then sat up. He smiled at Kaelyn. Cerulean still kissed his cheeks and forehead one after the other, and Gladamyr was turning more red than purple. Kaelyn laughed and so did her dream keeper.

"Hey Boss, that's enough. You don't want me to quote you the section on intra-office relationships, do you?"

"Since when have you ever been interested in the rules of the Crossing?" Cerulean teased as she ceased her attack of kisses.

"I've always been interested in the rules, Cerulean, just not that interested in following them."

Cerulean laughed, and Gladamyr slowly stood up. He reached his hand behind his back and felt the bandages that Kaelyn created.

"What did you two do?" he asked. "I mean, how did you. . .?"

Kaelyn shook her head, not knowing the answers.

"Kaelyn did it," Cerulean began. "She's some kind of healer or something. She healed your back, and she healed Cato's wings when they broke off."

"You healed Cato?"

"I don't know how," Kaelyn tried to explain. "I felt bad for him. He was obviously lost without his wings, so I—"

"Better to have left him alone. That pixie has nothing but hate in his heart, Kaelyn. He's sure to still have hate for you no matter what you have done for him."

"Oh, I wouldn't worry too much about Cato, Gladamyr. Kaelyn gave the fire pixie wings made of snow. They're rather beautiful wings, but if Cato ever uses his fire magic again, his wings will melt. I think a pixie would rather live without fire than flight."

Grinning, Gladamyr turned toward Kaelyn. "You really did that? You gave a fire pixie wings of snow?"

Kaelyn nodded, and Gladamyr lifted her off the bed, swinging her round. She laughed, and tears stung her eyes again. As Gladamyr pulled her in for a hug, Kaelyn again thought of her dad. He too would lift and spin her around when he was proud of something she'd done. She didn't want Gladamyr to lose his good spirit, so she forced the tears back and put a smile on her face.

Gladamyr put Kaelyn down and gazed around the room. Kaelyn thought he was surveying the situation, looking for all the possible ways for them to escape if there was ever a problem.

"Where are we?" The Dream Keeper asked.

"Aboard the Dreamer," said Kaelyn.

"The Dreamer?"

"Captain Bootie's ship?" added Cerulean.

"Loofyn?" A smile crept across Gladamyr's face yet again. "That old dog is still about? I thought he had been eaten by his pretend sea witches. Arr, got me leg . . . arr, got me hand . . . arr, got me—"

"No, Gladdie, they never got that, arr." Captain Bootie stomped into the room on his wooden legs. Parker followed behind and Kaelyn saw that hope had returned to him as well. They had their dream keeper back. Gladamyr and Captain Bootie embraced in a manly hug, with lots of back slapping and jeering at each other. Gladamyr complimented Captain Bootie on his added weight, and the captain joked about Gladamyr's run-in with death.

"How did you guys fix him?" Parker whispered to Kaelyn.

"I really don't know." Kaelyn hesitated. Parker

already thought she was weird, telling him she had magic powers would only make him think she was stranger still.

"I can tell when you're hiding something from me, you know. Your left eyebrow twitches. It did the same thing when you wanted to tell me about Dreams when we were at school but didn't know how to explain it."

"If I tell you, will you promise not to make fun of me?"

"Kae, have I ever made fun of you?"

She thought about all the times she had been teased at school. How all the girls called her names and brought her to tears with their words. She thought about all the times Parker had been there with the name calling. No, he never made fun of her. He watched, yes, but he never joined in with the others. Parker was different than Jason and Tiffany, even if he refused to see it. He was a nice guy.

"I have special powers," she mumbled.

"You have special powers?" Parker repeated, enunciating each word.

Kaelyn knew she shouldn't have told him. Now he was going to think she was a freak, and all the stuff they had done together that made them friends would just fade away into memory and never lead to anything—

"That's cool. What can you do?"

What? Kaelyn looked at Parker and shook her head. "You don't think that's strange?"

"If we were in the real world then yes, I would probably think it was strange. But then I would think it was totally awesome, and I'd plan on ways for us to team up and fight crime. But Kaelyn, we're in Dreams, and I think special powers are kind of common here 'cause I think I might have them too."

"What? What can you do? Can you heal things, like

me—you know make things appear and stuff?"

"What have you made appear?"

"Like bandages, and wings made of snow."

Parker laughed.

"What's so funny?"

"I was thinking you were going to tell me you could make weapons or warriors or something like that appear, not bandages and wings . . ."

Kaelyn remembered that right before she rescued Parker from the zombies there were statues of warriors protecting him. He had created them. She also thought back to when the wall of keys fell. A stone shield shot up from the ground and saved them from being crushed. Parker could create weapons and soldiers of stone. No wonder he laughed. She created wings made of snow and bandages. She might as well have told him she could make toilet paper appear. Now she did feel lame. She felt like he was teasing her for not creating things as great as he could.

"Hey, what's wrong?" he asked, obviously noticing Kaelyn's emotional state.

"Nothing!"

"Oh, come on, you don't go from smiles to fangs for no reason."

"Oh, so now I have fangs?" she snapped. "So what, I can't make a senseless army of stone, but I'm not going to rub it in."

"I'm not rubbing anything."

"Parker, when are you ever going to change? I am not the loser your friends think I am. Now that Gladamyr is better, I'm going back to Awake to get Zelda and your psychiatrist."

Kaelyn turned toward Gladamyr, who had been listening in on her and Parker's conversation for a while.

Cerulean was turning pink and Captain Bootie looked like a child in a candy store, wide mouthed and drooling. Apparently, the pirate didn't get much drama on the open seas. Kaelyn pulled the two keys from her pocket and handed them to Gladamyr.

"These are Zelly's and Dr. Gates' keys. I'm going to go get them."

"I'll come too," Parker said.

Kaelyn turned and glared at him. He just smiled back.

"I didn't do anything wrong, so stop acting like I just ran over your grandma. I think what you did for Gladamyr was cool. I can't heal people, and my stone army didn't even move."

And there you have it, world; Kaelyn has made a fool out of herself once again. Kaelyn about told herself to shut up, but that would only make her look even more unbalanced. Great, she had overreacted again and now she felt stupid. *You would think by now you would be used to it.* Annoyed with herself, she looked at Parker and tried to give him an apologetic smile, but he brushed it off.

"Glad to see you're back, Gladamyr," he said with a grin.

"Thanks. It's good to be back."

"Cerulean, Loofyn, please take care of our dream keeper until we get back. See that he doesn't try to die on us again." Parker smiled and Kaelyn couldn't help but smile too.

Gladamyr held out his hand with Kaelyn and Parker's glowing keys. Kaelyn felt Parker take her hand before they touched the keys. He squeezed and they were pulled away from Dreams, back to Awake.

"I don't know if this is such a good idea anymore," Zelda said, cleaning the cut on Parker's neck.

"What?"

"We have to, Zelly, the world is counting on us."

"Well, maybe they shouldn't." Zelda put a Band Aid on Parker's neck. "I mean, you said that Gladamyr is okay now, so let him and the others finish what needs to be done."

"Zelly," Kaelyn argued, "we don't even know what that is. That's why we're heading for No More. Cerulean thinks we can get answers there."

"And what will that lead to, Kae?" Zelda turned around and looked at her. Kaelyn didn't know what to say. Her aunt had never raised her voice to her. Even when Kaelyn had gotten upset in the past, Zelda had always remained calm.

"Zelly, we have to do this—"

"You don't have to do anything! Don't you see what it's like for me, Kae? I watch you go to sleep and minutes later cuts appear on your skin! It's like watching a scary movie. I'm just waiting for you to start levitating and shouting demonic things. I can't take it. I can't watch you bleed. I can't . . ." Zelda put her head in her hands and groaned.

"Zelly, what's wrong? You were all for this, and now you've changed your mind just because we get a few cuts?"

"Kaelyn," Dr. Gates began, "your aunt is right. It's getting a little dangerous. I mean, look at Parker."

"They're just cuts," Kaelyn said.

"I think they're cool!" Parker added.

"Well, you won't think they're cool when your mother sees them," Zelda snapped. "What if something else happens, like you're the one getting stabbed with a sword, or you're the one having the queen of hearts hacking your arm off? This is serious stuff, and it's starting to scare me. What if Gladamyr can't protect you? First it's the cuts, then the phone call, what else?"

"What phone call?" Parker asked. "Was it my mom? Am I in trouble?"

"No Parker, I told you, you both have only been asleep for a half an hour," Dr. Gates said.

"Then who was on the phone?" said Parker

"What did they want?" Kaelyn asked.

"Greg," said Zelda glancing at Dr. Gates, "I don't want to freak them out too."

"We're not scared," Parker said confidently.

"Zelly, what happened? We told you what has been going on in Dreams, and you've seen the cuts on Parker's neck and arms. You have to know this is real."

"I do know it's real, Kae, and that's why I'm scared. I lost your mom, and I don't want to lose you too."

Why did she have to bring up my parents? Kaelyn thought. *This has nothing to do with them.* She tried not to look hurt, but she could tell Zelda saw she had broached a forbidden topic. Kaelyn understood that Zelda was scared. Heck, Kaelyn was scared too, but there was no one else to help Gladamyr.

"My parents died from things totally unrelated to Dreams," Kaelyn argued. "And my dad wouldn't have me quit just because of a little blood and a scary phone call . . . Mom wouldn't have either."

"Zelda," Dr. Gates said, "I think they are going to do this with or without our help. It's better that we help them than let them attempt this on their own."

"Finally, a grown up with some sense," Parker cheered.

"Parker, don't test me right now, okay?" Zelda said, grabbing the bottle of alcohol. "If you'd like, I can add a little more of this to your cuts."

"*No-thank-you.*"

"Are you going to tell us about this phone call?" Kaelyn asked, ignoring Parker. Sometimes boys just act like . . . like boys.

Zelda sighed. "The caller ID said that his name was Edgar Huntley."

"Who's Edgar Huntley?" asked Kaelyn and Parker together.

"It's not who he is that worries us," Dr. Gates said. "It's what he said."

Kaelyn looked from one adult to the other, waiting for either of them to share what the mysterious Edgar Huntley had to say. Finally, Zelda said it. "He said to *stop dreaming or else.*"

"That's it?" Parker asked.

"Or else?" Kaelyn repeated.

"That's not much of a threat," Parker joked. "My mom says *or else* all the time, and it doesn't even faze me."

"You didn't hear his voice, Parker," Zelda said. "He sounded downright creepy. I pick up the phone and say hello, and he growls into the phone for us to *stop dreaming or else.* It was like hearing a ghost tell you not to sleep in your bed anymore."

Dr. Gates patted Zelda's shoulder and handed her a cup of tea, then sat down next to her at the table. Kaelyn noticed that Zelda's hand shook as she brought the cup to her lips. She had to help Zelda understand what was at stake. They needed her help. Fighting Fyren would be so much easier with adults. Zelda just needed to get past her fear of this phone stalker.

"Zelda," Kaelyn began in her best understanding voice, "let's say that this guy is for real, that he somehow found out about us entering Dreams, and he wants to stop us. So what? How can he hurt us? How can anyone prevent you from dreaming? We could just call the police or something and say he's harassing us."

"I called the police," said Zelda. "They told me they couldn't do anything unless it was a threat on our lives and that it probably was just a prank."

"That's probably all it was," Parker said. "I mean, me and Jason would prank people all the time—except we used codes to block our number. This guy's a total amateur."

"I don't think it was a prank," Zelda sighed. "I mean, he said to stop dreaming and that's just what you were doing!"

"I'm sure it was a prank," Kaelyn said, trying to drop the subject. This was ridiculous. Zelda's fears were totally overreactions to the cuts. *She watches too many scary movies.*

"Did you tell anyone other than us about entering Dreams?" Dr. Gates asked.

Kaelyn looked to Parker and they both shook their heads.

"I didn't trust anyone except you, Doc," Parker answered. "I mean, if I told Mom she'd think I'd gone crazy and try to get you to shoot me full of antidepressants or something."

"Parker, your mom has never asked me to put you on medication. Cut her some slack and try to open up to her more."

"Thanks, Doc, but this isn't a therapy session."

"It was just a prank call," Kaelyn said. "Maybe it was some whack job trying to scare you. I mean, the whole world isn't dreaming right now so maybe he was just telling you to stop sleeping 'cause he's not."

The room went quiet as everyone looked at Zelda. She gazed fixedly at her tea cup. Where was her strength today, Kaelyn wondered? She had never seen her aunt so weak before. A feeling of disappointment started to grow in her chest. Zelda had always been her hero. She was someone who never backed down. She was who Kaelyn wanted to be, but right now she was acting like . . . *me*, Kaelyn thought. *Zelda is acting like me.*

"Please, Zelda," said Parker, "a dreamling sacrificed himself so we could get your keys. It wouldn't have happened if I had trusted more in Kaelyn's plan than my own. Gladamyr has and will continue to protect us. But we need help to do it. Don't do this because we're forcing you to. Do it 'cause you want to help save the world."

Zelda continued staring at her cup for a while. Then she nodded her head.

"Okay, kids, let's do this."

"Really?" Kaelyn beamed.

"Sure." Zelda laughed. "I'm going to save the world. You know, I really hope people will believe me when I tell them about this later. No more Madam Zelda business. I'd be in the big leagues like Sylvia Browne and Belinda Bentley."

"You go from being freaked about a prank call to your career as a psychic?" Kaelyn asked.

"Hey, I think ahead, okay? Anyway it will never happen. The first person I tell this story to will tag me as a quack job."

"Too late for that," Parker mumbled, and Kaelyn took the opportunity to punch him in the arm. "Sorry, but it's what everyone else says."

"Well, the kids might say it but their parents don't," Zelda said. "How else do you suppose I have this house? I certainly didn't get if from the lottery."

"And here I thought you were psychic!" Dr. Gates teased. "What, you can't foresee the right numbers?"

"Baby, keep going on my profession and I'll give you some numbers."

Everyone in the kitchen laughed, and Dr. Gates let a yawn escape.

"Well, that about ends it here," Zelda said, standing up. "Time for some community napping—we'll all use my bed."

"'Cause it's bigger?" Parker asked.

"Because I'll sleep better."

"You'll need this," Kaelyn said, holding out the dreamstone. Zelda took it and held it for a moment in her hand as if weighing the power in the tiny stone.

"And we have to make sure we're holding hands, right?" she asked. Kaelyn noticed her aunt's face turn red as she glanced at Dr. Gates. Kaelyn smiled.

"Yes."

"You kids sure you don't need it?" Dr. Gates asked, indicating the stone.

"It's weird, but we don't need it anymore," Parker answered. "I mean, we did at first, but I don't know what happened to change it."

Dr. Gates eyed Zelda. "You sure you want to do this?" he asked.

"I told Kae I'd help her no matter what . . . plus I've been up since yesterday, and I really want a nap."

CHAPTER TWELVE
MAREMAIDS

Where is this hunk of junk you call a ship taking us?" Gladamyr asked jokingly. Captain Bootie harrumphed and tried glaring at him with his one good eye. The effect was probably opposite of what the pirate was trying to do and only made him look even crazier. Gladamyr looked at Cerulean, who thankfully had returned to her normal 'all business' self.

"We're heading for No More," she said.

"Whoa—"

"Before you tell me that No More is the last place we need to head, you must understand, Gladamyr, that a lot has happened since you passed out. The children have obtained powers—I don't know how. One minute I'm trying to get Kaelyn to help me strengthen my powers, and the next thing I know she is grafting wings on a pixie. And Parker, he can create statues out of stone—warriors. They are inanimate, yes, but with a little help they could come in quite handy."

Gladamyr agreed. Having an army of stone would be nice, especially if they ever had to fight against Fyren at a ground level.

"Does Fyren know about their powers?"

"I'm sure Cato has revealed what Kaelyn did."

"I'm not too sure about that." Gladamyr was thinking out loud. "Pixies like Cato are proud beings and would rather hide than reveal the shame of a mortal's assistance."

"Second to that, arr," Captain Bootie chimed in, "I never met a pixie who didn't think her own droppin's didn't stink."

"Well." Cerulean sighed in her emphatic way. "Let's hope Cato keeps his wings to himself. I doubt they'll connect the statues with Parker, but Fyren is very suspicious of the children having power."

"What makes you say that?" Gladamyr asked.

"He was scared of them."

"Fyren? Scared? Impossible."

"Gladamyr, you need to believe me on this." Cerulean took his arm. "The Mare was scared. He pulled Mab back from attacking the children, warning them about their bond."

Gladamyr agreed that what Cerulean said was very strange. In all the time he had known Fyren, he'd never seen the Mare pull someone back from killing a mortal. If anything, Fyren was the Mare that egged it on. At least, that was the case with Gladamyr. Thinking back to his youth, Fyren had encouraged Gladamyr to be as ruthless and uncaring as he possibly could. To hold back was to restrict yourself from being the best Mare you could be. There had to be a reason why he had shown fear.

"Do you know why he hesitated?" Gladamyr asked.

Cerulean shook her head. "No, I do not. One second he was holding Mab back, warning her not to attack, the next he was giving the death order. He said the children didn't know anything and couldn't hurt them."

"How could the children hurt Fyren?" Gladamyr wondered.

"This is why No More is so important," Cerulean continued. "No More holds the histories of our world. By finding the answers, we can find the way to defeat Fyren."

"Cerulean," Gladamyr said in a concerned tone, "no one has ever returned from No More. How do you know there is anyone even there?"

"I don't. But we're out of options, Gladamyr," Cerulean now picked up the commanding side of her voice. "Do you want to parade into the hall of histories? Perhaps that's the place we should go. It's only a few blocks down from the Crossing, and is probably surrounded by a million Mares and on fire, but at least people have returned from there. Going into one of Fyren's strongholds worked so well for us last time. Who will be torn to shreds this time? Loofyn, are you up to it? Anyone else? What, no takers?"

It was then that Gladamyr realized someone was missing from the room. Cerulean's pronouncement about someone being ripped to shreds echoed in his mind, and he slumped to the bed. *Oh no! Felix, where was Felix?* Cerulean must have noticed the change in him and she crouched down, trying to take back what she had said.

"I'm sorry, Gladamyr, I didn't mean to tell you this way. I know he was your friend, and you'd worked together so long . . . I . . . I'm just so . . ."

"Who did it?" Gladamyr heard himself say, as a flash of red started to edge into the corners of his vision.

"I'm not sure." Cerulean hesitated. "We all got split

up, and Felix had to take Parker. They were chased by Slither and some others, and the stihl . . . I really don't know what happened. Parker said that Felix barricaded him so he couldn't see . . ."

"Fyren must pay for this," Gladamyr growled.

"Gladamyr," Cerulean snapped, pulling his face to look into her eyes. The blue rivers that circled her dark irises were almost hypnotic and Gladamyr felt the red ebb away. "You need to remember that Felix was not the only dream keeper to suffer. Remember, I told you about the others I saw. Do not get in a rage about Felix. Think of the whole picture, not just the one. Felix died protecting Parker. Yes, Fyren will pay, but I cannot have you turning all Mare on me right now. I need you. Can you focus?"

Gladamyr nodded and then felt a cold hook press into his shoulder.

"Ye alright, Gladdie?"

Gladamyr nodded, but he didn't know how he was. The news of losing yet another dreamling hurt him inside. He thought of Allyon and all the others who had mysteriously disappeared since Fyren's overtake of the Crossing. So many gone! How were they to stop him? Gladamyr had proven just hours ago that he was no match for Fyren. He lost. Gladamyr barely escaped and, without Kaelyn's healing powers, he would have died. Died—the thought that eternity had an end disturbed him. Dreamlings called the humans mortal, because their lives had an end. Dreamlings lived on and on until they were forgotten, but even then they never died, at least, up until now. Where did they go after death? Was there a place for dreamlings to go, like the mortals believed there was a place for them? So many questions and no answers.

"No More will be good," Gladamyr said, pushing Cerulean back so he could stand. "If that's where the answers are, that's where we must go."

Cerulean smiled, and looked toward Captain Bootie, who gave a toothless, pirate smile.

"Well, it's a good thing too, 'cause I ain't about to make me ship move in circles, arr."

"I'll be surprised if this ship can get us there at all," joked Gladamyr, but at that moment the warning bells rang and the ship lurched to one side, forcing everyone but Captain Bootie to fall to the floor.

"There ye go, ye black-hearted son of a Mare, ye've cursed the voyage and now we be under attack!"

Gladamyr got a face full of salty water as a wave cascaded over the ship. Wave after wave threatened to sink the Dreamer. Captain Bootie took his place at the helm and barked out orders left and right, despite there being no one but Cerulean and Gladamyr to hear.

"Ready the cannons, ye scurvy dogs, arr!"

"He doesn't actually want me to ready a cannon, does he?" Cerulean shouted. "I don't know the slightest thing about cannons."

Gladamyr didn't know what they were readying cannons against. It didn't seem like they were under attack. It just seemed as though the Dreamer had sailed into a really bad storm . . . until a deafening blast sounded overhead and the center mast came crashing to the deck.

"Ye'll have to do more to sink me ship than that, ye scallywag!" Captain Bootie yelled. "FIRE AT WILL, ARR!"

The air was filled with the thunderclap of cannon after cannon blasting. Thick smoke rolled across the deck, and Gladamyr tried to see what it was they were fighting. But there was nothing but smoke and the short flashes from the ignition of cannon fire. Cerulean pulled on Gladamyr's arm, and he followed her up the steps toward Captain Bootie.

"What's going on, Loofyn?"

"Ye didn't strike me as daft, Madam Blue. This be an onslaught or, in other words, we be under attack, arr."

"I understand that!" she shouted back. "But who are we fighting against?"

Another ball hit the deck, and shards of wood and ash flew everywhere. Gladamyr pulled Cerulean down in a crouch and held her protectively. He flexed, and his back shifted into hard armor. He flexed again, and his arms and legs shifted into purple shiny chainmail.

"Blast thee, Maremaids!" Captain Bootie screeched as he shook his hooks at the sky. "Come about and fire again, arr!"

Maremaids? They were in a battle with Maremaids! Gladamyr had heard of Maremaids in stories but he never believed they actually existed. He rarely brought mortals to the oceans and when he did, they only dreamed of drowning. He would love to see what a Maremaid looked like. Was it true they were half fish and half beautiful women? Gladamyr slackened his hold on Cerulean so he could try once again to see their foe.

"Arr, there they be, Dreamer," Captain Bootie called, pointing his right hook. "Send them to Davey Jones!"

Gladamyr couldn't help it; he had to see what they looked like. He stood up and looked to starboard. There to the right of the Dreamer was a massive ship of sorts, resembling a large, pearlescent shell. It had portholes and sails much like a traditional ship, but was different because it had been created by things of the ocean.

Gladamyr shifted his gaze, looking closer at the craft, and then something glittery caught his notice and he had his first sight of a Maremaid.

She was something to behold alright, but a far cry from what the stories said. The Maremaid was part-mortal, part-fish, but there was no beauty about her. Her hair was like olive seaweeds jutting from her bony, thin skull that was pale and yellow. She opened her mouth to shout an order, and inside he saw many sharp rows of jagged teeth. Her fish part flopped and slithered as she moved about, squid-like tentacles and scales slapping the wet, slimy deck.

"Do you see them?" Cerulean asked, shouting above the sounds of battle.

"Ugly things," Gladamyr responded.

"Ain't any purtier up close neither, arr," Captain Bootie added. "Needs be losing them now, me thinks."

Captain Bootie turned the helm, and the Dreamer headed straight for the Maremaids' ship. The pirate shouted another order, and guns at the bow of the ship began to fire, blasting holes in the shell before it. The Maremaids returned fire. Balls hit the Dreamer with no mercy, ripping boards and sails. A fire broke out at the bow and Captain Bootie shouted for water. Then Gladamyr felt heat rise in his pocket as the keys came to life—Parker and Kaelyn were returning to Dreams.

Parker was thankful when the purple mist around him evaporated, placing him once again in Dreams. No offense to Kaelyn's aunt, but her bedroom was kind of dumb looking. The bed was huge, no doubt about that, but it was covered with at least twenty fluffy pillows and enough crocheted blankets to warm an army. The walls were covered with antique wallpaper or something, featuring large roses, and ornate picture frames with black and white photos. It basically looked like Zelda's bedroom belonged to an old lady—a really old lady.

"What the heck?" Parker shouted as he crashed to the deck of Captain Bootie's pirate ship. He glanced around, surveying what was going on. Kaelyn was next to him, looking bewildered. Zelda and Gates hadn't come yet, because Gladamyr hadn't given them his name personally, it would take them longer to fall asleep. *Better not bring them to Dreams just yet anyway*, Parker thought.

Captain Bootie's ship was on fire. Large buckets of water were being thrown on the flames by invisible hands, but it wasn't helping. Gladamyr, who had pulled Parker and Kaelyn down to protect them, got to his feet just as another cannon ball flew through the air and crashed into the steps behind his head. The Dream Keeper swung around, narrowly missing the shards of wood flying through the air. Kaelyn screamed and covered her head, and Parker moved in close, protecting her like a shield.

"What's going on?" he shouted.

"Maremaids!" Gladamyr called back. A huge wave rushed over the side of the ship, sweeping Parker and Kaelyn away. Parker crashed against the side of the ship, Kaelyn and the weight of water smashing into him. He choked and tried to bring himself to his knees. The ship rocked back and he tumbled over, rolling with Kaelyn to the other side of the deck. Parker knew he was going to hurl right there and then. He'd been fine on the ship before, but that was when it wasn't rocking back and forth like a crazed carnival ride.

Another wave rolled over the deck and Parker took

in a deep breath as he braced himself to be washed once again to the other side. Then he was lifted out of the water by a silver hook belonging to a grinning pirate. Captain Bootie had Parker in one hook and Kaelyn in the other.

"No time to be foolin' around, arr," he laughed. "We be at battle. Dreamer, now we got the fire out, get them Maremaids, arr!"

Parker pressed his hands to his ears, trying to silence the sudden cacophony of cannon fire. He would have loved to see what they fired at but the sight was either covered in smoke, water, or Gladamyr's trench coat. It didn't help that Captain Bootie had yet to put him or Kaelyn down.

"I can't see! Put me down," he cried, struggling to get free.

"I've heard they're not much to look at," Cerulean replied. Captain Bootie turned his hook and Parker fell to the deck with a rip of his shirt, but he didn't care. He was going to see a ship full of mermaids. He ignored Cerulean. She was probably just jealous—most girls got that way when in the presence of more attractive competition.

"Parker, be careful," Kaelyn shouted. Parker ignored her too; he knew what he was doing. The largest mast had been damaged but there was still another, and from a higher position he could see over the smoke. He climbed the rigging and found a point at which he could look over the smoke. Then he saw it.

It was an enormous glittering seashell—no, that wasn't glitter, the ship was being ripped to shreds. Ball after ball slammed into the shell, and its pearly pieces sprayed in every direction. Parker tried to see if there was anyone aboard the ship, but they seemed to have abandoned it. He waited, hoping for one of the beautiful creatures he'd heard about to peer over the deck, but there was no one. The ship got closer and closer. Parker panicked.

"Bootie, we're gonna hit!" he yelled.

Parker grabbed on tightly to the rigging. The Dreamer crashed into the shell, splitting the thing in two. Glittery fragments fell onto the Dreamer, resembling confetti. Parker looked down to see Kaelyn spinning round in the stuff like she was at a party or something. But something was wrong. It didn't feel right. Where were all the mermaids? Parker guessed they must have jumped into the ocean and swum back to their palace under the waves, but that didn't make sense. Why would mermaids be manning ships anyway?

"Where are all the mermaids?"

"Mermaids?" Captain Bootie frowned. "Who say anything 'bout mermaids, arr? We be fightin' MAREmaids, lad."

What the heck was a Maremaid?. Then something horrible caught Parker's eye, and he shouted a warning to the others.

"Arr, this be the fun part." Captain Bootie laughed as he pulled his wooden sword from his belt. The Maremaids flopped on board the Dreamer, and Parker felt his stomach turn. At the same time his back shivered from the scream of terror from—Zelda!

"Get back," Gladamyr called out. "Kaelyn, get her up the mast quick."

"I wanna wake up! I wanna wake up!" Zelda cried as Kaelyn pushed her up the rigging toward Parker.

"Hurry up, climb the ropes already! And don't drop the dreamstone or you'll really wish you were awake," Kaelyn said, pushing Zelda upward. "Ah!"

One of the Maremaids' tentacles grabbed Kaelyn's leg. It dragged her across the deck and wrapped its flabby pale arms around her. Kaelyn kicked and screamed, but it had no effect on the monster. Her frantic blows just bounced off the jelly-like skin of the Maremaid. Zelda let out a horrified cry when the Maremaid opened its mouth. It was going to eat Kaelyn! Gladamyr was there in an instant, shifting into a blob of purple goo that quickly worked its way between Kaelyn and the Maremaid. The fish thing let Kaelyn go, and with the help of its tentacles swallowed the Gladamyr goo-ball in one large, chew-less gulp.

The Maremaid grinned at Kaelyn and another tentacle reached out, grabbing her leg and bringing her to the deck. Suddenly the Maremaid exploded as Gladamyr shifted into a creature that was half-human, half-rhino. He looked for Kaelyn, checking she was alright, then charged three more Maremaids that had slithered onto the deck. Kaelyn looked up at Parker and gave him a smile. Parker felt something between elation and nausea as he looked down at Kaelyn lying in the remains of the exploded Maremaid.

Gladamyr shifted again, spinning round and round, his arms becoming swords that sliced the limbs, tentacles, and heads off the advancing Maremaids. In the blink of an eye he shifted into his flying creature shape and picked up Kaelyn as another Maremaid plopped on deck, tentacles swirling. The Dream Keeper shifted his backside and a long, spiked tail shot out from his back. He swung. The tail slashed across the Maremaid's chest. It fell back, convulsing, and black liquid oozed onto the deck. Gladamyr turned and flew Kaelyn up to Parker.

"Keep her safe for a minute, would you?" he asked, turning in mid-flight and dropping down on more

Maremaids swamping the deck.

"It wasn't my fault," Kaelyn said, looking embarrassed.

"Are you okay?" Parker asked. She nodded, and they both looked down. Zelda was still climbing the rope ladder, but she was out of harm's way.

"Kaelyn!" Zelda shouted, holding up her hand toward them. Parker reached down and helped her up the mast. Zelda pushed past Parker and threw one arm around Kaelyn.

"Are you hurt? Did it injure you?"

"I'm fine," Kaelyn said.

Parker turned his attention back to the action below. Gladamyr, Cerulean, and Captain Bootie were making mincemeat out of the Maremaids. Literally. It was like watching three barbarous sous chefs preparing a sushi buffet. The sea creatures seemed to lack hand-to-hand combat skills and were looking like . . . fish out of water. Gladamyr shifted into his normal shape but kept the sword-like arms. Cerulean had somehow found a real sword and was pretty good at fighting two Maremaids at once.

Dreamer helped too. Ropes dropped out of nowhere, wrapping themselves around the Maremaids and dragging them toward Captain Bootie, who wasted no time beating them with his wooden sword or catching them on his hooks.

"What the heck are those things?" Zelda demanded..

"Maremaids."

"Mermaids, those aren't mermaids," she huffed. "Where's all the singing and stuff? Those things are nothing like Ariel!"

"Mare-maids, Zelly, not mermaids," Kaelyn corrected. "We don't know what's going on either, we just got here too. It didn't take you long to fall asleep."

"Kae, I haven't slept in two days. Of course it didn't take me that long. I thought we were out of danger. I thought we were—"

"LAND . . . LAND!" Parker called. "LAND HO!"

"Parker, you don't have to shout it like that," Kaelyn yelled back.

Parker grabbed Kaelyn and Zelda and pulled them tight against the mast. He braced himself for an even bigger crash. With all the smoke and the fighting, he didn't think anyone was guiding the ship. Not even Dreamer could have been paying attention because the rocky island was just seconds away.

"PULLBACK, Arr!" Bootie shouted.

But it was too late. The Dreamer hit and everything, including mortals and dreamlings, lurched forward. Kaelyn pitched outward, slipping from the rope rungs. Parker barely managed to untangle his arm and catch her by the wrist, but his hand was sweaty and she was slipping too fast. Suddenly, a stone corkscrew slide erupted from the deck. Kaelyn fell onto the stone slide and rolled down it. She landed on the remains of several dead Maremaids. Another enormous wave swept over the deck and all the Maremaids' remains washed away with the water. Gladamyr rushed to Kaelyn. He pulled her clear of the water and looked up at Parker, giving a thumbs-up.

Cerulean was looking around for more Maremaids, but once the Dreamer touched land they seemed to vanish. Captain Bootie, who had been thrown quite forcibly by the crash, was just getting to his stilts and trying to adjust his hat, which seemed to have taken on more water than the ship.

"I said 'pull back' blast it! Ain't anyone steering this

here blasted ship, arr?"

Parker smiled at Zelda. "Welcome to Dreams."

"I wanna wake up," she mumbled. Parker looked at Kaelyn and they both laughed.

"Where did all the Maremaids go?" Kaelyn asked, noticing that even the black tar-like blood they left had vanished too.

"We be on land now, arr," Captain Bootie answered, slamming his wooden legs down hard as he walked toward the bow of the ship. "The Maremaids can't survive on land, only in water."

"So we made it to No More?" Parker asked, taking the opportunity to ride down the stone slide.

"Aye," Captain Bootie nodded, "but I reckon we best not stay long. I smells a foul wind."

Kaelyn looked out over the strange island they had landed on. It seemed to fade in and out like the whole island was ready to disappear into nothingness. She thought about what No More was. Captain Bootie was right. The island smelled weird, musty or moldy. She crossed over to Parker and without even thinking, took his hand. Parker didn't pull away. He actually gave a gentle squeeze. *Is he as scared about this place as I am?* she wondered.

Captain Bootie interrupted her thoughts. "Gladdie, ye go do yer business on shore and I will get this here ruddy ship back on the sea, arr."

"Cerulean," said Gladamyr, "do you have any idea where we need to go?"

"There should be a keep or something at the center of each of the No More islands. At least, that's what's written in the retirement manual."

"Why on earth would this place be talked about in a retirement book?" asked Zelda. She was still sitting up in the ropes and didn't look like she was about to budge. "I mean, not your best location for a timeshare."

"Dreamlings *are* immortal, madam," Cerulean said. "When we want to die, we come here to fade away. As long as we can remove ourselves from Dreams . . . or try to be forgotten, then we can fade away."

"So you come here to die?" Kaelyn was horror struck. This was a horrible place. No wonder it smelled bad. It was the smell of death and decay. Not the gross kind like rotting meat, but the smell of rotting wood.

"You just said you were immortal," Zelda said. "If that's true, how come you can kill each other? I thought you couldn't kill something immortal."

"Creatures like the Maremaids will have their energy regenerated in time, and will be the loathsome things they were before I killed them," Gladamyr answered with a smile. "Now, if you will allow me, Zelda, I will help you down."

"You must be Gladamyr?"

"One and the same."

"Remind me to thank you later for getting my niece involved in your mission to save the world. It really makes me feel good to know she can count on friends such as you."

"I will," Gladamyr said seriously.

It didn't take long for Gladamyr to fly up to Zelda and bring her down next to the others. Zelda ran to Kaelyn and threw her arms around her. Although Kaelyn was happy for the hug, she didn't like the fact that Parker had to let go of her hand.

"Did you not say there was another adult mortal?"

Cerulean asked.

"He must be having trouble falling asleep," Zelda replied.

"Let me help you with that problem," Gladamyr said solemnly. "Zelda, I'm going to share with you something very special. When I tell you this, you will have the power to enter and leave Dreams as you wish. There will also be a bond formed between you and me, one that will produce unknown powers in you. Are you ready?"

"Will it hurt?"

Parker snorted and Kaelyn immediately came to Zelda's defense, elbowing him. He smiled at her and then unexpectedly took her hand. Kaelyn's chest filled with a flutter of emotions. *Maybe Parker really does like me . . . oh, get over yourself. Have you forgotten you're a loser? No wait, a fat loser . . . please leave me alone for once . . . Kaelyn, one day you'll realize that you should've been listening to me from day one. Without me you are a no one. Oh wait, you are a no one . . . just go away!*

"You okay?" Parker whispered.

Kaelyn nodded, giving a half-smile. She didn't know why she always had to make herself feel so bad whenever something nice happened for her. Why was there a voice inside her head constantly telling her she was a failure? She thought about pulling away and letting go of Parker's hand, but he had been the one to take hers, not the other way around. *There is nothing wrong with hope!* Kaelyn shouted inside her mind, praying to silence the monster within.

"My name is Gladamyr," the Dream Keeper said.

Zelda repeated his name as if it alone was magical. Gladamyr smiled, and Zelda held out her hand.

"I'm Madam Zelda Creighton, psychic mage and your personal guide to the spirit world."

Kaelyn heard Cerulean snort and warning bells sounded in her head. Zelda hated skeptics and Cerulean had announced her stand with her snort.

"You wanna say something, Blue?" Zelda asked, eyeing the fairy.

"I'm sorry, I mean no disrespect. I just don't believe in your kind."

"*My kind?*" Zelda repeated, offended. "You're certainly one to talk. I'm speaking with a woman with blue skin and a pair of oversized wings. Now that is something to believe in."

Captain Bootie snickered, and Kaelyn knew she had to convince Cerulean and Zelda to get along.

"Does your world not have things like prophecy?" Kaelyn asked.

"Our world has had its share of dreamlings pretending to give out what they called prophecy, but they never amounted to anything," Cerulean answered, standing up straight.

Gladamyr stepped in. "Not true. Allyon made the prophecy of Mab's fall. He said a mortal girl would defeat her, and it happened."

"Yet Mab is still around?" Cerulean argued. "If Allyon did in fact give a prophecy, then he should have seen this all come about. Why not a prophecy about Fyren? Why not a prophecy . . . something to show how to defeat him?"

"There is!" Kaelyn shouted.

Everyone turned to look at her. She was excited, and she shouldn't have shouted so loud, but she'd tried before to bring up the prophecy Zelda had given her but it just never was the right time. Cerulean had set up the topic perfectly.

"What prophecy?" Parker asked, looking hopeful.

"It happened just after I got back from Dreams the very first time. I was in the kitchen and Zelly was telling me about some all-night ghost marathon show she had been watching."

"*Ghosts and Psychics,*" Zelda added with a smile. "Great show! There is this team of psychic investigators that go into these really spooky houses, mostly on the east coast because you know, they're older and stuff. And they set these surveillance cameras and then try to communicate with lost souls that still inhabit the grounds of the old houses. It's very scary, but kind of cool at the same time. I never miss an episode. I love it."

Everyone stared blankly at Zelda, including Captain Bootie, who Kaelyn was sure would get along great with her aunt. Kaelyn didn't know how to continue. If Zelda had just kept her mouth shut, maybe they would believe Kaelyn when she told them that the prophecy came from the quack job who *loves to watch* a darn psychic ghost show.

"It is a pretty cool show," Parker helped. "My mom and I watch it sometimes."

Kaelyn looked at Parker and tried to give him a silent 'thank you'. Then she took a deep breath and continued. "Yeah, so Zelly was telling me about the show, and I was leaving to get to school early to find Parker. And Zelly goes to say goodbye and all of a sudden her voice changed. It got really deep, and she said, '*Seek the web from the unknown friend; it will be the key to the shifter's end.*' I knew it was a prophecy because I hadn't told Zelly about Dreams yet."

"That is *not* a prophecy," Cerulean said. "Zelly, Zelda, whatever, was just—"

"Just what?" Zelda asked, getting in Cerulean's face. "I don't like your attitude, Blue. Go on, finish what you were going to say. I dare you."

"This isn't helping," Gladamyr said, stepping between the two.

"Nay, Gladdie, leave them be. Let's see 'em wrestle, arr."

"Zelda, please," Kaelyn said, taking her aunt's arm.

"Kaelyn's right," Parker said, speaking loudly. "You two need to get along. Look, Kaelyn has told me before that Zelda is the real deal. And I believe her. This is what you wanted, Cerulean; a prophecy that tells us how to defeat Fyren."

"That prophecy says nothing of the sort," Cerulean corrected. "Kaelyn said a *web* is the *key*. Do you even know what it's talking about?"

"No," Parker said softly, but his face changed. "But I'm a gamer, Cerulean, remember, and gamers believe in prophecy. Heck, that's how most games go—"

"This is no game," the fairy interrupted.

"No, it's not. But games do help you to think strategically, and prophecies are used all the time in games. Kaelyn was given the key to defeat Fyren. Sure we don't know what that is, but we're here on this stinking island and that's one more thing we can try to find an answer to."

"Parker is right," Kaelyn added. "Look, I know that my aunt may seem a little quirky—"

Cerulean snorted. Zelda glared. The fairy glared back, straightening her posture even more.

"Quirky is just how she is, and I love her—she's the real thing. Please Cerulean, you're my bond too. Please try to believe me that what she said was not fake. She told me that the key to Fyren's end was a web. Is there any weapon in this world that is like a web?"

"There be a net, arr," Captain Bootie said.

"But would a sea net be able to hold down Fyren? He'd just shift out of it," Parker said, shaking his head.

"Gladamyr?" Kaelyn asked, noticing the Dream Keeper's silence. Gladamyr was just staring at Zelda with a look of shock or disbelief. Kaelyn's voice shook him from his daze. "Are you alright?"

"Yeah, I'm fine. I just . . . I want you to know, Zelda, that I believe you have given us the key to end this war. You are a prophetess."

"A prophetess, really?" she said, giggling. "Well move over Sylvia and Belinda, here comes Zelda the Prophetess."

"Cerulean," Gladamyr said, in a serious tone, "we will need to find answers about this web as well when we reach the keep. Loofyn, I didn't plan on staying on this island long. How long till you can have Dreamer back in the water?"

"Not long, arr."

"Good. We all need to hurry. Cerulean, if you can take Zelda, I can carry the children."

Cerulean nodded without argument.

"Wait!" Gladamyr pulled a key from his pocket and Dr. Gates appeared in a swirl of purple mist. "Looks like you'll be taking the children. Dr. Gates, I presume?"

Dr. Gates nodded but Kaelyn thought the guy looked like he was about to wet himself.

"Zelda, take his hand!" she said.

Zelda quickly took Dr. Gates' hand and immediately his expression changed. He still looked scared, but he seemed like he was handling it better.

"Have we met before?" Gladamyr asked, noticing Dr. Gates' slight nervous shake.

"I was very young . . ."

Gladamyr's face fell, and Kaelyn swore he was about

to cry. The Dream Keeper knelt down and shifted to make himself smaller and less threatening. He said in that soft, sweet voice that reminded Kaelyn of her father, "Gregory, I am so very sorry for what I put you through. I hope one day to earn your forgiveness, but until that day I offer to be your bond. My name is Gladamyr, and I am a dream keeper."

CHAPTER THIRTEEN
THE CRYSTAL TABLE

Gladamyr was leery about being on the island. It just felt wrong. And if they stayed too long they, like so many dreamlings before them, would fade away. It also felt strange carrying Dr. Gates, or Gregory, as he knew him as a child. He remembered that Fyren had arranged for the boy to be brought nightly to the same part of Mares so that Gladamyr could practice on the child. He had tried to perceive Gregory's thoughts and shift into what the boy feared most. Gladamyr, however, wasn't as talented as Fyren and was never able to accomplish mind reading. He ended up just shifting into various shapes, feeding off the terror they inflicted. Oh, how wrong he had been.

"There's not much to this place, is there?" Zelda called out.

Gladamyr agreed. The island was very odd. There was no shore line; the Dreamer had smashed into a line of rocks that flung the ship atop the vacant beach. There were no plants, trees, buildings or dreamlings anywhere. It was just a vast wasteland of nothing but fog and dark volcanic rock.

"I somehow expected to see more," Dr. Gates agreed.

"Where did you say we were going?" Zelda asked.

"There is supposed to be a keep of some sort at the center of the island," Gladamyr answered. "When dreamlings come here to fade, their memories are supposed to be written down and placed there. Cerulean thinks this is the only place to find out what Fyren is trying to do."

"By reading someone else's memories?" Zelda asked sarcastically. "That could take forever! I mean, you don't even know what you're looking for and she wants to read a bunch of autobiographies?"

"Zelda's right," Dr. Gates called out through the wind. "Isn't there someone we can ask? Someone who might know more than we do?"

"I'm sorry, but I do not believe there is." Gladamyr didn't know what else to say. The adults had even more questions than the children and he felt he was proving to be horrible at giving answers. He simply knew too little. Then Cerulean shouted from behind that she spotted something up ahead, and Gladamyr shifted his eyes to focus on what it might be.

It was a looming tower that protruded from the volcanic rock like a nail. The sight of it was foreboding. It did not look welcoming at all. The inner tower was as black as ebony with slate grey archways that piled high, one upon another in a circular pattern. It was finished off with five sharp turrets that jutted out at the top. Gladamyr heard Parker make a joke about the dark tower and something called a hobbit, but the Dream Keeper didn't understand.

"Looks like a five star hotel," Zelda jeered.

"More like a three," Dr. Gates corrected.

Gladamyr put the couple down and shifted back to his regular form before landing. Cerulean alighted with Parker and Kaelyn seconds after, and the group looked up at the massive thing that was hopefully the answer to everything.

"So do we knock or just go in?" Parker asked with a small chuckle.

"I'm glad someone finds this inviting," Zelda replied.

"It's not that bad," said Kaelyn. "I mean, imagine it standing by a waterfall and a rainbow, and it's quite nice."

"Anything looks nice next to a rainbow," Zelda argued.

Gladamyr took the lead by boldly walking up to the door and knocking.

"You really think anyone lives there?" Dr. Gates asked.

"It states in the retirement book that the keep does have a keeper," Cerulean answered.

"Poor guy lives in the middle of nowhere with no one to talk to. Oh great, he'll be loads of fun," Parker said. Kaelyn gave him a small shove, and Gladamyr had to smile. The way the two mortal children acted was very entertaining. He wondered if all boys and girls acted this way to each other, or if Parker and Kaelyn were an exception.

"Be nice," Kaelyn scolded. "He might hear you and get grumpy. Besides, dreamlings probably come here all the time to die, and so he gets plenty of conversation, I'm sure."

"Sure . . ."

There came the sound of a large plank being removed from behind the door, and soon the large door cracked open.

"What is wanted?" asked a deep, ancient voice.

"We have come seeking answers from the keep," Gladamyr replied.

"Who seeks these answers?"

"I am the Dream Keeper, Gladamyr."

There was silence for a while and Gladamyr felt anxious, wondering if they were somehow in trouble. He looked toward Parker and Kaelyn, and they signaled the others to be watchful. The door slowly opened. Gladamyr tensed and prepped his body to shift into something to shield the mortals, but the only thing behind the door was an old man.

"Are you a dreamling or a mortal?" Gladamyr asked, for the old man did not appear to be a dreamling at all. Dreamlings were different in that their skins shone with various colors, or their faces had different shapes, but this gentleman looked so human that Gladamyr had to ask. The man was old, really old, with a white beard that touched the floor. His skin was more than wrinkled, it was pleated. He wore a long, red robe with a small, gold cord around his waist, and he held a thin, tall walking stick.

"I am neither. I am Era."

"Yes, but are you a dreamling or a mortal?"

"Ask him if he's a wizard," Parker whispered, and was shushed by Kaelyn and Zelda.

"Again I say: I am Era. What is wanted?"

Seeing that the question would never get answered, Gladamyr stated their business. "We have come hoping you can help us find answers to some questions regarding the shifter Fyren. He has taken over the Crossing and imprisoned all the dream keepers. He has stopped the mortals from entering Dreams."

"And he's trying to kill us all," Parker added. "We need to know how to stop him."

"You already have the answer to that, child," Era said, motioning for them to enter the tower.

Gladamyr looked from Era to Kaelyn, wondering if the prophecy Zelda gave her was in fact the way to defeat Fyren. A cold chill ran up his spine. Zelda's prophecy had said that the web was the key to the shifter's end. But Fyren wasn't the only shifter in Dreams. What if the prophecy was not the way to kill Fyren, but the way to kill Gladamyr? Shaking the horrible thoughts from his mind, the Dream Keeper entered the tower followed by the others. With a loud echoing sound, the door closed.

Gladamyr and his friends followed Era past an entryway to a set of spiral steps. Era walked up just enough for everyone to be on the staircase, then he stopped. The stairs started to move, winding like a screw, moving them higher and higher with great speed.

"This is cool," Parker shouted.

"I'm going to be sick!" Zelda complained.

"It's like an escalator, Zelly, you're fine," soothed Kaelyn.

"Escalators don't spin you in circles."

"Kaelyn," said Cerulean, "I recall you said she'd be of some use. All she has done since coming into Dreams is complain."

"You want me to be of some use?" Zelda snapped. "Blue, I will take your wings off and shove them down your throat! Shutting your bossy face would be plenty of use!"

"Come now, ladies!" Dr. Gates tried, getting between the two before someone got pushed off the staircase.

"She started it!" Zelda growled.

"I'll be happy to finish it too."

"This is not the place and time for you two to be acting like—"

"Cut it out, Zelly, you're embarrassing me!"

"This is so cool!" Parker cheered.

"Do you know who I am, mortal? I demand more respect!"

"Respect is something earned, lady!"

"Ladies, please!" Dr. Gates continued. "Ladies. . ."

"ENOUGH!" Gladamyr roared. His shout echoed down the shaft, repeating over and over. The group behind him fell completely silent. Cerulean went down a few steps, distancing herself from Zelda, who even with Gladamyr's glare was tapping her chest and acting cocky. Then the staircase stopped, and Gladamyr turned to see they were in a large room containing vast numbers of books.

"Wow!" Kaelyn said. "It's like the world's largest library."

"You think a bunch of old books are cool?" Parker asked.

"As a matter a fact, I do. And don't go playing like you don't. I believe I ran into you once coming out of the library."

Gladamyr smiled as Parker blushed. Era walked slowly over to a large, crystal table that had seven crystal chairs around it. Gladamyr followed behind and instinctively surveyed the room as he did so. There were many rows of shelves and no doorways to different rooms, unless they were hidden somehow. Only one window—he'd sit by the window. The staircase, it seemed, was the only exit.

"You are safe for a time, Gladamyr the Dream

Keeper," Era said as he sat down.

"For a time?"

"You and your party seem to be a group plagued by trouble, so I cannot imagine it being long before it finds you."

"He's got us pegged, doesn't he?" Parker laughed as he sat down at the table.

The others followed Parker, and Gladamyr slowly sat down last. As he did so, a gust of air seemed to flood out from the table. Gladamyr was ready to back out of his seat when Era spoke.

"Do not be afraid of the table," he said. "At this table, dreamlings sit to write out the knowledge they gained before they fade away. It holds many secrets and, for you perhaps, some answers. But I must caution you to not give it any more information than you need to obtain your answers, for it is through this table that your fading will start."

Gladamyr didn't know what to say. It seemed from the warning given that any speech would take life away. The answers they sought came at a heavy price. He looked at Cerulean, and she smiled reassuringly back. Parker and Kaelyn smiled at him too, waiting for him to begin. Gladamyr thought about what to ask.

The thing that puzzled Gladamyr most was what Cerulean had told him when he rescued her from the Crossing. She had overheard Fyren say that he was trying to restore Mares, but the statement made no sense. Was he trying to break down the barrier to mix the realms? No, that would not be restoring Mares. Then what? *Think, Gladamyr! If something needs to be restored then it has to have been taken—but Mares wasn't taken, it's still there . . . Think . . . restore, replace—bring back?*

"Who is Mares?" Gladamyr asked. Everyone at the

table looked at the Dream Keeper in surprise, and he knew why. *What in Dreams was he asking that for?* But the table responded to the question, and its crystal surface seemed to shatter into a billon cracks that formed into definite shapes. As the scenes played out on the table, Era spoke of the creation of their world.

"When the world was new and all things created were upon it, it was then that the first mortals dreamed. But this was before Dreams existed. Somehow, their combined consciousness created two beings. One was named Favor, full of beauty and love; and the other, Mares, a being formed of ugliness and hate. The mortals welcomed their creations with open arms and Favor gladly shared her warmth. But Mares did not care for their affection and fled before the mortals, hiding himself away in depths of the Earth.

"The mortals discovered that their creations had great powers. Favor was able to create beautiful life and so she covered the Earth with grasses, flowers, shrubs, and trees. Mares' power was to destroy, and he killed the beauty that Favor created. This pained the mortals greatly, for Mares spared nothing that was beautiful or lovely.

"Each night the mortals dreamed, and more beings arose from their consciousness; some good and some bad. The good ones looked to Favor to guide them and the bad beings looked to Mares to rule them. Soon, Mares tired of taking beauty from the mortals. He wanted to enslave them and make himself their ruler. He rallied his followers to war, but he failed.

"Favor, who loved the mortals, would not let him harm them. By her own sacrifice she spun a spell that trapped both her and Mares in a place removed from the world of the mortals. In order to trap Mares forever,

Favor had to bind him to herself, creating two realms in which all the entities the mortals created could live. This was the creation of Dreams.

"The spell allowed mortals to visit Dreams each night in their sleep, and as they dreamed, their consciousness created dreamlings to inhabit the world of Dreams; the good looked to Favor and the bad to Mares.

"It is important to keep a balance in Dreams. All things must have their opposite. Should the balance of Dreams tip too far, the spell that binds Favor and Mares together will break and Mares will be free to unleash his horror upon the mortals once again."

"Fyren really is trying to destroy the world—both worlds!" Kaelyn said, horrified. "We have to stop him, Gladamyr! We have to!"

She looked to the Dream Keeper who, after the experience at the crystal table, was slumped against a book case. The one question he asked took much out of him. He looked sweaty, like he had run ten miles. She glanced at Cerulean, who was completely silent. Maybe the story of her world's creation was new to her, and her mind was overloaded.

"Give them a minute, honey," Zelda said, touching her shoulder.

Kaelyn turned to Zelda and tried to smile. Zelda looked nice holding hands with a guy. Not that Kaelyn didn't like Zelda all to herself, but she knew how happy her mom and dad had been to have each other. In the short time that Dr. Gates had been around, Zelda was acting different. She snapped a lot at Cerulean, but Kaelyn thought that must be because she wanted Dr.

Gates all to herself. Who knew? Maybe Zelda's irritation just came from being stressed. Whatever it was, one thing was clear. Zelda was falling for the doctor.

"We should ask this thing more questions," Parker said, still sitting at the table.

"Parker, you saw what it did to Gladamyr," Kaelyn said. "I really don't think we should mess around with it."

"But—"

"Kaelyn's right, Parker," Dr. Gates said. "We learned a lot from that one question. I think we should talk about what we learned and then—"

"All you ever want to do is talk! Gosh! Can you try not being a shrink all the time? Now isn't the time to talk. It's time for *him* to talk." Parker gestured at Era, who just sat and stared fixedly at the table, awaiting another question. Kaelyn was about to say something like 'that was rude' or 'Parker!', but Zelda beat her to the punch.

"Parker, that wasn't nice. Greg does a lot for you, you know."

"And here I thought you were going to say it was rude to talk to Era that way," Kaelyn mumbled. *Yep, I think she's falling for the guy.*

"I want to know how to use my powers," Parker said.

"Parker, NO!" Kaelyn rushed to the table. She tripped and fell forward, her arms and chest slapping the table. A rush of wind exploded from the crystal surface and she felt pain pulling at her. Somewhere in her mind, behind all the shouting from the adults and screaming from Parker, she heard Era speak the instructions.

"You must look within yourself and create the balance. When all things are in opposition, then you will be able to control your gifts."

Kaelyn thought she had shattered the crystal, but the cracks reformed into one great unbroken whole. She looked up and Parker's head was back, his eyes rolled up. He was shaking like he was having a seizure of sorts, and panic took Kaelyn.

She turned to Zelda. Dr. Gates had dropped Zelda's hand and moved toward Parker, but he became lost in a dream. Zelda, who still had the dreamstone, ran over to him and quickly took his hand. This broke the dream and they ran to Parker. The second Zelda and Dr. Gates touched his shoulder, Parker was fine. He looked at the adults and then at Kaelyn, and smiled.

"Well, that wasn't too bad," he said, a grin spreading on his face. "We know now."

"Parker Bennett, if Fyren doesn't kill you I will do it myself!" Kaelyn scolded.

"Parker, that wasn't very smart," Dr. Gates said, pulling him away from the table. "Didn't you see what it did to Gladamyr?"

"I'm fine," Parker said, laughing. "I mean, it hurt at first, but now I'm fine. So what, I gave a few minutes of my life to the table?"

"Not just yours, buddy," Zelda said seriously.

"I'm fine, Zelly, really," Kaelyn said. She felt fine. Like Parker said, it only hurt for a second and then she knew how to use her power.

But what the heck was that supposed to mean anyway, 'look within yourself and find balance?' It means you need to let your better side shine more . . . You don't shine, you blacken . . . Everything needs its opposite, Kaelyn, everything, even you—can't be all sweets and treats all the time. Sometimes you need edge . . . and sometimes you need to be more positive! Great, Kaelyn thought. She was going crazy because she was always arguing with herself. Perhaps when Dr. Gates was alone, she could ask him if that was normal. It would have to be totally confidential, of course.

"I still think you should have thought it through a little more, Parker," Zelda went on. "I mean what would your mother thiiii—AHHH!" Zelda bent forward and put both hands to her forehead. She screamed and fell to her knees. Dr. Gates quickly grabbed her shoulders so he didn't lose the connection to the dreamstone, but he seemed more concerned for Zelda than anything.

"Zelly! Zelly, what's wrong?" Kaelyn asked, running to her aunt.

"THEY'RE HERE!" Zelda cried. She hunched forward and started coughing. The urge to cough tickled the back of Kaelyn's throat too, but she tried to ignore it. Then Parker and Dr. Gates started to cough.

"What's going on?" Cerulean asked, moving close to them. "Zelda, what do you mean they're here?"

"They're here—they're here! A thing with spiders, and oh—Cough! —Cough!" Zelda tried to speak but the coughing continued.

Kaelyn's stomach lurched and she turned to see the spiral staircase began to spin. Someone was coming up the stairs! Parker suddenly fell to the floor in a fit of coughing.

"How do you know who it is?" Cerulean demanded. "Who is coming?"

"I saw it . . . in my—" Zelda collapsed. Dr. Gates pitched forward, his body slapping on the floor.

"Zelly!" Kaelyn cried, and coughed. She lost the strength in her legs and suddenly sat down.

"Gladamyr, what's wrong with them?" Cerulean asked.

Kaelyn too started to cough. She felt as though she

couldn't breathe and her mind was getting cloudy.

"I hear them coming, Gladamyr!" Cerulean called, looking down the staircase. "Where is Era? Where is Era?"

Kaelyn looked over toward the crystal table, but the old man was gone. They were trapped. The only way out was the staircase, but who is to say where it led? This feeling of suffocation—she felt as though something was terribly wrong. Gladamyr pulled out their four keys and they were glowing red hot.

"You have to leave. Something is wrong in Awake."

"Gladamyr, they're coming . . ." Zelda whispered, then she closed her eyes.

"Zelly!"

"Gladamyr . . ." Dr. Gates moaned.

"Parker!" Kaelyn cried, as he fell down lifeless. She tried to crawl to him, but she couldn't move. *What the heck is going on?* She tried to move toward Gladamyr, who had touched Zelda's and Dr. Gates' keys to their skin. They vanished back to Awake, but Kaelyn had no energy. Gladamyr raced over to Parker and touched him as well, and Parker disappeared in a swirl of purple mist.

"Gladamyr, look out!" Cerulean cried, as spiders poured out from the staircase. There were thousands of them, all shiny and black. They crawled all over Cerulean's body and she froze in fright. The spiders moved in on top of one another until they formed the outline of a man's body.

"Don't try anything if you want her to live," the Mare clicked.

"Minyon, if you—"

"What—do what? Tell me so that I might do it." Minyon laughed and clicked at the same time, and Kaelyn felt nauseous as well as lightheaded. The spiders wrapped around Cerulean like a thick black moving rope. She whimpered and Gladamyr tensed.

"We don't have to do this," Gladamyr began. "Think of it, Minyon, bringing back Mares will only destroy our world—"

"NO! Fyren says we will go to Awake like it was in the beginning. We will rule over the mortals. We will be gods."

"Fyren cannot guarantee that. How do you know what Mares will do when you let him free? He could be happy just to kill us all—"

"No, Mab says Mares has agreed to let us be rulers as well."

"Minyon—"

"I did not come here to argue with you, Gladamyr!" Minyon clicked furiously. "I came to get her, so that in return we can have you."

"What does Fyren want with me?" Gladamyr asked, poised to attack.

"To break the barrier the spell requires a sacrifice. The heart of Mares must be killed at the heart of Favor."

The heart of Mares! Gladamyr was the heart of Mares! No wonder Gladamyr believed he was capable of such horror. Kaelyn recalled Dr. Gates sharing with them the pictures of the monster that tortured him when he was little; Kaelyn knew that Gladamyr was nothing like that. The Gladamyr she knew was kind-hearted and cared for others. If he didn't care, then why would he be trying to talk Minyon out of destroying everything? Gladamyr loved both Mares and Favor.

"And you came for Cerulean?"

"For collateral," Minyon clicked with a laugh. "She will be released with all the others when you meet Fyren in Éadrom."

"Others?"

"All the other dream keepers and dreamlings we had to take into questioning." Minyon smiled. Kaelyn nearly threw up at the sight. The coughing had stopped but she still felt lightheaded, and now dizzy like she'd been given a funny medicine.

"What makes you think I will even let you down those stairs?" Gladamyr said with a tone of contempt. Minyon laughed, and Kaelyn tried to sit up slowly so she could back further away should Gladamyr shift suddenly.

"I have been instructed to tell you that after the third moon falls, Fyren will kill a dream keeper for every quarter hour that passes until you arrive in Éadrom."

Kaelyn watched Gladamyr slump down. The Dream Keeper wasn't going to fight. He would not let Fyren murder so many just because he wanted to fight. But what of the bigger picture? If Gladamyr gave in to Fyren's requests, what would happen to Dreams? And what about all of the billions of mortals in Awake? Kaelyn couldn't stomach the thought of so many lives under the control of this one being.

"You have my word that I will be in Éadrom as Fyren requests," Gladamyr spat.

Minyon laughed and clapped his hands with delight. "Good boy . . . good boy!"

"Let her go! You don't need her to get me there."

"Oh, but we do, Gladamyr," Minyon said, gleefully clicking. "She will be the first to die."

Then Minyon's spiders untangled his face and moved to cover the lower half of Cerulean's body. A particularly large spider crawled up her neck and planted itself right across her mouth so she couldn't speak. She just looked at Gladamyr with terrified, tear-filled eyes as the spiders carried her down the staircase.

Kaelyn coughed again, and Gladamyr looked at her. He too had tears in his eyes, and she couldn't bear the thought of what must be inside the Dream Keeper's mind. Everything was being taken from him, and he knew his life was a curse from the beginning. He was only created to be killed so that Mares could rise again and destroy all mankind.

"We will find the web, Gladamyr," Kaelyn said, trying to be strong. "We will stop this before anyone has to die."

"Oh, little Kae," the Dream Keeper said, "if only that were true."

And with a touch of his hand, she was whisked away from Dreams in a swirl of purple dust.

CHAPTER FOURTEEN
THE SLEEPWALKER

G ET UP! WAKE UP!" Someone was screaming in
Parker's head. "Greg, I can't get them up. They
won't—" Coughing erupted in his ears. He tried
to open his eyes but he couldn't.

He breathed in and immediately wished he hadn't.
He sat up, coughing uncontrollably. Each time he tried
to gasp for air he inhaled a cloud of smoke. Was he in
Dreams? No, Gladamyr had sent him back. If he wasn't,
then where was he? This seemed like a nightmare.

Someone yanked on Parker's arm and he was
dragged off the bed and onto the floor. He started to
struggle and get up, but was pinned to the ground.

"Stay low," a raspy voice said. It took Parker a
second to realize it was Dr. Gates. Again he tried
opening his eyes. They stung but he wiped them with his
shirt. He was in Zelda's bedroom. Everything looked the
same as it did before except the haze of grey smoke.

"Zelda, we have to get out of here!"

"I can't wake her up," Zelda cried.

"Get her onto the floor! Parker, help me open the
window."

"We need to get out," Parker roared. "The house is on fire!"

"The stairway is blocked. We have to jump out the window."

"Jump out the window!"

"Don't argue with me! Help me with the window."

Parker crawled after Dr. Gates toward a large oak dresser that sat below the windowsill. With one quick motion, Dr. Gates cleared the dresser from the array of knickknacks, picture frames, and an antique lamp. They all crashed to the floor, some items shattering as they hit. Parker caught a glimpse of a picture of Kaelyn with her parents. She had to be about five years old, but she was happy and beautiful. He turned to find her. Zelda was pulling her body toward them. She still hadn't woken up. Something was wrong. Kaelyn should have woken by now.

A rush of energy infused Parker and he stood up, tearing the lace drapes away from the window. He unhooked the latch and pulled up. The window was stuck. Dr. Gates pushed him aside and tried forcing the window open.

"It won't budge," Dr. Gates groaned.

"Move!" Parker picked up the lamp off the floor and hurled it at the window. The sound of a distant siren sang a duet with the shattering glass. Parker turned back to Kaelyn and tried lifting her. His legs crumpled under her weight.

"Let me," Dr. Gates said, lifting Kaelyn into his arms.

"Zelda, grab the blanket and put it over the glass so you don't cut yourselves."

Zelda ripped the comforter off the bed and hung it out the window. She looked out and gasped. "Greg, it's too far. I can't jump that far."

"I'll go first," Parker volunteered. "I'll show you. It will be okay."

Parker moved to the window and saw what Zelda feared. The drop wouldn't be that easy. There was snow, but not enough to impact any fall. If they were lucky, no one would break their legs.

"Maybe we can just wait for the firemen?" Zelda suggested.

"There's no time," Dr. Gates argued. "Parker, you need to just do it. Jump!"

Parker thought for a second about what Zelda had said. The firemen would have a ladder. They could easily get to them. He could hear the sirens. They had to be close. But then another sound pricked Parker's ears. It was the sound of a roaring fire. He turned to look at the door and could see an orange glow framing it. Dr. Gates was right. They had no time. Without another thought, Parker climbed onto the windowsill. He took in a deep breath of the cold fresh air and prepared himself to jump.

Just do it, he told himself. *It's not that far up . . . shut up—yes it is . . . you need to get out. The house is on fire . . . just do it!* Parker pushed himself forward and his foot slipped. He tumbled outward and did a summersault in the air. He felt his stomach churn with vertigo as his back hit the soft snow.

"About time!" Dr. Gates yelled. Parker got to his feet and hobbled away from the burning house. Zelda jumped next, landing the same way Parker did.

"Greg, hurry!" she called. Parker pulled her back away from the house. The fire was like a lion roaring. It licked up the side of the house as if it were alive. Soon it would reach the window. There was a strange intake of air as if the inferno inside the house was breathing. Dr. Gates straddled the windowsill with Kaelyn in his arms. He pushed off and Zelda's room exploded. Fire reached out the window, grabbing for Kaelyn and Dr. Gates. Parker and Zelda were pushed back by the wave of heat rushing from the house. Parker could see nothing but fire as Zelda screamed.

"Kaelyn!" Parker shouted, seeing her eyes open. He had been so worried something serious was wrong with her. She looked around and started mumbling something, but he didn't give her time. "You're okay. We're in the hospital. Some crazy dude set your aunt's house on fire but everyone is fine. Zelda and Gates are just down the hall, filling out police reports."

"Excuse me, young man," a nurse said as she pushed past him to check on Kaelyn.

Parker watched as the nurse checked all the tubes and things sticking out of Kaelyn's arm. Then she glared at him. He glared right back.

"Should you be in here?" she asked, looking him up and down.

"Yeah, she's my *best friend!* And we were just in a *fire* together."

"Hmm . . . well, I'll let the doctor know you've both woken up. And I'll see if he has released you to be out of your room, young man."

"I'm fine," Parker snapped. He was sick of the people at the hospital. For crying out loud, they had just been through a fire. He would have thought someone like that would get a little compassion from others, but n-o-o-o. They were all too tired to show any sort of kindness whatsoever.

The nurse glared at Parker a second longer, then turned once again to Kaelyn. "If you feel you are fine without it, you can probably remove the mask, but if you start feeling short of breath, I want it back on. I'll be back shortly to check on you again."

Parker waited as the nurse took her time leaving the room, then he turned to Kaelyn. "What happened? I heard Cerulean say that someone was coming up the stairs or something."

Kaelyn pulled the mask from her face and sat up. "Did you really mean what you said?"

"What? Yeah, your house is totally wasted. They said it's uninhabitable."

"No, what you told the nurse."

"Yeah, I'm fine, see?" Parker spun around with his arms extended. He smiled and gazed at her, but she still acted like he hadn't answered her question. What had he said to the nurse? *Yeah, she's my best friend!* Wow, he really did say that, didn't he—was it true? That was what Kaelyn was asking him—if they were friends. What would Tiffany think? Forget about Tiffany, what would Jason say? *Then again, who cares?*

"Yeah, Kae, if it's okay with you."

Kaelyn smiled and Parker couldn't help but smile too. He didn't know what else to say. He'd never had a girlfriend before—heck, Kaelyn was the only girl he had ever actually hung out with. Kaelyn laughed and Parker joined in, and they continued like that for a few minutes until the doctor came in. He asked Parker if he could step out for a minute and get Zelda so the doctor could speak with her.

"I'll be back, Kae," Parker said.

"Okay."

Parker ran down the hall to the nurses' station where Zelda and Dr. Gates were speaking with a police officer. Zelda looked like she had been crying, but now she stood straight as a board. The posture reminded Parker a lot of Cerulean. Cerulean, Gladamyr—he needed to know what was going on in Dreams. Why did grownups have to be so—grown up about things? He and Kaelyn needed to get back to Dreams.

"And you said that he called the house about an hour before the fire?" the officer asked, scribbling in his notebook.

"That was the name that showed up on the caller ID, yes," Zelda answered.

"And do you know this man, had any dealings with him—perhaps as a client?"

Zelda shook her head.

"So you called the police after the call because he threatened you . . . how so?"

Zelda paused and glanced at Dr. Gates.

"It was his tone that sounded threatening, officer," Dr. Gates answered for her. "I know you have a lot of paper work to fill out, but we would like a break for now. Zelda needs to check on her niece."

"Yes, yes . . . I'm sorry about your home, Ms. Creighton."

The officer walked away and Zelda turned to Dr. Gates, who put his arms around her. Parker about turned around, but he remembered the doctor wanted to speak with Zelda. He cleared his throat, interrupting them.

"Parker, is Kaelyn awake?" Zelda asked, wiping new tears from her eyes.

"Yeah, the doctor wants to talk to you. He's in with Kaelyn."

"Oh, thank God!" Zelda quickly walked past Parker toward Kaelyn's room. Dr. Gates watched her as she went. The doctor put his hand on Parker's shoulder, and they walked slowly behind.

"Is she okay?" Parker asked.

"I think she'll be fine," Dr. Gates said quietly. "Zelda's lost practically everything. Kaelyn too. That house used to be Zelda's grandmother's, she and Kaelyn's mom grew up there. It's like having all your memories taken away from you all at once."

Parker thought about what it would be like to lose everything all in one fell swoop. His clothes, games, toys, house. But Kaelyn and Zelda lost even more than that— they lost everything that reminded them of their loved ones who had died. The thought was horrible.

"Where are they going to stay?" he asked Dr. Gates.

"The officer said there are several charity operations to help families in this situation, but that it's nicer for them to be around loved ones—like family."

"I think Zelda and Kaelyn are all that's left of their family."

Dr. Gates nodded his head.

"They can stay with me and my mom for a while," Parker said, excitedly.

Dr. Gates laughed. "I know you want to help, but you need to let Zelda make this decision. And speaking of your mom—no one can get hold of her. She's not at her office and she's not answering her phone."

That was weird. Parker's mom didn't leave anywhere without her phone. And if she wasn't at work, then she had to be at home.

"Did you call the house?"

"Yes, and she didn't answer. They sent a police officer over to bring her to the hospital, but no one was home." Dr. Gates paused, looking at the floor before he continued. "Parker, the hospital won't release you to me or Zelda. We aren't legal guardians. I had to call your father—"

"What? Tell them I'm fine! I can just go home with you. Mom's probably stuck in traffic somewhere and her phone's dead."

"Parker, I know you don't get along with—"

"It's not that I don't get along with him. It's the fact that he's never there. He probably won't even come."

"He said he was on his way . . . Parker, look, it's only to get you released. You want to stay here until your mom comes?"

"Yes."

"You don't really mean that. If you were fine staying here, you'd be in your room. Not out in the halls."

Dr. Gates was right. Parker didn't want to be in his room. He didn't even want to be in Awake. He wanted to get back to Dreams so he could help Gladamyr. *I guess it doesn't matter who takes me home.* It was surprising that his dad even had time to come and get him.

The doctor exited Kaelyn's room and he smiled at Dr. Gates as he passed. Parker took the opportunity to go see Kaelyn again.

"Kae, we need to get back to Dreams," he said as he walked in. He heard Dr. Gates quickly shut the door before anyone heard them talking about a world outside their own. *Probably a good thing,* Parker thought. *Wouldn't want to end up on the psych floor.*

"I know," Kaelyn said anxiously. "Minyon's taken Cerulean, and Gladamyr is being forced into . . ."

"No!" Zelda said loudly. "I don't want you kids going back there. It's getting too dangerous."

"Zelly!"

"Come on!" Parker whined.

"No, and that's it. Kae, we almost died in a fire. Don't you see this is getting over our heads?"

"That's not our fault, Zelly," Kaelyn said, sitting up in bed. "Gladamyr needs us. Cerulean needs us. They're going to kill her, Zelly. They're going to kill a dream keeper every fifteen minutes until Gladamyr agrees to sacrifice himself to Fyren—and he's going to do it!"

"What?" Parker couldn't believe it. "Why would Gladamyr do that?"

"Then let him, Kae. You are more important to me than Gladamyr or that fairy," Zelda said, tears filling her eyes again.

"Her name is Cerulean, Zelly, and she's my friend."

"We've lost everything, Kaelyn!" Zelda sobbed, "Everything! Your mama's clothes, her pictures, her diaries—all the stories she wrote in her little notebook, her pictures—they're all gone."

"They're just things. Gladamyr is a person."

"They were my sister's!"

Dr. Gates went over and held Zelda as she sobbed freely in his arms. Parker looked at Kaelyn, who had tears in her eyes. Again Parker thought about losing everything, and the idea was hard to comprehend.

"Zell, it's okay," Dr. Gates soothed, holding her tightly. "It's okay. Those things were just memories of her, but she is still in your heart . . . you still have her in your heart."

"We should never have dreamed . . ." Zelda sighed.

"No, we must keep dreaming," Dr. Gates said pointedly. "Kaelyn and Parker are right; they need to get back to Dreams."

"No, I'll lose Kae too . . . I'll lose her too."

"Kaelyn has proven far more capable than you give

her credit for. You need to let her go, Zell. The world is in their hands. We made a mistake. One of us should have stayed behind so we could watch out for danger here. Somehow, someone from Dreams was controlling that man."

"The guy who burned down the house?" Parker asked.

Dr. Gates nodded. "The police offer said they found him sleeping under the tree in the back yard. He was covered in gasoline. When they finally got him to wake up, he said he didn't know what was going on, and the last thing he remembered was taking a shower this morning."

"He's probably lying," Zelda spat.

"Or being controlled," Kaelyn added.

"A sleepwalker," Parker said, sounding eerie even to himself.

"A sleepwalker," Dr. Gates repeated, nodding his head. "The point is that we were warned. He called us himself, and we were the ones who didn't take it seriously enough to leave one of us to watch. Now that we know, we need to be more careful."

"I still don't want Kae to go back," Zelda said, sitting on the bed holding Kaelyn like she was about to run away.

"Zelly, I have to."

Zelda shook her head and cried even more.

"Zelly, you know that mom would want me to do this. She wouldn't want me to let Gladamyr kill himself. It would be for nothing. Even if he does sacrifice himself, Mares will reenter our world. Zelly, we will lose even more than a house full of a bunch of pictures and diaries. We will lose everything."

Zelda nodded her head and held Kaelyn tightly.

Parker thought Zelda was going to argue again, but she didn't. She breathed in deep, wiped the tears from her face, and put on a look of determination.

"You remind me so much of your mama," she said, kissing Kaelyn's forehead. "Greg, how long till they'll make us go?"

"We probably have at least until Parker's dad comes. But I think we can distract them if we try."

"Distraction is my middle name," Zelda said. She stood up.

Parker smiled and winked at Kaelyn. They were going to do this. They were going to go back to Dreams and stop Fyren together. Together—that was it. Parker had been trying to figure out how to make his powers work. The stupid riddle he received from the crystal table made no sense. He needed Kaelyn to make his powers complete. He had the power to create the stone. Kaelyn had the power to give it life.

"Parker, what is it?"

"I think I know a way to save Gladamyr."

"Well then, you two better get at it," Zelda said proudly.

Parker climbed into the hospital bed next to Kaelyn and took her hand. They both laid back and whispered Gladamyr's name. Nothing happened. *Oh no, we're too late!* Parker immediately thought, but slowly the purple mist filled his eyes, and they entered Dreams.

"Captain Bootie?" Kaelyn asked, looking up at the pirate. "Where's Gladamyr?"

"Blast ye, bugger said he be off to kill Fyren," Captain Bootie said, pulling Kaelyn to her feet with his hooks.

"What?" Parker spat as the pirate lifted him as well.

"Gladdie left me yer keys and told me to head as far away from Éadrom as I could."

Kaelyn stared up at the night sky, but couldn't tell where in Dreams they were.

"Tell me you didn't listen," she said hopefully.

"Me little lady, no one tells me where to steer me ship. I knew Gladdie would want ye away from Éadrom, but I also knows that ye two are here to help. Éadrom is just yonder, arr." Captain Bootie pointed his right hook ahead and smiled.

Kaelyn squealed with delight and threw her arms around the pirate, giving him a kiss on the cheek which turned his whole face a deep red. Parker whooped loudly and ran to the bow of the ship, hanging out over the side to try and see land.

"Thank you, Captain," Kaelyn said.

"Ye're most welcome, miss."

"Now, Parker, what is this brilliant plan you've come up with?"

Parker turned and smiled. Then he sat down on the deck and spoke rapidly, moving his hands. "Well, I thought a lot about that dumb riddle the table gave us, and I think it means for us to work together to use our powers. It said we must look within ourselves and create a balance. I think that means we need to be thinking clearly. You know, focus on the thing we want. I don't know about you, but sometimes I argue with myself . . ."

"Really?" Kaelyn sat next to Parker and beamed. "I argue with myself all the time. Sometimes I feel like I'm two people trapped in the same body. One of me wants to be strong, and the other wants to be weak. I guess finding the balance is getting the two to get along so my mind can be clear enough to focus on what I want."

"Exactly! I've noticed that about you, you know. Like how you seem all sweet all the time, but then I hear that you totally ripped Tiffany apart."

Kaelyn blushed and tried to hide her face.

"No, Kae, that's fine—because that's who you are . . . and I like that."

Parker paused and looked at her. It seemed he wanted to say something, just didn't know how. "Kaelyn," he began quietly. "Remember when you told me how you knew who you were, but that I didn't?"

"I'm sorry. I was really upset at—"

"No, you were right! I didn't know who I was. I didn't get it until . . ."

"Felix?"

Parker nodded. "Not just Felix. When I went back to Awake, the firemen were pulling us out of the house. Everyone was awake, but you. I thought you might have been really hurt or something, and it worried me—a lot. I thought about you and Felix and . . . and all the stupid things I had done because I was more focused on being someone else. I never told you, but I'm the reason Felix died."

"How can you say that? It was his choice to fight."

"Had I been looking for the right keys, it would have been, but I was looking for Jason's key."

"What?"

"I thought that if Jason came to Dreams I could have him help, but more importantly, I thought that if he knew the reason I was hanging around you, he wouldn't think I was just—"

"Hanging out with a loser?"

"No . . . yes . . . but I don't think that way anymore! That's what I'm trying to say. Kaelyn, I don't care what

Jason thinks, or Tiffany, or anyone else. I like you, and I don't care if they call me a loser, too. I want to be with you. When I'm with you I can be myself, and I don't have to worry what you'll think about me . . . most of the time you just tell me what you think about me anyway."

They both laughed and Parker took Kaelyn's hand. She smiled at him and stared into his big, puppy dog brown eyes. He had changed. Kaelyn really believed that if they were to go to school tomorrow and Tiffany or Jason said something mean to her, he would actually speak up for once—perhaps even take her hand.

"Don't ye stop now," Captain Bootie called, "It be getting good, arr."

Kaelyn blushed even harder and hid her face. Parker laughed. It was getting awkward. Kaelyn almost thought Parker was about to kiss her, and she didn't know what to do. They had kissed before, but that was when they needed to get away from the zombies. This would be a real kiss, and her first.

"Anyway," Parker laughed, "like I was saying, before Captain Interruption said anything. I think I've found a balance within myself. I mean, think about it. The times I was able to create those things was when I was either trying to protect you, or save myself, but it was always easier when it was you."

"Aww!" Captain Bootie cooed.

"Loofyn, this is an A and B conversation. C your way out!"

"Looks like wooing to me, lad."

Kaelyn had to laugh. They were about to fight against the most dangerous thing in all the world, but they were still laughing. *At least we know you still have your humor,* Kaelyn's inner voice said without its usual mocking tone. *What's this—a compliment . . .? Well, you seem to be doing rather well for yourself . . . Thank you, I'll take that as a compliment, too.*

"This isn't a show, pirate!" Parker said, sounding annoyed.

"Just ignore him," Kaelyn whispered.

"Aye, aye," Captain Bootie said, climbing up the stairs to the ship's wheel. "I'll leave ye alone. But mind, ye have just minutes till we reach Éadrom, arr."

"So, your plan?" Kaelyn said, getting them back on course.

"Right," said Parker. "So we have balance, and we are thinking clearly, so we can use our powers. The next part said that when all is in opposition—heck, that's now, you know—good versus evil. I think once we get to Éadrom, we find out where Fyren is. Then I create an army of stone soldiers, and you bring them to life. We stop the Mares, and Gladamyr can stop Fyren, and we'll all be saved."

"Great plan, but how is Gladamyr going to stop Fyren?" Parker thought for a moment then his face brightened. "Era told us we already had the way to defeat Fyren."

"Zelda's prophecy?"

"A web, we need a web."

"I've thought and thought about it too, but Parker, I can't think of anything that's a weapon that looks like a web."

Parker and Kaelyn were silent for a while, and then Captain Bootie shouted out over the ship.

"Perhaps ye need to think of something that's not a weapon, arr."

"Well, that's dumb," Parker said loudly. "What good is something to fight with if it's not a weapon?"

"No, Loofyn is right. We should at least try."

"Fine. What are things that are webs?"

"Me net," Captain Bootie offered.

"Yes, thank you, you've mentioned that before I think," Parker snapped.

"Parker, be nice. He's only helping."

"Sorry."

"Okay, a net. A spider's web—"

"Thought of that, too. There's the internet—the world wide web ..."

"What be that, arr?" Captain Bootie called.

"If you're going to be a part of this conversation, why don't you come down here so you don't have to keep shouting?"

"Who be steering the ship, lad?"

"As if it was a problem before he went up there," Parker hissed.

Kaelyn wasn't paying any attention to the two arguing. She was drawing a web with her figure along the deck. Strangely, she seemed to leave a slight imprint in the wood with moisture from her finger. She drew a circle with lines crisscrossing through it, then other lines connecting the crisscrossed ones together, bringing them into the center like a spider's web. The image reminded her of something she'd seen recently, but she couldn't quite pick it out.

"Why don't ye try focusin' on the other part of the prophecy, arr," Captain Bootie suggested.

"Why don't ye try focusin' on the other part of the prophecy, arr," Parker mimicked.

"No, he's right," Kaelyn said.

"It was just to seek it from a friend," Parker answered back, "or an unknown friend—I think."

An unknown friend, Kaelyn thought, *who is the unknown friend? Someone who could possibly be a friend, but you didn't really know . . . Tiffany? Oh, please, don't gag me . . . Jason? He hates you, and once he learns you've stolen his best friend . . .* Kaelyn looked at the web she had drawn. She licked her finger and drew a feather sticking out of the bottom of the circle. Now it looked like Lena's dream catcher.

"A dream catcher!" she shouted, finding the answer.

"A what?"

"A dream catcher . . . that's it! Lena, remember Lena?"

"Wasn't she the girl leaving your house?"

"Yes! She showed me a necklace she was wearing with a dream catcher on it. She said that her grandmother gave it to her to protect her from bad dreams."

"Yeah, I've seen them. They have feathers and stuff on them."

"Yes," Kaelyn said happily, "but it's what they're for that's important. Bad dreams are caught in the web, and when the sun comes up, the rays from the sun kill the bad dream."

"And you think Lena is the unknown friend?"

"Yes," Kaelyn nodded. "Lena and I have a lot in common. I was thinking that it was just bad timing for her to come over because I wasn't focused on becoming her friend. I was focused on getting back to Dreams. But this is it, Parker! We need to make a dream catcher and somehow get Fyren in it. Then we need a sun . . ."

"Loofyn, when does the sun rise in Éadrom?" Parker asked.

"Oh, now ye wants me in the conversation, arr?"

"Loofyn!"

"It be night this season in Éadrom."

"Night? Season?" Kaelyn and Parker asked in unison

"Aye, Éadrom has seasons, arr. Night be this

season."

"Wait a minute." Kaelyn jumped to her feet and looked up at the sky. She tried to find the moons that she'd seen when they first came to Éadrom, but they were gone. She made out just the slightest bit of moon setting on the ocean. "Minyon said that Gladamyr had to be back to Éadrom before the setting of the moons. If the moons are setting, the sun must be coming up right?"

"Aye, but not for hours, maybe days. Not be its season."

"But the dream catcher won't work without the sun!" Kaelyn stomped her foot on the deck.

"Kae, it's okay. We'll think of something."

"Better think fast. We be here, arr."

The Dreamer came to life, throwing down ropes and pulling the great sails up. Captain Bootie shouted an order, and Kaelyn and Parker heard the anchor being dropped. They had made it to Éadrom. Kaelyn reached out with one hand, and Parker took it. In her other hand she held the dreamstone. She tightened her grip around it, hoping it would give them the strength they needed to get through the night.

"If all else fails, we can at least say we tried," Parker said, trying to cheer her up.

"If all else fails, Fyren wins," Kaelyn whispered.

"Don't forget Gladamyr, Kae," Parker said, turning her to face him. "Loofyn said he was going to kill Fyren, which means Gladamyr wasn't going down without a fight. And we're going to help Gladamyr give all the fight he wants to Fyren. So we don't have the sun—so what? We will have a stone army . . . and we'll have each other."

Kaelyn looked into his brown eyes, and they

reassured her that they wouldn't fail. Parker believed it, and it helped her believe it too. They had Gladamyr ... they had each other.

Just then Parker pulled her in close and hugged her. Kaelyn hugged back. They would not fail! They had each other—they had love and friendship, and that was enough to stop any nightmare.

CHAPTER FIFTEEN
THE DREAM CATCHER

Gladamyr took a few minutes to rest after his flight back to Éadrom. He thought a great deal about how he was going to fight Fyren, but he hadn't come up with any possible ways that would actually work. It seemed to him that there were so many dreamlings bent on bringing Mares back that even if he did kill Fyren, another dreamling would just take his place as executioner—Mab perhaps, or even Minyon. The only way to stop Mares was not to go at all. But Gladamyr couldn't do that.

He thought of the other dream keepers, dreamlings who devoted themselves to the mortals they served. They were the best of everything in Dreams and if Fyren killed them, all that was good in Dreams would be gone.

And then there was Cerulean. He thought of her— she was beauty mixed with the fierceness of a work horse, and he loved her for it. Every time she had brought him into her office he had secretly liked it. It amused him to watch her face turn that shade of red that clashed with her blue hair when she got angry. To love her was impossible. He was of Mares and she was of

Favor, but wasn't that what life is—opposition? She was his match no matter what differences they had between them. When he went out of control, it was she who calmed him. How could he let Fyren murder her? How could he just hide away as Fyren cut her with that black sword of death? The answer was he couldn't—and he'd shown that to Fyren.

Gladamyr had rescued her from the Crossing, and had given Fyren the thing he needed to get Gladamyr to come to him. Fyren had been hunting for a weakness, and Gladamyr had shown it.

"AHH!" Gladamyr shouted, angry with himself. *Control yourself,* the voice of Cerulean seemed to say. *This is not helping.* It was odd that Cerulean had become the voice in Gladamyr's head. It used to be Fyren ordering him to be unmerciful, then Allyon telling him it wasn't what he was born as that mattered, but what he chose to be. Now the voice was Cerulean's, the voice of the dreamling he loved. Love? Was love even possible for a Mare? Wasn't it a contradiction of his very being? He was the heart of Mares after all, and Mares had been removed from love. Yet here Gladamyr was—a Mare who loved.

He looked out over the ocean and saw the last moon dipping below the water. His time was up. He had to go to Fyren now. Gladamyr shifted his arms once more, and although they were tired and strained from his flight, he lifted himself high into the air and flew over the city of Éadrom.

The sight was something to see. It was as if every Mare in Dreams had come to watch the fall of Favor. The city roads and walkways were filled with dreamlings. There were thousands of them, and Gladamyr could barely see gaps between them. The thought of having to fight them all was daunting, but he would do it to save even the worst dream keeper. Gladamyr looked toward the center of the city where a large garden had once sat atop a tall hill. Fyren's dreamlings had stripped the garden of all its beauty and left it a wide arena with a stage for the spectators to watch the sacrifice about to take place.

It sickened him to see the dream keepers all linked together with a black cord, no doubt created with Mare magic to keep them from running away. Then he saw Cerulean. She was strapped to a stone altar at the front of the stage with Fyren behind her, holding his sword at his chest while he waited for the moon to disappear beneath the waves. Gladamyr wouldn't keep him waiting. He dove forward, speeding toward the stage. At the last minute he shifted his body midflight, and landed just feet from Fyren.

"I knew you'd come," Fyren said, his wide grin gleaming in the firelight.

"Don't flatter yourself," Gladamyr hissed.

"Dear me, it seems you've forgotten that I have the upper hand. I can still have her executed."

"Touch her and you will wish you'd never heard my name."

Fyren laughed. Backing away and raising one bone hand to the crowd, he said, "Patience my friends. Our wait will soon be over. Now, Gladamyr, you won't mind one of us checking to see if you have any keys . . . wouldn't want you leaving too soon."

Gladamyr held his arms away from his body and Twister, a wind Mare, stepped forward to search him. The Mare motioned with his hands and wind blew all over Gladamyr, feeling in every crack and crevice of his form. With a disappointed sigh, Twister stepped back down off the stage. Fyren snarled and gestured toward the altar. "Release the fairy and put her with the dream keepers. We will not see her killed today."

The crowd booed with disappointment as Minyon sent several spiders from his body to cut the black cords that bound Cerulean to the altar. Once the last cord got cut, Cerulean leaped from the altar and stomped on the spiders, bringing Minyon to his knees in pain.

"Gladamyr, go!" she cried, as Slither and Somnus grabbed her and carried her toward the dream keepers. "Go—let me die! You can't let them do this! It's immoral!"

Iniga slapped Cerulean across her face and tied a gag over her mouth. Gladamyr had to restrain himself so the red hate wouldn't seep into his eyes. He needed to remain focused.

He watched as they linked the black cording around Cerulean's hand, connecting her with the other dream keepers. He looked at them all, sadly bound, appearing like all hope was lost, and was about to look away so as to not feel like them when he saw him. The dreamling stood out from the other dream keepers because he was one of the few who refused to bow his head. He had been badly beaten, and his face was covered with deep cuts and bruises, but still it was Felix. He smiled at Gladamyr.

"Shall we begin?" Fyren asked, motioning with his bone hand for Gladamyr to lie on the altar.

"Yes, we shall." With a shift of his body Gladamyr spun around, knocking his arms into Fyren and sending the Mare crashing into his cronies. Fyren quickly rose to his bone feet and raised the sword over his head.

"I thought you might want to go down fighting," he said.

Gladamyr turned to see Iniga throw out a stream of molten rock that steamed as it hit the ground. Then Somnus, Slither, and several other Mares began pushing the dream keepers close to the lava.

"Oh, it won't kill them, but they will wish they could fade," Fyren said joyfully. "NOW LIE ON THAT ALTAR!"

Gladamyr glared at Fyren, and then something else caught his attention. The crowd began to scream. The noise started off in the distance but got louder and louder as panic spread. Gladamyr shifted his focus toward the outline of the city, where an army of large stone warriors were cutting through the dreamlings blocking the road like tissue paper. He strained his eyes and looked behind the stone army. It was Parker and Kaelyn!

"Brought your little friends, I see," Fyren said. Gladamyr smiled at Fyren and the Mare snarled back at him.

Gladamyr felt a surge of hope. He had told Loofyn to take the keys and not let the kids back into Dreams, but he should have known the pirate was . . . well, a pirate. More shouting erupted from the crowd as some dreamlings saw it as an opportunity to fight; not everyone in attendance, it seemed, wanted to bring back Mares.

Fyren roared and Gladamyr turned, expecting to dodge a blow, but Fyren wasn't charging him. The black blade sank into Cerulean's body, and she tried to cry out from behind her gag. The blue fairy fell to her knees as Fyren pulled his wicked blade from her torso, and Gladamyr felt the rush of anger fill his mind. Red—hot, fiery red engulfed his vision.

Parker swung the sword Captain Bootie had given him like a pro. He had played so many video games that wielding a sword came naturally to him. Kaelyn, on the other hand, did better with holding the dreamstone and sending a blast of air at the oncoming Mares. He guessed that was pretty cool too. Captain Bootie wasn't doing too badly either. Having two hooks instead of hands could be quite helpful in a battle.

"Parker, we need to get to Gladamyr!" Kaelyn shouted.

"I'm trying my best," he called back, dodging an angry blow from an evil-looking thing throwing pieces of broken statues. "What do you suggest? I can't walk any faster through these things."

"How about a car, or something?"

"A car?"

"We are blocks away from that hill! It will take forever to walk there, especially with having to—"

Kaelyn was cut off, forced to aim a very large blast of air at a group of ferocious wolves that had gotten hold of one of Captain Bootie's wooden legs. The wolves rolled away, leaving the wooden leg. Captain Bootie crawled toward the thing and reattached it, swearing such words even Parker thought were bad.

"I got it!" Parker focused as he thought of a large horse—no, a war horse. He focused his mind and the energy zapped out of him, creating a stone war horse that stood eight feet tall.

"Awesome!" they both said in unison.

Kaelyn reached her hand forward and touched the dreamstone to the horse's long mane. It instantly came to life, but this time the horse wasn't stone, but real. The massive creature was golden brown with a long white mane and tail. It reared back on its hind legs and let out a war cry. Parker grinned and turned to Captain Bootie. "Mind giving us a hook?"

"Parker!"

"What? I was being politically correct. He doesn't have any hands, Kaelyn."

"Aye, lad." Captain Bootie put his hooks down and Parker used them to climb atop the horse. Then Kaelyn did the same and scooted in next to Parker. Parker liked the fact that Kaelyn had to wrap her arms around his waist; it made him feel even more like a knight. Sword in hand, he pressed his heels into the horse's side, willing it to go, but it just stood there.

"Did it turn back into stone?" Parker asked.

"Have you ever ridden a horse?" said Kaelyn.

"No, but how hard can it be? I've seen movies, Kae. You hit it with your heels and you guide it with its reins."

"Aye, lad," Captain Bootie laughed, "and ye can also slap its rear, arr."

With a swing of his arm, Captain Bootie slapped his hook across the war horse's backside. The beast charged forward with a cry that would send fear into most, and Parker held on tight to the reins, guiding it through the crowd of fighting dreamlings and stone warriors. Kaelyn gripped Parker tightly with one arm and with the other shot off blasts of air into anything in their way.

"Look Parker, the Favors must be fighting back."

Parker looked at the crowd as they sped by. Kaelyn was right! There were dreamlings fighting dreamlings. It gave Parker a sense of hope that not everyone wanted to follow Fyren. Some dreamlings had sense; just nothing to rally behind.

"I see Gladamyr!" Kaelyn cried as they approached

the hill. Parker saw him too, and his stomach churned. Gladamyr was fighting Fyren, and he looked evil. Parker thought of the pictures that Dr. Gates had drawn when he was a little boy. The beast with spikes kind of resembled what Gladamyr looked like now. The shock of Gladamyr's appearance took the focus off where the war horse was heading and they were much too close to the two fighting shifters. He pulled back on the reins, and the war horse pawed to a stop.

Kaelyn climbed down and ran over toward the stage on which Gladamyr and Fyren were fighting. Fyren was rapidly shifting into different forms, but he continually kept hold of the black sword. Parker joined Kaelyn and saw what she was planning to do.

"You think that'll work?"

"I'm going to try," she replied, holding out her hand and sending a blast of air at the sword. It fell out of Fyren's hands, but he shifted and caught it with another hand that formed somewhere else. A blast of fire erupted right in front of Parker and Kaelyn, and a small stone wall appeared, blocking the flames. Parker and Kaelyn turned to see several Mares advancing.

"Oh, great!" Parker said, readying his sword.

"Parker, look!" Kaelyn pointed behind the Mares.

Parker focused his eyes past the Mares and the fire and saw an endless line of dream keepers tied together. They were being forced into what looked like a stream of lava, but they were fighting. Then Parker saw Felix and his heart leaped. He thought of all the games he'd ever played and all the movies he had seen where the hero went charging into battle. They always seemed to cry out some sort of battle cry, and he felt that he should as well. Lifting his sword above his head, he charged the Mares.

"GLADAMYR!"

Kaelyn followed behind Parker, crying out the same battle cry and shooting explosions of air at the Mares. She watched as they fell back, or were taken out by Parker's sword. It was like all the power of Favor was with them as they fought through the Mares and over toward the dream keepers. The war horse was not satisfied with just standing around either. It charged too, running down several Mares as it leaped over the small river of lava.

Kaelyn was the first to reach the line of dream keepers. She stared at several of them, trying to see how to untie the black cording that bound them, but the rope burned when she touched it.

"What is it?"

"Mare magic," a dream keeper with only half a face said. Kaelyn looked at her with a feeling of empathy and disgust. Then she held out her dreamstone.

"I hope this works." She cut through the cording and it fizzled like a fuse down the line, allowing the dream keepers to break free of their bonds. They wasted no time pulling their worn, beaten bodies out from their prison, and they too began to fight the Mares.

Kaelyn watched as several dream keepers fell on Minyon, ripping spiders from his body like hair off a cat. The Mare screamed in agony. It took six dream keepers to bring down the snake thing, but they succeeded and even pushed the werewolf into the lava in the process. Kaelyn searched for Parker and spotted him just past the stone wall he'd created.

She ran to him and saw that he was fighting back to back with—Felix! The Dream Keeper was alive! The two were spinning around, their backs together. Felix conjured roots from the ground to tie around their enemies so Parker could hack at them with his sword. Kaelyn was about to smile when she saw the slumped shape of something blue lying next to the steps leading to the stage where Gladamyr and Fyren continued to fight.

"Cerulean!" Kaelyn ran to her bond. Parker must have heard her because seconds after Kaelyn reached the fairy, he was at her side.

"You can heal her," he said reassuringly, "like you did Gladamyr. You can heal her."

Kaelyn nodded and tried to focus on the healing magic she knew was in her, but the steps started shaking and a loud, evil growling came from the ground. It was as if Mares was again fighting with Favor, and he wanted his freedom.

"Parker, we don't have time. This has to stop."

They both looked to the stage where the endless battle between the two shifters continued. Fyren would shift and claw at Gladamyr, only for him to shift and bite back. No one was gaining the upper hand, but the moment Fyren found a way to use his sword it would literally all be over.

"The web?" Parker asked.

"But without the sun it's pointless."

"A dream catcher doesn't necessarily need the sun to catch a bad dream, only to destroy it."

Parker brought Kaelyn in close and she held onto him.

"We have to do this together!" she called over the thunderous growling noise.

She pressed the dreamstone into his palm, and then began to think of a large web. She laced the golden cords together in her mind, linking them one by one like a net.

The closer she got to the center of the web, the smaller and smaller she linked the cords. Then she opened her eyes and cried out Gladamyr's name.

Gladamyr heard his name and the blinding red slowly ebbed out of his vision. He tried to focus, but he was so tired. His muscles ached from the effort of shifting. And it was harder and harder to do each time . . . the red . . . He heard his name again. He saw Fyren swinging. He backed away and shifted, turning his midsection into vapor, and the blade swung cleanly through. Fyren roared with frustration.

"Gladamyr!" It was Kaelyn's voice.

The red blinked away, and the Dream Keeper looked above him. An intricate golden web was descending upon them both. The kids had found the web! They had found the way to stop the shifter.

Gladamyr parried Fyren's next attack and tried to move out of range of the web, but Fyren followed him. There was no way for Gladamyr to escape the web without Fyren following. He had to stay, he had to . . .

The web is the key to the shifter's end. The prophecy sounded like a death chant repeating over and over inside Gladamyr's mind. It would be the key to the shifter's end—to his end. Gladamyr thought about leaving, clearing himself from the web's fall, but he couldn't. He had to keep Fyren there. He took one last moment to look at his friends.

Parker and Kaelyn were holding Cerulean and looking up at him. Kaelyn had tears running down her face and she shouted something, but he couldn't hear. He knew they too wanted him to get out of the way, but this was the way it had to be.

With a shift of his body, Gladamyr charged Fyren again. He used all the strength he had and gripped the Mare around the waist. Fyren tried to shift, but Gladamyr held tight to the wrist of Fyren's sword hand, making it impossible for Fyren to shift without losing his sword. Gladamyr sprang upward with Fyren in his grasp just as the golden web came down. The golden cords stung as they touched Gladamyr's skin, and Fyren cried out so loudly his ears bled. Gladamyr smiled as the sword dropped from Fyren's hand and hit the stone stage, shattering like glass.

"You're a fool," Fyren hissed. "You think by killing me you'll stop me? Mares will rise, Gladamyr, and you will be the one to bring him back."

"I will never help you."

"You already have." Fyren smiled and began to shift. Flesh covered his bone frame and he began to shrink down. Soon Fyren was a little girl hunched over and crying. She wore a pale pink dress. *Pink. Little girls always wore pink when they slept.*

"Don't hurt me," the little girl cried. "Please don't hurt me."

The little girl looked up at Gladamyr with doleful eyes. He recognized her at once. She was one of the first mortals he ever saw. Was this the same girl that created him so long ago? He remembered her screaming as his talons sunk into her skin. He remembered sending her back to Awake covered in blood.

This was his nightmare.

Gladamyr reached out his hand to touch the child. To tell her he was sorry for everything he'd done. To tell her he would take it all away if he could. His hand was inches from her face when the child's smile turned cold and her eyes lit with flame. A tiny hand with a shard of black onyx thrust forward. Gladamyr never felt the pain. Light exploded above him.

The little girl turned her eyes upward and her shape shifted back into Fyren's. He screamed as the light from the web's golden cords burned into his bones, turning his form to ash. A sudden gust of wind blew through Fyren and he vanished in a swirl of dust. The shard of black onyx clattered to the ground and Gladamyr closed his eyes.

He could feel the light touching his skin too. It burned, but not painfully. It felt like his body was being immersed in a hot tub of water. The red anger that he was always aware of in the back of his mind vanished. It was replaced by love—overpowering love. His heart was burning with the knowledge that he knew how to love. That even he, a Nightmare, was capable of such a pure thing.

Gladamyr smiled. If this was death, then it was wonderful.

Parker held onto Kaelyn as she cried out Gladamyr's name once more, and tried to reach out for him. The golden web fell upon the two dreamlings, and Fyren screamed. Without warning the ground stopped shaking and light—glorious light—broke free from the ocean as the sun began to rise over the city of Éadrom.

"NO!" Kaelyn cried.

Parker turned and the golden web burst into white light that blinded him. He shut his eyes and pulled on Kaelyn, who struggled to break free. She cried "no" over and over, pushing against Parker. Then she stopped and turned into him, sobbing into his chest. Gladamyr had truly sacrificed himself.

"I didn't mean for him to get trapped . . . I tried to warn him."

"Kae, he knew what he was doing . . . He knew . . ." Parker began to cry too. He couldn't help it. He hadn't known Gladamyr all that long, but the Dream Keeper was his bond. He was like a brother, and Parker loved him. He held onto Kaelyn, and they cried together.

"We were supposed to win, Parker," Kaelyn choked out. "We were supposed to win."

"We did win, Kae. We won it for him."

"Winning is supposed to make you feel better."

Parker agreed, but it didn't make him feel any better. If he ever won another game in all his life he would think about this moment. How the greatest win in his life was also the greatest loss. But not all was lost. He had Kaelyn and Felix and . . .

"Cerulean," Parker remembered. "Kaelyn, can you heal her?"

"I don't know," she said, pulling back and wiping her face. "Gladamyr's wasn't this bad. I can try."

Parker watched as Kaelyn put her hand on Cerulean's wound and pressed hard against the silvery blood. She tightened her eyes, and she felt the magic working within her. He felt it—like rushing wind, the energy escaped from Kaelyn and entered into Cerulean. Parker closed his eyes, and he too tried to focus his energy, not on Cerulean—he didn't know how to heal— but he concentrated on giving more power to Kaelyn.

Parker felt the dreamstone, still pressed into their palms, grow hot as if the very thing they were doing would melt the stone. He opened his eyes and light, blue light, poured out of Kaelyn's hand. The silver blood drained back into Cerulean's body, and Parker felt a smile spreading across his face.

"Kaelyn, it's working! It's working!"

Parker looked at Kaelyn, and she looked hopefully at Cerulean, who still lay there motionless. "Is she . . .?"

"The blood is all gone and there's no wound . . . Cerulean?" Kaelyn asked. "Cerulean?"

"Gladamyr?" Cerulean moaned.

She was alive! Kaelyn had done it!

"Kaelyn, Parker?" Cerulean opened her eyes. "Where's Gladamyr?"

Parker didn't know what to say. Kaelyn squeezed his hands, and the tears fell once more.

"Where's Gladamyr?" Cerulean repeated shakily, tears filling her blue eyes.

"I'm right here."

Parker looked up to see their dream keeper hobbling down the steps to Cerulean's side. He stooped down and held the blue fairy in his arms. The two dreamlings kissed. Kaelyn threw her arms around Gladamyr's middle, and the Dream Keeper set Cerulean on her feet. Then Parker too wrapped his arms around his bond.

"How did you . . .?" Kaelyn asked.

"Gladamyr!" Parker pulled back and wiped his wet face. Gladamyr looked different somehow, as if all his sadness had left. "We tried to warn you. We didn't mean for you to—"

"It's alright. I'm fine now."

Parker tried to believe him, but he could tell that something was different about him. He looked worn out, and yet he looked happy.

"I see you somehow made it out of another horrible situation without getting killed," Cerulean said, taking a break from kissing him.

"I have no idea how I did it," Gladamyr shrugged. "I felt it burning me, but it felt good. I thought I was dying, but when I opened my eyes I was still here. I don't understand. It killed Fyren and I'm as much of a Mare as he was."

"But you're not just a Mare," Parker said beaming. "You're a dream keeper . . . our Dream Keeper."

"It's in your heart, don't you see?" Kaelyn pressed her hand on Gladamyr's chest. "It's in here that really matters. Not what you appear on the outside. Inside you are as good as they come. That is why you survived. I know it. Lena said only good dreams escape the web."

Gladamyr pulled them all in once again, and they hugged for what seemed an eternity. Felix came over and slapped Gladamyr on the back. He too received a hug, and they laughed and joked about the battle they had won.

Several dream keepers came and bowed low to Gladamyr, paying their respects for what he had done. It seemed the death cry of Fyren scared the other nightmares back to Mares. Only Favors and dream keepers were left in the city. Once those left in the city had congratulated Gladamyr, Captain Bootie came hobbling, leaning on a strange dreamling with two faces. It was the strangest thing Parker had seen yet—a dreamling with two faces on the same head. One face was a beautiful woman and the other was a green thing that looked like it was dead or something.

"Looks like you finally found your shape," the woman side said sweetly.

"Jaynus!" Gladamyr put out his hand, and the dreamling shook it and smiled.

"You're looking well."

"She ought to now," Captain Bootie laughed. "That

no good Mare side needed a little sense knocked into him, arr—I was glad to oblige."

"Yes," Jaynus said, smiling again. "I see Loofyn hasn't lost his love of fighting—and you too it would seem, Gladamyr."

"I only fight when I need to," Gladamyr replied. He motioned for Parker and Kaelyn to step forward. "I'd like to introduce you to my bonds, Parker and Kaelyn."

Jaynus bowed politely while Gladamyr searched the pockets of his trench coat. "Ah, there it is. You can have this blasted thing back." He handed the dreamling what looked to Parker like a sand dollar. "That thing has brought me nothing but bad luck since the moment you gave it to me!"

"Did I say luck?"

"You said good fortune!"

"And what do you call this, dream keeper?" Jaynus lifted her hand and spun around. "You have saved our world, you and your bonds. That, Gladamyr, is just a shell. They say it holds special powers and brings good fortune, but I really believe it is the person who holds the shell that has brought that. Keep it if you will. It was a gift, after all."

"Thank you, Jaynus," Gladamyr said humbly.

"Since we be givin' gifts, take these rutty things off me, arr." Captain Bootie held out his right hook, and four keys hung from it; two iridescent and two glowing hot.

"I guess it's time for us to head back," Kaelyn said, disappointed.

"We'll come back just as soon as we can get back to bed though," Parker added.

Cerulean pulled Kaelyn in for a warm embrace and thanked her for everything. Then she turned to Parker and gave him a kiss. Parker blushed and Kaelyn squeezed his hand. Felix patted Parker on the shoulder, and Parker threw his arms around the dreamling, who laughed. Gladamyr took the keys off Captain Bootie's hook and placed them in his pocket. Captain Bootie saluted the kids, and Gladamyr knelt down next to Parker and Kaelyn.

"You two have given me more than I ever thought could be given to a dream keeper. You have given me a reason to hope. This war is not over. Allyon is still missing, and there will be others to follow in Fyren's footsteps, but I know I can count on my bonds to help.

"Parker, you are a boy who is becoming a man. Remember that the choices you make not only lead you in a direction, they make you who you are. Make the right choice and never be afraid to be yourself."

"I will," Parker said, giving Gladamyr a hug.

"Little Kae, my Kaelyn, I couldn't thank you enough for saving my life, but you have also shown me love. Remain true to yourself, your whole self, and never fear to dream."

"I never have since I met you," Kaelyn said, kissing him on the cheek.

"Until we meet again," Gladamyr said as he pulled out their keys and touched their faces. A soft lullaby played and the purple mist spun them back to Awake.

CHAPTER SIXTEEN
DREAMNAPPED

Zelda hadn't stopped hugging Kaelyn since they came back to Awake, and Kaelyn thought she was going to have bruises later. They held a short, quiet victory party in the hospital elevator as they went to meet Parker's dad. Dr. Gates gave each of them hugs and said he would see them all later. He was going home to shower, and then he would meet them over at Parker's. He thought it was time to bring Parker's mom in on all the details of Dreams, and he didn't want to look like a man who had been through a fire when he did it.

"Always the professional, Greg?" Zelda asked flirtatiously.

"Always, Madam Zelda."

Kaelyn and Parker rolled their eyes and followed Zelda into Parker's dad's car.

"I find it weird that your mom isn't answering her phone. She always answers her phone," Parker's dad said, putting his phone once again to his ear.

"I'm sure it just died. She probably forgot to charge it or something. If you want to just drop us off, I'll be fine."

Kaelyn could tell Parker didn't get along all that well with his dad. And she saw why. Since arriving, his dad had made three phone calls and sent who knows how many texts. His car was pretty flashy and Zelda always said to never date a man with a flashy car. "He either works too much or he wastes his money."

"I can't wait to wash my hair. It smells like a fireplace," Zelda moaned. "I can't believe I am out in public looking like this."

"This is coming from a lady who wore an afghan to school today," Kaelyn whispered to Parker. The two started to laugh. Zelda eyed them suspiciously but didn't say anything.

When they finally made it to Parker's house, his dad said he would wait out in the car and they could let him know if Parker's mom was home.

"Sure, Dad." They all piled out of the car. "See what I mean?" Parker said to Kaelyn. "The man is more attached to his phone than I am to my limbs."

"I'm convinced cell phones are going to give people cancer one day," said Zelda as they walked up the steps. "Ahhh, it's freezing!"

"Don't you have a cell phone?" Parker asked.

"Yeah, but I never use it. Unless it's an emergency, or for long distance, or to text with, or—"

"Zelly!" Kaelyn said, laughing.

Parker fumbled with his keys for a moment before opening the door. They all went inside and Zelda 'awwed' over the warmth of the house.

"Mom, I'm home," Parker called out. "Mom?"

Kaelyn looked around the living room as Parker went off to check the other rooms. The house was like a museum. Everything was so clean and organized. It was nothing like Zelda's house. Zelda made herself right at home, grabbing a fuzzy throw off the couch and wrapping it around her. Kaelyn was about to sit on the couch when she heard Parker screaming in the other room.

"Mom! Mom! Kaelyn, MOM!"

Kaelyn ran into the room and saw Parker stooping over his mom, who was on the floor.

"She's not . . . she . . ." Parker cried.

Kaelyn and Zelda rushed over and Zelda immediately checked for a pulse. "She's alive . . . she's just sleeping," she said, looking up at them.

Parker sat up and stared at his mom.

"I don't understand. Why won't she wake up?"

"Parker, look!"

Kaelyn pointed at the immaculately vacuumed, carpeted floor. Parker's mom had traced three letters in the carpet as if they explained everything; they read: MAB.

The prison's iron grate slid open and Liz knew she was about to die. The monstrous Mare crawled down the steps and raised the stinger attached to its thick scorpion tail. Liz tightened her muscles, preparing for the pain she knew was coming. The Mare plunged the stinger down. The poison hurt at first, as it always did, but soon the numbing took effect and Liz crumpled. She didn't move. Not even a flutter of an eyelash. Mab clearly wanted her paralyzed, but with eyes open.

The monster moved out of the way so the thirty or so small creatures that Liz thought looked like garden gnomes could climb down the steps into the prison. Three of the gnomes looked Liz over, making sure she was in fact paralyzed. One checked her eyes, opening the right eyelid a bit wider so Liz could see more clearly. The other gnomes lifted Liz's body and followed the monstrous Mare up the steps, avoiding the swaying, scorpion tail.

Liz watched as the halls turned from darkened stone to ornately decorated walls of marble and gold. The further the gnomes carried her, the more beautiful the halls became. Liz dreaded every moment. She knew that the further she went from the safety of her prison, the closer she got to Mab. Strange carnival-like music played from the room they approached, and Liz tried to think about something other than what she feared was about to happen. She thought of Parker, and how the last thing she had done was to ground him, and how she never told him about what happened so long ago. How she never taught him how to dream.

"If it pleases her majesty, I would like a break," a shaky voice said.

"It does *not* please me," the shrill voice of Mab shouted back. "You'll stop when I tell you to stop—and I want more items juggled! You there, toss the clown something sharp. I want to see if he can catch it without losing another arm . . . aw, my guest!"

Liz tried to take the room in as she was turned about by the gnomes, but there was so much to see. It was a throne room with high ceilings and tall columns. Dozens of creatures lined the perimeter, but to focus on one was impossible. In the center of the room was a clown wearing a red polka-dot suit. He was juggling three rubber chickens and a meat cleaver with one hand. The clown's other arm was missing, the sleeve tied off with a large orange bow tie. Liz felt pity for the clown when she saw the tears that had ruined his make-up, making him look like a psychotic serial killer.

The gnomes moved Liz's immobile body forward, turning her toward the throne.

There was Mab. Her throne looked like it was made of diamonds. It sparkled as if it belonged in the throne room of heaven, not in Mab's palace. The queen was the most beautiful woman Liz had ever seen in her life, but it was a cold sort of beauty that made her look fierce. Mab's dark hair was pulled up in an elegant style, accentuating her thin neck that was dripping with diamonds. Her crown was oversized and her gown looked like it belonged in a bank vault. The millions of diamonds and precious stones adorning the gown glared light into Liz's eyes. Liz tried to blink but her eyelids remained open, tears now spilling down her face.

Mab smiled and stared at Liz for a moment, before she sighed.

"This look of terror on your face is exhausting me. Satyral, fix her."

Liz felt panic once more as the monster with the scorpion tail turned around, grinning with rows of teeth. He turned back to Mab. "Of course, your majesty."

In one swift motion the stinger stabbed into Liz's back. She felt searing pain shoot up her spine and hit her head like an explosion. She didn't have control over her throat but she knew she was screaming.

The numbness ebbed from her body and the pain took over. Liz thrashed uncontrollably as the poison coursed through her veins. Her lungs felt as though they were collapsing. She couldn't breathe. *Control . . . take control . . . it hurts . . .* Liz focused on her lungs and she breathed. Slowly she tightened into a ball and began to cry.

"Idiot, Manticore. I still want to communicate with

her!" Mab roared.

Another stab of the stinger and fresh hot pain followed. A ringing sound screamed in Liz's ears and her eyes felt as though they were about to burst. The numbing followed and her body relaxed. The poison stilled her muscles. A slight tremor of adrenaline coursed in Liz's blood, making her tremble, but she could tell Mab liked that. Liz was able to turn her head and watch as the Mare with the tail, the manticore, took a space next to another monster by the wall. Liz turned back to Mab and scowled.

"You were so much prettier as a child," Mab said mockingly.

Liz said nothing. She knew that any reply would only reward her with punishment, and Mab certainly knew how to punish.

"Now then, I know I promised you a swift execution; however, I'm afraid my plans have changed. You see, that horrible spawn you created has somehow killed Fyren."

A gasp sounded from around the room and Liz noticed the small collection of spiders that rested on the arm of Mab's throne droop as if bowing in sorrow. Mab patted the arachnids as if comforting them, and the gesture churned Liz's stomach

"Yes, I know, I know, my subjects, this news is very sad." Mab turned toward the creatures lining the room and Liz was reminded of a minister addressing a congregation of sinners. "I know what you feel in your hearts. You feel emptiness and hate. That hate turns you to the desire for revenge. You want justice. Very well. I will give you revenge! I will give you justice! Loyal subjects of Faerie, this woman—this filthy mortal is to blame. She's responsible for the abomination that has taken place this day. But let us not forget what she has done in the past. No! She will pay for those grievances too. The filthy mortal before you is responsible for Fyren's death. What would you have me do to her?"

The crowd around the throne room erupted into a cacophony of cheers and pronouncements of torture and death. Liz saw magical creatures both beautiful and magnificent, as well as the dark and ugly, call out for her execution. She didn't understand. She hadn't killed anyone. Was Mab trying to blame her for something she hadn't done? What was her crime? This wasn't a fair trial. Mab was acting as accuser, judge, and jury.

"My loyal subjects, please," Mab said, lifting a gentle hand to quiet the creatures. "Fyren was mighty and it's a crime to let this woman live, but I would ask you this: would a mere execution satisfy the depth of damage this mortal has wrought on our world? I say no! A quick death would not satisfy Fyren, and it does not satisfy me. I will make her pay, but the sentence will be drawn out. The pain will be intolerable and this filthy mortal will beg me to kill her."

Mab stood up and addressed the dreamlings with a more prophetic stance. "Fyren is gone, but you forget that you have me. I am your queen. I was here long before Fyren ruled the Crossing. I know what is to be done and I will see that Mares is brought back to his glory. And you . . ." Mab turned to Liz, an evil smile playing across her lips. "You, my pet, will be the key."

The dreamlings cheered. A little man in green who sat at the base of Mab's throne popped up and did something that looked to Liz like an Irish jig. The crowd cheered again and the little man fell to his knees, worshiping Mab's feet. Liz looked around at the creatures, trying desperately to figure out what was going on. She didn't understand. What was the spawn she had created—who was Mares—how was she a key to his return?

"Oh, now you look confused, little peasant. Is your collar not working? You there," Mab pointed at a creature that was half-man, half-goat. "Check her collar. I need to know she can see clearly."

The goat man raced over to Liz and checked the thick collar around her neck. Liz knew what it was for. Without the collar she would simply dream. Mab didn't want Liz distracted. She was here to settle a score.

"It's secured just fine, your majesty."

"Then why isn't she . . . oh . . ." Mab began to laugh and soon others joined in, following the queen's lead. The little man in green was rolling on the ground, clutching at his stomach and laughing. "My, my, my, you didn't know that your very own son has been gallivanting through Dreams? Well, little Lizzy González, he has, and once he finds out that I have you, he will try to rescue you . . . And when he does . . ."

Mab stepped down from her throne and pulled something small and dark from beneath the lining of her blouse. She marched toward Liz, who flinched, but Mab sidestepped her and drove the dark thing into the clown, who cried out in horror.

"I DID NOT TELL YOU TO STOP JUGGLING!" With a turn of her wrist the clown crashed to the floor, evaporating in a cloud of dark dust. "Have I made my point, peasant? Satyral, throw her back in the dungeons. Let her wait for Parker to come."

End of Book One

The Story Continues in Book Two:
THE DREAMSTONE
Available 2014

ABOUT THE
AUTHOR/ILLUSTRATOR

Mikey Brooks is a small child masquerading as an adult. On occasion you'll catch him dancing the funky chicken, singing like a banshee, and pretending to have never grown up. He is the author/illustrator of several books including *Bean's Dragons* and the *ABC Adventures series*. His art can be seen in many forms from picture books to full room murals. He loves to daydream with his two daughters and explore the worlds that only the imagination of children can create. THE DREAM KEEPER is his first novel. He looks forward to sharing many, many more. Mikey has a BS degree in English from Utah State University and works as a freelance illustrator. He is also one of the hosts of the *Authors' Think Tank Podcast*. You can find more about him and his books at:

www.insidemikeysworld.com

IF YOU LIKED THIS BOOK
PLEASE LEAVE A REVIEW AT:

AMAZON.COM

BARNESANDNOBLE.COM

GOODREADS.COM

FOR SIGNED COPIES OR MORE
INFORMATION ON OTHER BOOKS BY
MIKEY BROOKS VISIT:

INSIDEMIKEYSWORLD.COM

SWEET DREAMS

Made in the USA
San Bernardino, CA
16 December 2016